Laney started to reach for Sam, but Caleb stopped her.

"I've got this," he said, lifting Sam easily and holding him against his shoulder.

Her little boy sighed and snuggled his face against Caleb's throat.

A look flashed across Caleb's face that Laney couldn't quite decipher. It was a combination of surprise and tenderness and something else she'd never seen there before. Joy, maybe?

Carrying Sam, Caleb turned away, heading for the barn. She followed slowly, watching the way Caleb adjusted his gait to compensate for the additional thirty-five pounds he was carrying. He held Sam tightly, and she knew that if he was in danger of stumbling, he would fall on his wounded leg before he would let Sam hit the ground.

She realized that if she wasn't very careful, she could fall in love with him.

Dear Reader,

Sweetsilver, Arizona, is the home of Delaney Reynolds and her son, Sam, an adventurous four-year-old who is crazy about all things cowboy. Laney is a high school teacher and, in summer, a wildland firefighter. She and Sam have recently moved into their new home, which is right next to reclusive rancher, Caleb Ransom. Laney's biggest challenge is keeping her son off Caleb's property.

Caleb chose this ranch in the Sonoran Desert to raise cattle and horses and to heal from the physical and emotional wounds he'd received while deployed as a soldier. He simply wants to be left alone.

Sam has other ideas. The curious boy is unable to resist visiting Caleb and his animals, especially his dog, Bertie, who becomes Sam's instant best friend. Whenever Sam shows up, his attractive mother is never far behind, making it impossible for Caleb to have the solitary existence he desires.

Like most Americans, I love the cowboy mystique. There's something so appealing about a rugged outdoorsman who spends much of his time alone, or with his animals, honing skills such as roping, which most of us will never master. I thought about that continually as I was writing *Her Lone Cowboy* and I tried to do justice to the cattlemen who helped shape our country.

I hope you enjoy Caleb and Laney's story, my first Harlequin Heartwarming book, and will visit my website, patriciaforsythebooks.com, to see what else I've written. Also, drop by heartwarmingauthors.blogspot.com to meet other Harlequin Heartwarming authors.

Happy reading,

Patricia

HEARTWARMING

Her Lone Cowboy

Patricia Forsythe

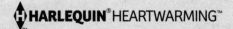

Recycling programs
for this product may
not exist in your area.

ISBN-13: 978-0-373-36730-6

Her Lone Cowboy

Copyright © 2015 by Patricia Knoll

Printed in U.S.A.

www.Harlequin.com

If it hadn't been for a seventh-grade teacher who told **Patricia Forsythe** that her story characters were, well, crazy, she probably would never have become a writer. She didn't think that was such a bad thing. After all, she has a large, extended family of decidedly interesting and unusual people who provide ideas and inspiration for her books. In Patricia's opinion, that only makes them more lovable and worthy of a place in literature.

A native Arizonan, Patricia has no concept of what a real winter is like, but she is very familiar with summer. She has held a number of jobs, including teaching school, working as a librarian and as a secretary, and operating a care home for developmentally disabled children. Her favorite occupation, though, is writing novels in which the characters get into challenging situations and then work their way out. Each situation and set of characters is different, so sometimes the finished book is as much a surprise to her as it is to the readers. She is the author of many romance novels for Harlequin and Kensington Books and currently also self-publishes ebooks. She is thrilled to see the publication of *Her Lone Cowboy*, her first Harlequin Heartwarming novel.

Visit the Author Profile page at Harlequin.com for more titles.

This book is dedicated to
Roz Denny Fox and Vicki Lewis Thompson,
my good friends, who have been such a source
of encouragement, friendship and joy
that words can't express my gratitude.

CHAPTER ONE

WHAT WAS THAT? Caleb Ransom pulled on Cisco's reins and brought the horse to a stop. He stood in the stirrups and looked across the pasture to where he'd seen something black moving along at a steady clip. Was it a dog? A coyote? One of the barn cats?

Whatever it was, it was heading toward Addie and her new filly.

Caleb's eyes widened when he identified the little boy he'd seen hanging over the fence the past couple of days—and the boy was moving straight for the most overprotective mare Caleb had ever seen.

Sitting back down, he spurred Cisco into action. They galloped across the field, Caleb leaning forward in the saddle, urging his horse on.

WHERE WAS HE?

Delaney Reynolds hurried down the front steps of her house and made a frantic sweep of the front yard.

"Sam!" she called, as she had been calling for the past five minutes. Her son was one fast-moving four-year-old. He'd been equally fast at three, two and one. He had walked at nine months and she hadn't had an easy day since. Her dearest hope was that she would be able to bring his adventurous nature under control and he would live to grow up.

His favorite hangout was the rail fence between her property and the one next door, whose owner kept cattle and horses. Sam was desperate to make friends with those horses. She had warned him away and threatened that he would find himself sitting in the "naughty chair" in the corner of the kitchen for a very long time if he disobeyed, but she had the sick feeling that his enthrallment with the horses had overcome his fear of forced immobility.

Laney climbed the fence and from the top rail, gazed out over the pasture, searching for Sam.

A hundred yards in front of her she finally saw a little black cowboy hat bouncing through the tall brush and grass toward a mare and her baby. Coming from the opposite direction was a horse and rider, heading straight for her son.

"Sam!"

Clamping her hands on the fence rail, she pushed off and ran, arms pumping, feet pounding.

CALEB KNEW THAT if he didn't reach the kid before he got to Addie's foal, there was a good chance the mare would turn aggressive. She hadn't let Caleb near her foal for the first three days of its life and still watched him nervously, hooves dancing and head tossing when he came close or approached with a less-than-soothing voice. There was no way she would let this pint-size stranger touch her filly.

Caleb's advance, at right angles from the child's, would spook Addie, but there was nothing he could do about that. He could only hope that if she spooked, it would be away from the little boy.

As he'd expected, the sound of Cisco's pounding hooves caught Addie's attention. She lifted her head and swung it around to see what was going on. Her gaze fixed on Caleb and Cisco, but then, unerringly, her attention focused on the little boy who was closing in fast. She shook her head vigorously, then lowered it, a sure sign she was going to head-butt the child. Snorting, she pawed the ground.

Alarmed, Caleb saw that the boy was oblivious to the danger he was in because he wasn't stopping or even slowing down. Addie, used and abused by drug smugglers and then abandoned, pregnant, in the desert, was already wary of people. Caleb couldn't begin to guess how she might react to this kid, but he expected it wouldn't be good.

Addie moved to stand between her baby and this small, determined human.

Before she could take more than a step toward the boy, though, Caleb was there, reins in his right hand, left arm outstretched, leaning over in the saddle as far as he could. He clamped his right leg against Cisco's ribs as he bent, hoping that his weakened muscles would hold and not cramp up on him. With a mighty swing, he snagged the little boy by the back of his shirt and swept him up in front of him.

The kid shrieked in alarm as he was swung up and set just behind the saddle horn.

Caleb kept Cisco at a gallop as he wheeled around and away from Addie.

When they were far enough, he pulled his horse up, set the little boy on the ground and dismounted. Cisco, always happy to eat, ripped up a mouthful of grama and began chewing the grass placidly.

Caleb dropped Cisco's reins, then took off his hat and clapped it against his leg. It wasn't dusty, but he needed to do something to calm himself. He knew that turning this kid over his knee and paddling his little butt wasn't an option. His heart was still pounding and alarm prickled along his nerve endings as he thought about what could have happened to the boy.

He placed his hat on his head and took several deep breaths. When he could trust himself to speak he said, "What were you doing?"

To his surprise, the boy took off his own cowboy hat and clapped it against his leg. Then he resettled it on his head just as Caleb had done and took a few deep breaths, too. Caleb would have thought the boy was mocking him if he hadn't had such a solemn expression on his face.

Finally the kid said, "I wanted to see the pony."

Caleb didn't bother to correct the child's misconception by telling him the difference between a pony and a week-old filly. He had a more important goal in mind.

"You're trespassing," he said.

The kid's big brown eyes grew indignant. "Not trepsassing," he said then frowned. "What's trepsassing?"

"Being where you're not supposed to be."

"I was visiting."

"You could have gotten hurt."

The kid gave Caleb a look that appeared to question Caleb's sanity. "That little pony couldn't hurt me."

"Her mother could and she would have, too, if I hadn't come along and grabbed you."

The little boy's face lit up and he gave a little hop of excitement. "That was fun! Can we do it again?"

"No!"

Stymied, Caleb stared down at the boy. He didn't seem scared or even intimidated. He thought the whole terrifying episode had been fun!

The boy tilted his head back to look up

at him and then stuck out his hand. "My name's Sam," he said. "Me and my mom live over yonder."

Yonder? Who had this kid been talking to? Caleb put out his hand to shake Sam's but before they made contact the noise of someone crashing through the brush caught his attention. He looked over to see a woman racing toward them. She barely seemed to notice the greasewood and acacia branches that whipped against her legs and plucked at her jeans and shirt as she ran. When she saw that Caleb knew she was there, she slowed to a fast walk, her chest heaving with the effort of fighting for breath. She lifted a hand in acknowledgment.

As she neared, Caleb had the chance to observe her. She was tall, maybe five-eight, and more full-figured than skinny. Her hair was dark brown shot with sorrel red and pulled back into a ponytail that swung as she moved. Her features were strong, with a straight nose and full lips. He would call her good-looking rather than pretty, if he was going to call her anything—which he wasn't. He could tell right away where her son had gotten his big brown eyes.

Because he found himself admiring her looks, he scowled at her. He didn't want this kind of complication, didn't need it and didn't need this woman and her kid right next door. He'd liked it when the old Reynolds place had been empty and forlorn. It suited his purposes—and his disposition—just fine.

"Thank…thank you for gr-grab…bing him out of the way," the woman said, gasping for breath as she hurried up to them. She pressed a hand to her side where she must have developed a cramp. "I…I didn't realize what was happening. I th-thought you didn't see him and might run him down… then I saw that mare and colt."

Against his will, Caleb was touched by her concern for her son and by the flush of exertion on her cheeks.

"It's a filly," Caleb said.

She blinked and her head drew back. "Oh, of course, a filly." She looked at him for a couple of seconds as if she expected him to say more. When he remained silent, she turned to her son, going down on one knee in front of him and grasping his shoulders so that he was forced to look at her.

"Sam, what did I tell you about leaving our property?"

He screwed up his face. "What's property?"

Her eyes narrowed. "Don't you try to be tricky. I've told you many times in the past few days that our property is our house and yard and that's where you're supposed to stay."

The little boy turned his head, avoiding his mother's firm gaze. "Maybe I forgot."

"Maybe?"

He jerked his small thumb toward the mare and her foal. "That pony wanted me to come play."

"How do you know that?"

"'Cause I just know," he said stubbornly.

She sighed. "Never mind what the pony wants. *I* want you to stay in our yard." She forced him to keep eye contact with her for a few more seconds. When his gaze skittered guiltily away from hers, she said, "We'll talk about this at home. You're going to be in time-out."

"Aw, Mom," Sam said in an injured voice, sticking out his bottom lip and crossing his arms over his chest.

She turned to Caleb and held out her hand. "I apologize for my son. I'm Delaney Reynolds—Laney to my friends—and this is Sam. You're Caleb Ransom, right?"

Caleb looked down at that hand—long-fingered with unpolished nails. It looked competent, as did she. Deep inside him something stirred, reacting to the intensity of her. He hadn't experienced this emotion for a long, long time, but he knew it for exactly what it was—longing.

He kept his arms firmly at his sides until her open smile faded.

She finally dropped her proffered hand to her son's head.

"Yes, I'm Caleb Ransom," he acknowledged with a nod. "This is my property. Your son could have been in real danger."

Again her head pulled back at his curt tone and she stammered out an apology. "I realize that and I'm very sorry…"

Caleb tilted his head toward Addie. "That mare doesn't like anyone coming around her foal. She'll hardly let *me* come near. If Sam had gotten too close, she would've head-butted him or, worse, kicked him."

Her face had been flushed from running, but now it paled. "I…I didn't…"

"Have either of you ever been around horses before?"

"Yes, of course." Her arms came up to cross over her chest, mimicking her son's stance. Caleb decided not to see how charming that was.

"Then you should have some idea how dangerous it is for a little kid like this to run up and surprise a mare. You don't have any idea what could happen, do you? Which is why you need to stay on your own property."

Anger sparked in her eyes.

Good, he thought. Maybe that meant she'd stay away.

"We will certainly stay on our own property," she said, reaching to take her son's hand. "Won't we, Sam?"

Silence. Both adults looked down at the bent head hiding under the black hat. Laney cupped her son's chin, lifting his face so that his eyes met hers. His brow wrinkled and his nose crinkled as he gazed at his mom.

Caleb wondered if the little guy was trying to figure out how to sound as though he was agreeing with his mom without really agreeing with her.

"Won't we, Sam?" she repeated.

"Okay, Mommy," he said.

She looked up and met Caleb's gaze. "Thank you again for saving my son's life. We'll stay off your property and leave you alone."

"It's best if you stay out of this pasture," he said, emphasizing this point. She, and this boy, disturbed him. "Be a good idea if you passed that along to your husband, too."

Her dark eyes flashed angrily. "I'm not married. Goodbye, Mr. Ransom," she said, turning and pulling her son with her. The boy went willingly enough, but after a few steps, she swung him up into her arms, transferring him smoothly to her hip, her head bending close to his as she walked, his short legs bumping against her with each step.

Caleb wondered if she was reminding her son to stay off the neighbor's land, or if the two of them were discussing what a mean old grump he was. Either way, he didn't care so long as they left him alone.

He swung onto Cisco's back, ready to ride away. It was impossible for him to keep his eyes off the pair of them, though. Their heads were close together, her dark hair shining in the sun. She strode confidently ahead, her arm holding the boy safe. They were a solid unit of two.

Suddenly, Sam twisted in his mom's arms, whipped off his hat and lifted an arm to wave at Caleb.

"I'll see you later, Mr. Ramson," he called, mangling Caleb's name. His big brown eyes, shock of dark hair and wide grin were like a punch to Caleb's gut. He nearly doubled over in the saddle.

Memory washed over him, making his breath cut through his lungs like a sharp blade. With iron will, he shoved the image that had seared his mind back to the place where he kept it secured. Still, it was several long seconds before he could wrestle the image of desert sand, hot sun and the face of a grinning little boy into the vault. Finally he straightened and gathered Cisco's reins into his hands.

He'd worked long and hard to get this peaceful little corner of the world, and he wasn't going to let them disrupt it. He clucked his tongue and headed Cisco toward home.

Fifteen minutes later Sam was still sitting in the time-out chair, stealing sidelong glances at his mother and punctuating the air with aggrieved sighs. For her part, Laney had almost stopped shaking from the combination of fright for her son and anger at her neighbor.

"The man certainly has the right to his privacy," she muttered as she trimmed shelf paper to fit a kitchen cabinet. "But does he have to be so rude?"

"Maybe he needs to sit in the naughty chair," Sam said brightly. "I could go tell him."

Laney pointed a purposeful finger at him. "You stay right where you are, young man. You're not going anywhere."

Sam frowned and settled down with another sigh. He spread his knees out to each side of the small chair seat and leaned over to look underneath it. Then he started to kick a leg with each foot, thump-thump, thump-thump, thump-thump in rhythm.

"Wish I had somebody to play with," he said, peeking at his mom. She didn't respond. "I wanna play with Logan and Shane."

"You'll see them soon enough."

"Does Mr. Ramson have kids?"

Laney paused and glanced at him. Sam

had scooted so far forward on the chair and stuck his head so far under the stool that he was in danger of landing on his head.

"It's Ransom," she corrected him. "Now, Sam, sit up straight." When he complied, she said, "And I don't know if he has kids for you to play with."

"He looked mean."

Laney wasn't sure what to say. She didn't want Sam to be afraid of their neighbor, but she didn't want him to be a pest, either. She certainly wanted Sam to stay on their property. It was impossible to keep him safe if she didn't know where he was. Raising a boy was a bigger challenge than she'd ever anticipated.

Sam was right. Ransom *did* look mean.

"What's that guy's problem, anyway?" Laney muttered. She finished lining the shelf, stacked the plates neatly inside and closed the door with a satisfied snap, then ran her hand over the worn surface of the birchwood.

The cabinets were probably much older than she was, no doubt original to the house, which had been built in the early 1950s by her great uncle, Calvin Reynolds, and left to her when he passed away last year. Everything about the place showed its age, but it was solidly built, the roof was only a few years old and her dad, brother and friends had gotten together and surprised her with a new paint job, inside and out. Somehow, they'd known her favorite colors and which ones to paint on the walls of which rooms. That had probably been her mom's influence, since she and Vivian had spent hours discussing décor, design and color choices.

But best of all, the house was hers; security for Sam and for her. Now the money she'd been spending on rent for that apartment in town could go into savings and into Sam's college fund, where most of the child support money from Sam's father went. It was another brick in the solid foundation of protection she was building for her son.

She had a good job—two good jobs—friends and family. She had a retirement fund, life insurance and a will giving custody of Sam to her brother Ethan and his wife if anything should happen to her. Now she had a house and land. There was a good pasture she could rent out to a neighbor if she wished, with a small freshwater

stream—a rarity in southern Arizona—that
dried up or just trickled most of the year but
ran full during the summer monsoon rains.
She remembered playing in the creek as a
child and hoped to give Sam that same pleasure in a few weeks—if she could keep him
in one piece until then.

She was grateful for the financial security she now had and for the family members
who had stood by her, helped and supported
her throughout her life and throughout every
stupid mistake she had made. They had
showed her love and compassion every day
of her life. They had also ingrained in her
the belief that God had put people on earth
to help each other.

She glanced up guiltily, her gaze traveling
to Caleb's pasture, which she could see from
her kitchen window. Maybe she should give
some consideration to showing her neighbor
some compassion.

Caleb Ransom. She had barely given him
a moment's thought since she'd moved in,
but now that she'd met him she couldn't get
him off her mind.

Laney tried to think back over what she
had heard about him. She had been so busy

with her move that she hadn't given much thought to any of her neighbors. She already knew Chet and Karen Bartlett who lived in the first house nearest the road and had named their lane after themselves. Their son had been in her English class—she taught high school in Sweetsilver. It was a town where everyone knew everyone else, but few people knew Caleb Ransom.

Bartlett Lane dead-ended at his place. Anyone who went that far was only going to his ranch. In the few days she'd been in her house, no one had passed on their way to see Caleb. No one seemed to interact with him except maybe Don Parkey, the local vet who took care of everyone's animals—unless Caleb doctored his own animals as she knew many ranchers did.

Either Caleb was naturally a grump or he was a deeply troubled man. And she had seen something in his eyes, a spark of... something that had both puzzled her and drawn her to him. He'd extinguished that spark with a frown, but it had only ignited her curiosity about him.

In spite of his attitude, though, he had saved Sam's life. He didn't want her and

Sam to trespass, but she felt she owed him gratitude for saving her adventurous little boy. And then there was that insatiable curiosity of hers that she probably shouldn't feed—but knew she would.

Laney glanced over at her son, who had now moved off the chair except for the tip of his big toe, which was still touching one of the legs. She knew she should warn Ransom that today's visit probably wouldn't be the last he'd receive from her son.

Sam must have felt her gaze on him because he looked up. All Laney did was point to the chair and he climbed back on with another wounded growl.

Ignoring his theatrics, she returned to the cabinet and took down a bowl. She knew how to make a terrific chocolate cake.

CALEB LOOKED INTO the pot of chili he'd been attempting to make and wondered what had gone wrong. Maybe he'd put in too much chili powder. Except that it wasn't red like chili powder. It was dark, really dark, and resembled industrial waste. He had to eat it, though, or go into town and buy a meal, which meant being around people—something he wasn't willing to do. Meeting his neighbor and her kid today had fulfilled his quota of socializing for the month, unless Don Parkey showed up with another half-dead horse.

Resigned, he took a bowl from the cupboard and used a coffee cup to ladle out a generous portion. He knew he couldn't go without eating. He'd learned that in Afghanistan when he'd been on patrol for hours with no food and very little water. Light-headedness didn't allow good decision-making. He only hoped this chili didn't taste as bad as it looked, but he was afraid that it probably did. Grabbing a spoon from a drawer and two cold beers, because it would take more than one to choke down this stuff, he sat at the table, took a deep breath and dug in.

The first mouthful gagged him and brought tears to his eyes. Salt. He'd put in way too much. And he'd put in chili powder, all right, along with a big dose of cayenne. Caleb dropped the spoon and stared down at the mess.

"Face it, Ransom. You can't cook. You'll be eating canned and frozen for the rest of your life, or worse, army surplus MREs," he said. Even the Meals Ready to Eat he'd hated the most had tasted better than this.

He looked across the kitchen to where his dog, Bertie, a mystery mix of breeds, lay sleeping. As if the animal could read his thoughts, he raised his head and gave Caleb a look that clearly said, "Don't even think about it."

"You're not interested, either, huh?"

Before Caleb could give any more thought about what to do, Bertie lumbered to his feet and emitted a low *woof* to indicate someone was coming. His duty done, he collapsed back onto his rug and closed his eyes.

Caleb's chair scraped on the linoleum as he stood and went to the window. It couldn't be Don; he never showed up this late in the day. Through the uncurtained window, he saw a well-traveled Jeep pull up. After a few seconds his new neighbor and her son stepped out.

The little boy looked around, spied a stick on the ground and picked it up. He waved it around for a few seconds, then tossed it in the air with a whoop of laughter and watched it land near the porch.

"No," Caleb grumbled. His gut roiled.

Hadn't he been clear that he didn't want company? What kind of woman came back for more? And brought her child. A desperate one? A crazy one?

Or, the most unthinkable prospect, one who wanted to rescue him?

"Oh, man," he said, running his hand through his hair and looking around. He couldn't pretend he wasn't home. The light was on and his truck was out front. If she looked in the kitchen window, she'd see him standing there, gaping at her.

He watched as she opened a back door of her Jeep and carefully took something off the seat. When she straightened and slammed the door with a swing of her hip, he saw that it was a cake. A chocolate one.

His traitorous stomach growled in anticipation.

He walked to the front door and opened it. Sam bounced up the steps and greeted him with a big grin.

"See, Mr. Ramson?" the boy said. "I told you I'd see you later. Mom says this is later, but it's not tomorrow yet. 'Cause I checked."

Flummoxed, Caleb looked down at the eager little boy. He'd cleaned up since their encounter in the pasture. He carried his cowboy hat and he wore a pair of blue shorts and a bright red T-shirt with a bronc-riding cowboy on the front. In place of the boots, he wore sandals and his thick hair had been inexpertly slicked down and combed. No doubt, he'd done it himself.

He looked so happy, healthy...whole, that a huge lump formed in Caleb's throat. Well, he'd shoved away the memory earlier that afternoon and he wasn't going to let it surface now. He glanced away from the boy and into the half-apologetic face of his mother.

She had changed clothes, too. Instead of the jeans and T-shirt she'd worn to chase her son across the pasture, she wore a simple, sleeveless blue dress that buttoned up the front and fell in a swirl of skirt to below her knees.

Laney gave an ironic little twist of her lips. "Before you say anything, yes, you made it clear that you don't want company or trespassers, and I'm not ignoring what you said, but I came to thank you again for keeping Sam from getting hurt."

Caleb looked at the sincerity in her eyes and the gentle curve of her lips. Her face looked ready to break into a smile with the tiniest encouragement from him. He glanced down at Sam, who returned his regard with a big, innocent grin. The scent of chocolate nearly sent him to his knees.

Caleb wanted to take the cake from Laney and shut the door.

"I know seeing him in danger of being attacked by your mare probably scared you. Whenever he scares the life out of me, I feel snappy, too." Her smile widened, lighting her eyes, inviting him to share her rueful humor at her son's actions.

This woman was willing to credit him with an excuse for his rudeness.

Behind him, he could hear Bertie's nails clicking on the linoleum. "A dog!" Sam shrieked, scooting past Caleb and into the living room, even as his mother tried to call him back. Laney hurried after him, trying to make a grab for her son, but was hampered by the cake she still carried. Focused on the little boy, she shoved the cake at Caleb, who had no choice but to take it.

Before Laney could pull Sam away, her son fell on Bertie like a long-lost best friend.

He threw his arms around the animal's neck and gave him a hug.

Bertie turned his head and gave the boy a lick on the side of the face that sealed their bond. Laughing, Sam wiped his cheek. "He likes me. I want a dog," he told Caleb with a sigh. "But my mom says I'm not ponsible."

Puzzled, Caleb looked at Laney, whose cheeks had reddened. "Responsible," she answered his unspoken question.

"What's his name?" Sam asked. He sat back on his heels to admire what he certainly considered to be the most beautiful animal on earth.

"Bertie."

Sam buried his face in the canine's neck. "I love you, Bertie."

"I'm sorry about this," Laney said. "Come on, Sam. We need to go and leave Mr. Ransom alone." She indicated his big rancher's hands. "I hope you like chocolate cake."

He looked down at the thick swirls of frosting. All he wanted was to be left alone, to stop her and her son from trespassing.

If he took this cake, he'd be taking a step forward he wasn't ready to take.

For the second time that day.

CHAPTER TWO

"WE WOULD LOVE to join you," Laney told him with a warm smile. All right, so he hadn't exactly invited them in to join him, but he hadn't kicked them out, either. She was thrilled. This was going much better than she had anticipated given their earlier encounter.

He stood there, staring at her openmouthed for a moment. Then, abruptly, he turned toward the kitchen.

Laney's gaze followed him. This was the first time she'd seen him walk a few steps and she noticed that he did it with a pronounced limp that favored his right leg. She wondered if he'd had this since birth or if he'd been in an accident. Somehow, the stiffness with which he walked told her he was still getting used to this change in his body and she wondered if it was a fairly recent injury. But she knew she couldn't ask.

Earlier, she'd been too frantic about her son to really notice the man, and then she'd been furious with him and his rudeness.

Now, as she watched him, she saw that he was a few inches taller than she was, putting him at maybe six feet. His face looked tough, she would even say hard, but she hadn't really been able to get a good look at him earlier because the sun had been in her eyes and his face had been shaded by his hat. She had thought his eyes were filled with shadows, but maybe she'd been attempting to give him characteristics that would account for his prickly attitude.

Glancing around, she saw that Sam was busy scratching Bertie's stomach. The dog had rolled over onto his back and hung his paws in the air. His head lolled to the side and his tongue protruded in cartoonish contentment. Sam looked equally ecstatic. Knowing he would be therefore safe for a little while, she followed Caleb from the room.

Laney looked around Caleb's kitchen without appearing to be examining it as closely as she was. The house was about the same age as hers, but nothing here had been upgraded or freshened up. The wallpaper was a splash of huge flowers in avocado green and harvest gold à la 1970s. The appliances had to be that old, too, as was the worn linoleum. The kitchen was squeaky clean, though.

On the scrubbed top of the wooden table sat a bowl of some dark substance and two beers.

She turned to him in consternation. "Oh, we've interrupted your dinner."

"It wasn't worth eating." Caleb set the cake down on the counter, found some small, mismatched plates and opened a drawer. He took out three forks, gazed at his collection of knives and then at her.

"Any one will do," she said with a smile. "Would you like me to cut it?"

"Sure." He handed over a knife and while she cut the cake, he removed the bowl from the table.

"What's wrong with the chili?"

"You could recognize what it was?"

Her eyes twinkled. "The beans gave it away."

"I guess I'm not much of a cook. It looks weird and it's way too salty—and too full of cayenne."

"If you have a potato, you can cut it up

and simmer it in the chili. Remove it when it's soft and it'll take out some of the salt. If you've got more diced tomatoes, you can add those, too. They'll help the appearance and the taste and water down the saltiness—though probably nothing will tone down the spiciness." She handed him a plate. "And while it's simmering, you can enjoy a chocolate cake appetizer."

For the first time his eyes met hers. She saw that they were dark gray like the sky before a summer rainstorm. Sadness and regret lurked in them. She'd been angry at him because he'd been rude to her and Sam, but the torment she thought she'd seen in his eyes at their first encounter and again now told her his moodiness came from deep pain. His expression was wary and guarded. As she looked at him, really seeing his features for the first time, she noticed the scar that ran down the side of his face and ended at the right corner of his mouth. What had happened to this man? Her heart filled with compassion.

He must have sensed what she was thinking because he glanced away. "I'll try that," he said. "Like I said, I'm not much of a cook."

He set his plate down, grabbed a potato

from a bin beneath the sink, scrubbed and sliced it and put it in the chili pot, along with a can of diced tomatoes.

Laney placed small slices of cake on two other plates and called Sam in to join them. He came, bent at an awkward angle, half dragging, half walking with Bertie, his arms still wrapped around the long-suffering animal's neck. "Can Bertie have cake, too?"

"No, dogs can't eat chocolate," Laney said. "It's bad for them."

"Can I have his piece?"

"No."

Sam's arms fell away from Bertie's neck and dropped stiffly to his sides. "Why can't I have two pieces?"

"It's not your cake. Mr. Ransom is kindly sharing it with us. You can have one piece." She waved the plate gently in the air. "Or you can have none." She hid the plate behind her back.

His bottom lip started to jut out but Laney gave him a steady look that helped his decision. "One," he said as if he'd thought of it himself.

"Good choice. Wash your hands."

"Where's the bathroom?"

She looked questioningly at Caleb, who pointed the way, and Sam skipped off in that direction.

Laney considered following and assisting him, but knew she needed to give him a little bit of leeway without hovering. When she heard the sound of water running, she turned back to the kitchen table.

As soon as she did, Sam broke into a loud, off-key rendition of the alphabet song.

She winced. "Sorry. There's something about running water that always makes him want to sing. I taught him the ABC song and told him he had to sing it all the way through while washing his hands. That made him love water, I guess. He would *live* in the shower if I'd let him." She pressed her lips together as she realized she'd shared way more than he could possibly want to know.

Caleb's eyes were steady on her face. "He's quite a kid."

She rolled her eyes. "You have no idea. I sometimes have the horrible feeling that he's already smarter than I am."

Caleb smiled; a lift of the lips that curled up more on the left. Laney realized that the scar must have changed the way he smiled, stiffening the right side of his mouth. It was crooked and endearing. Her heart gave an unaccustomed flutter.

Disconcerted, she turned away. Sam shut off the water and quit his song in midsyllable. He dashed into the kitchen and clambered onto a chair. "I'm ready!" he sang out as if the world had been waiting breathlessly for his return. "Can I have some of that?" he asked, pointing to the beer. "Uh, please?"

Taken aback, Caleb said, "No."

"Samuel John!" Laney said.

The little boy divided a confused look between them at what he clearly considered to be an overreaction. "What *can* I have to drink?"

"I've got lemonade. It's powdered." Caleb gave Laney a questioning look.

"Lemonade would be great," she said, not able to imagine having beer with cake.

Caleb took two tall glasses from the cabinet, looked at Sam's small hands, put one glass back and removed a plastic juice glass. After filling both glasses with ice and lemonade, he brought them to the table, stopping to give his chili a stir.

When Caleb joined them, Sam picked up

his fork and said, "My mom makes cake real good. But you have to use a napkin to wipe your face. It's rude to lick off the frosting. I used to do that when I was a little kid." His eyes narrowed as he looked at Caleb. "You're not gonna lick off the frosting, are you? 'Cause that'll make my mom mad. You *don't* wanna see her get mad."

"Sam…" Laney said in a warning tone.

He gave her another questioning look, wondering what he'd said wrong *this* time.

"I'll remember that," Caleb said, his eyes meeting Laney's. He picked up his fork and took a bite of cake. "He's right. It's good."

Pleased, Laney ate her own piece. The three of them sat in companionable silence. She thought this was a very domestic scene for three people who had been at odds a couple of hours ago.

"Are you settling into your house okay?" Caleb asked awkwardly. Small talk was clearly not his forte.

He reminded her of one of her freshmen students, giving a presentation in front of the entire class for the first time. She decided to take pity on him since teachers are accustomed to taking charge of a conversation.

"Yes. We lived in a small apartment before, so we didn't have much to move in and it was easy to get settled. There are still some things I want to do." She launched into a description of her plans for her house, which she realized couldn't possibly interest anyone but her, but as she talked, she saw him relax.

"We're gonna put pictures of cowboys on my wall in my new room," Sam announced. "Can I put your picture on my wall? You and Bertie?" He glanced down at his new best friend, so he missed the look of consternation that flashed across Caleb's face.

Laney couldn't imagine what had caused their new neighbor to look like that. She felt as if she was picking her way through booby traps, careful not to get caught by one or to let her son get hurt. And yet there was something about the way Caleb looked at Sam that told her he would never hurt the boy—a sort of sad longing mixed with regret. And it clutched at her heart to see that Caleb could only look at Sam for a few seconds before glancing away.

"We've got plenty of cowboy pictures, Sammy," she said. "If you've finished your cake, why don't you take your plate to the sink so I can wash it before we go?"

Sam hopped down to do as she asked, then hurried back to Bertie, who had pulled himself to his feet. The dog walked into the living room with Sam trotting along behind.

She turned back to their host, whose haunted eyes followed her son. This was a troubled man. It was clear to her that coming here had been a mistake. She had done the neighborly thing, but it was over now. From this point on, she and Sam would keep their distance.

She stood and said brightly, "Sam and I had better be on our way. I'll wash these dishes up before we go."

"No, that isn't necessary. I'll take care of it." Caleb surged to his feet, his right leg twisting awkwardly. His breath hissed from between his teeth and he reached out to grab the back of his chair, but it skidded away from his grasping fingers. He would have fallen if Laney hadn't leaped to his side, wrapped her arm around his waist and braced herself against him.

There was nothing for Caleb to do except put his arm around her shoulders. She heard his ragged breath rasp in his throat as he tried to gain control over the surge of pain she knew must be racking his body. His arm spasmed and his hand gripped her shoulder. When she looked up, she saw that sweat had popped out on his face.

Turning carefully, she reached for his chair and pulled it close so he could sit. It took him a minute, though, because he had to rest all his weight on his left leg as he stretched out his right. A tight, pale line appeared around his mouth when he clamped his lips together—probably to keep from crying out in pain.

Turning, she grabbed another chair, pulled it close and then bent to lift his leg. Holding the back of his knee with one hand and his ankle with the other, she gently raised his leg to rest on the chair. She knew he probably would have protested if the pain hadn't obviously stolen his breath.

"Thank…thank you," Caleb said when he could get air back into his lungs.

"Can I get you anything?" she asked, stepping back because she instinctively knew he would hate it if she hovered.

He shook his head, his eyes avoiding hers.

"Then I suppose Sam and I had better go. I have to read him *Goodnight Moon* and then half a dozen books about cowboys before he goes to sleep…" Her voice trailed off. The man clearly wanted to be alone and she was only prolonging things. "Well, good night."

Caleb's eyes finally turned to her, guarded and full of pain. She fought the urge to bustle around getting him an ice pack or a hot compress for his leg—to do something to help. She mustn't, though. He didn't want her help and he certainly didn't want her pity.

"Thank you," was all he said.

She didn't know if it was for the cake, the visit, for catching him so he wouldn't fall or because she was finally leaving. Feeling as if she was abandoning him, she turned, crossed into the living room and collected her son, scooping him up from his place beside Bertie and setting him on his feet.

"Time to go, sport," she said brightly, capturing his hand. "Say goodbye."

"Aw, Mom. Me and Bertie was gonna…"

"Say goodbye," she repeated, sweeping him toward the door.

"Goodbye—"

The word was barely out of Sam's mouth before she whirled him out the door and closed it behind them. She hustled him across the porch and down the steps to the Jeep, lifted him inside and strapped him into his booster seat. She jumped in behind the wheel, fastened her seat belt and had them on their way within seconds.

"Is somebody chasing us, Mom?" Sam asked. He tried to twist to look behind them. "Is it the bad guys?"

She laughed and hoped it sounded genuine. "No, of course not. It was time to go, that's all."

"Oh, okay." He sat back. "I love Bertie," he said with a sigh of happiness.

"Okay, but you don't go visit him without being invited." She didn't know how to tell him that such an invitation almost certainly wouldn't be forthcoming. All she could do was hope he'd forget about Bertie if she kept him busy with other things.

Her neighbor wanted to be left alone to deal with whatever was bothering him. She would respect that and she would do her best to make sure Sam understood.

As she turned into her drive, though, she

wondered how recent the injury to his leg was and how it had happened. Although she was pretty sure it hadn't been that long ago, the faint scar on his face wasn't new. What on earth had the man been through?

CALEB'S EYES JERKED open with a start, his right hand flying out to search for his rifle. When his hand didn't close on the familiar stock, he came fully awake, his heart pounding as he tried to make sense of his surroundings. He didn't need his gun. He needed to find that kid—the little dark-haired boy with the big grin who'd invaded his dreams. He shook his head, trying to free himself from the image of the child waving then disappearing in the flash of a fireball. He groaned, trying to orient himself.

Home. He was home at his own place, not on guard or on patrol in Afghanistan, not sleeping on the ground beneath a Hummer with O'Malley's stinking feet near his face.

He started to turn over, but a strong twinge from his bad leg had him falling back against the pillows with a sharp breath whistling between his teeth. After several minutes the spasm passed and he was able to sit up, massage his tortured leg for a while, then turn to put his feet on the floor and sit with his elbows resting on his knees, his head in his hands.

When the pain subsided, he lifted his head to glance at the clock. Midnight. He'd only been asleep a couple of hours. It was those blasted painkillers. Whenever he had to take them, as he had right after Laney and Sam had left, they knocked him out, but then he'd jerk awake too soon, sure he was back in a war zone. He'd be half off the bed, looking for his soldiers, before reason would kick in and he'd know where he was.

Most of the time he could keep the memories at bay, but often they'd plague his sleep, coming in nightmare form, seeping under his defenses like smoke curling beneath a closed door. He knew if he opened the door, the memories would blaze up in a flash fire to consume him.

Taking a painkiller before he slept almost always triggered the nightmares, but they came more often when he took nothing at all.

Caleb rubbed his palms over his face, shoved his feet into the worn-out slip-ons he kept next to the bed and then stood cautiously, waiting for his leg to become accustomed to his weight once again, before walking through the house to work out the stiffness. Down the hall, past the two empty bedrooms, he moved into the living room, where he stood in front of the big window—uncurtained because he had no clue how to go about buying drapes and had no desire to learn.

As he stared out at the yard, he heard coyotes, the bothersome pack that roamed the area and had probably been responsible for the disappearance of many domestic animals. No doubt, the predators had dens in the nearby Mule Mountains, where they hid out, waiting for some unsuspecting cat or jackrabbit to happen by—

A sudden scream split the air, sparking a shiver up Caleb's spine. That sound wasn't made by a coyote, but he didn't know what *had* made it since he'd never heard it before.

It came again, high and sharp. It wasn't human, but it ignited a memory of a fire fight, of Mack, wounded, fallen, clutching his side as he tried to swallow cries of anguish that would attract more enemy fire to their position.

Memories overwhelming him, Caleb rushed to the door, grabbing his rifle on his way out. He didn't know where the attack would be coming from, but he was ready. Crouching, moving stealthily, he slipped off the porch and hunkered down into a shooting stance as far as his bad leg would let him. His gaze swept the yard then the area beyond.

He saw something ahead of him, moving through the low bushes, too fast and steady to be a man doing the belly crawl. What was it?

The creature turned its head. Caleb saw the flash of yellow eyes. It wasn't human. But what was it? Confused, he stepped forward. The crack of a stick breaking under his foot snapped in the air and jerked Caleb back to reality.

Whatever he'd seen in the yard disappeared with a gentle whoosh of sound.

He shook his head, trying to clear the cobwebs, working to recall why he was standing out in the yard in his underwear. He glanced down. He held a piece of one-by-two-inch board, the one he used to prop open the living-room window.

Hands falling to his sides, he stood for a minute, concentrating on his breathing, letting his waking nightmare dissipate as he shoved the memory back into the mental vault where he kept it under lock and key.

His gaze moved out past the yard and the barn to the pasture where he'd encountered Sam and Laney earlier, then beyond to their house where a porch light speared the darkness. He couldn't even see the outline of the house, only the glow of the light, a faint beacon of reassurance.

Reassurance? He didn't need reassurance. He needed to be left alone.

He lifted the board, holding it up in front of his face. He'd thought it was his rifle; that he was going to protect his home with it.

No. He couldn't be a neighbor. It wasn't time yet.

He turned back to the house with a sound of disgust, returned the board to the sill of the window, which he double-checked to make sure it was closed and locked.

Bertie, asleep on his favorite rug, raised his head as if willing to commiserate, but then apparently decided that Caleb was doing a good enough job of being miserable on his own. He dropped his head on his paws and sighed.

Caleb looked down at the old dog. "Yeah, buddy, that's how I feel."

He wandered into the kitchen and poured a glass of water. Leaning against the sink, he drank it down, grateful for the miracle of clean, good-tasting water, so unlike the filtered, never-quite-right stuff they'd had in Afghanistan.

Like all the other military personnel, they'd consumed bottled water by the gallon, along with electrolyte drinks. When he'd come back to the States, he'd never been able to get enough clean water into him and he still drank more than he ever had in his younger years. He set the empty glass down and stood with his hands gripping the edge of the sink. The memories were close tonight and he couldn't seem to shove them away as he usually could. He'd been back for more than a year and a half, but as his mother had said, he'd left the war but he'd never really come home.

Pushing away from the sink, he wandered

back to the living-room window and stood, arms crossed over his chest, staring into the darkness while he thought about his new neighbors.

"What do you think, Bert? You think she ever had a husband?"

He glanced down. Bertie's gentle snores told him that this man's best friend couldn't have been less interested.

In spite of that, Caleb continued with his speculation. "Did the guy abandon her and Sam? Didn't care that he had a wife and kid?"

Caleb's eyes narrowed as he thought it over. "Maybe she was impossible to live with." He straightened, his arms dropping to his sides as another thought came to him. "Or did she always want to be a single mom so she got some clinical assistance?"

He ran his thumb along the stubble on his chin. "Nothing wrong with that, Bert. But, nah, I don't think so. I think…that I'm losing my friggin' mind."

Caleb admitted he was out of his element and had been for a while.

At one time he'd had an unerring sense of direction, a built-in compass that could point him the right way even if it was pitch-black outside and only safe to move a few inches. Now he tried to defend his home from night noises with a stick and stood staring at his neighbor's house.

And he didn't even care about his neighbors.

He turned, headed back to bed, giving in to the twinge in his leg that told him he'd been on it too long and ignoring the one in his gut that told him he was a liar.

BY THE NEXT afternoon Laney thought she may have convinced her son that he wasn't to visit Caleb, or Bertie, until he was invited. She had left him inside to play with a building set he was using to make a replica of Caleb's place.

Sam had only seen the yard and the house, but in his imagination it contained endless corrals made of snap-together pieces of plastic fencing, as well as a barn of cardboard and masking tape.

With a few minutes to herself, she decided to take a break from organizing her house and get her turn-outs ready for the coming fire season. During the summers when school was out, Laney was a wild-land firefighter, a member of Fire Team 8, currently an all-woman group that fought wildfires during the summer. There had been men on the team in the past and there probably would be again, but right now, it was all women who, like Laney, had families and additional jobs. The money from fighting fires paid for both necessities and luxuries.

She spread her coat, pants and boots out on the patio attached to the back of the house and examined them closely for damage. Her fire boots appeared to be in good shape, as did her coat, but there was a rip in her pants caused when she'd fallen over a log last summer and snagged them on a broken branch. She thought she could mend it.

Laney stepped back into the house for her sewing kit, calling out to Sam as she went.

"Sam, everything okay?"

Silence.

Whirling around, she hurried to his room. His construction project lay scattered across the floor, but he wasn't there. His black cowboy hat was gone from the top of the dresser where he left it when he wasn't wearing it. That told her exactly where he was headed. He was so taken with the whole cowboy mystique that he wouldn't have left without that hat if he had gone to visit Caleb and Bertie, and she was sure that was exactly what he had done.

He had probably only left a few minutes ago, but she knew from long experience that he could move like the wind when he wanted to. If she took the Jeep and hurried, she might make it to Caleb's house before Sam did. Having his mother greet him when he arrived would be an unpleasant surprise that might make him think twice about going over there without permission again.

"And maybe pigs will fly," Laney muttered as she ran to get her keys. "So much for keeping our distance from Caleb Ransom." She had tried to impress on her son that their neighbor wanted to be left alone, but clearly she hadn't succeeded.

Laney knew that in this rural area, neighbors often had to depend on each other, but Caleb didn't want that. She thought he was probably embarrassed that she had seen him in pain last night, had seen him weak and vulnerable. Having Sam pop up there again, with her chasing him, might make things even more strained.

That wasn't her biggest worry, though. She was most concerned that Sam had gone back to the pasture where Caleb kept his horses. She ran out to the fence, climbed up to balance herself on the rail and scanned the area for the mare and her foal. She spotted them quite close by with no little black cowboy hat bouncing toward them, so she knew Sam probably wasn't in the pasture.

"Thank heaven," she murmured, jumping down and running for the Jeep.

Starting the engine, she wheeled out of the drive and headed for the Ransom ranch.

Only a few yards down the single-lane road she had to squeeze past a car pulled over and stopped partway in a ditch. Driving past, she saw that someone was inside so she stopped, jumped out of her car and hurried back to ask if the driver had seen Sam.

When she recognized the driver, her steps slowed and her heart sank in dismay, but she forced a smile. Monette Berkley had been her neighbor in the tiny apartment building where she and Sam had lived in town. She was a busybody, a long-time social worker employed by Arizona's newly revamped and name-changed Department of Child Safety, and she delighted in spying on her neighbors.

She was a definite oddball, but Laney didn't think she meant any harm—although she couldn't imagine what the woman was doing out here, and there was no time to find out. As she approached, she noticed that Monette's appearance, always haphazard, was approaching sloppy. Her hair slid out of a loose topknot and the front of her blouse was stained with what looked like coffee.

Leaning over, she said, "Hello, Monette. Did you see my little boy on the road?"

"Your little boy? You mean Sean?"

"Sam," Laney corrected. "Yes. He's the only little boy I've got."

"What's he doing off by himself?" the woman demanded, her dark eyes narrowing suspiciously. "Why aren't you watching him?"

"Monette!" Laney cried in exasperation. "Did you see him?"

"No," the woman answered, looking miffed. "I only stopped a second ago. Did he run away?"

Laney whirled around. "Of course not. He probably went to visit the neighbor."

Or at least the neighbor's dog, she thought, rushing back to her car.

Monette called out to her, but Laney ignored her as she put the Jeep in gear and sped down the road to Caleb's driveway.

CALEB MOVED CAUTIOUSLY toward the front door where he'd heard scuffling noises and then a soft knock. Since his leg had seized up on him last night, he'd been moving much more carefully, trying to handle the pain and outlast the muscle seizures without resorting to more of the painkillers the doctor had given him. Aside from making him woozy and giving him nightmares, they'd probably caused him to stand by his window gawking at his neighbor's house. Besides, the pills didn't really cure anything, so why bother with them?

He finally reached the door and swung it open, his curious gaze at eye level. Seeing no one, his focus swung down to right above knee height where Sam Reynolds grinned up at him.

"Hi, Mr. Rasmon."

"Ransom," Caleb corrected automatically.

"Ransom. Can Bertie come out and play?"

Sam's huge smile and big brown eyes begged him to agree.

From behind him Bertie shuffled up, tail wagging and mouth open in his own big, doggy grin. He wiggled past Caleb to greet his new best friend, giving Sam a lick on the cheek that sent the eager boy into peals of laughter. Sam threw his arms around Bertie's neck and sighed blissfully. "I love you, Bertie."

These two were made for each other, Caleb thought sardonically, stepping onto the porch. He leaned against the doorjamb and crossed his arms. "Sam, does your mom know you're here?"

Into Bertie's furry neck, Sam mumbled something that sounded like "Maybe."

Caleb wanted to pull the boy away and get down at eye level with him, but his weakened right leg wouldn't let him do that. And if he fell, he might land on the boy. Instead he reached down, cupped Sam's chin and brought the boy's face up until their eyes met, the way he'd seen Laney do the day before. He tried to make his voice sound as firm as hers had without resorting to his army sergeant's voice.

"Sam," he repeated, "does your mom know you're here?"

"Sorta."

"Sam…"

"Maybe, sorta."

"That means no, doesn't it?" Caleb said then jerked when another thought jolted him. "Did you come through the pasture? The same pasture where Addie and her filly are? That I told you to stay out of?"

Sam wrinkled up his nose and squinted as if he was thinking about it. "You mean where that pony is? No. I came on the road. I 'membered the way."

Caleb threw his hands in the air. "That's just as dangerous. What if a car had come along?"

"I woulda moved," Sam responded as if he was talking to someone who wasn't too bright. He went back to petting Bertie, who was eating up the attention.

Caleb stared at him. As an only child of parents who had both worked long hours, he knew what it was like to be lonely and to need distraction, but this had to stop. Why didn't his mother keep him away? He was still trying to figure out what to say when he became aware of a vehicle on the road. A rooster tail of dust kicked up behind Laney's fast-moving Jeep and gravel scattered as she turned into his drive. Caleb could see her sitting forward, peering anxiously over the steering wheel, and then visibly relaxing when she saw Sam standing on the front steps with Bertie and Caleb.

On the lane behind her, he saw another car slow at his gate, wait for a few seconds, then turn around and head back the way it had come. Caleb didn't have time to ponder who that could have been because Laney was headed straight for them.

Sam turned to see his mom's fast-approaching car. "She looks mad."

"Ya think?" Caleb fought the urge to laugh at the crazy situation. He didn't want them here, didn't want to get caught up in the struggle between this lovable kid and his attractive mother. He knew the more he saw of them, the more he was going to get pulled in.

He was adamant about not getting pulled in, he reminded himself. He had every-thing carefully planned, exactly what his life would be like and who would be in it—or not.

Laney stopped the Jeep and jumped out. She strode over to the steps; her gaze never leaving Sam, whose face was buried in Bertie's accommodating neck.

"Samuel John Reynolds, what do you think you're doing?" she demanded.

"Visitin' Bertie and Mr. Ramsun."

"Ransom," Laney and Caleb said in unison. Their gazes met and skittered away from each other.

"You weren't invited. Go get in the car. We'll talk about this at home when I've had time to calm down."

Sam looked at her for a second. "Bertie wants me to stay."

"*I* want you to go. Now move," she said, tilting her head toward the Jeep.

That ended any argument. Sam trudged toward the car. She turned back to Caleb with a look of consternation. "I'm so sorry. I promise I'll find some way to keep him off your property."

Her gaze went to his leg as if she wanted to ask him how it was.

Questions, sympathy, pity were things he

didn't want. He straightened, belying his need to lean against anything for support.

He looked her straight in the eye. "Keep him off my property."

With a nod, she went back to her Jeep and got her son and herself inside in record time. She started the vehicle, turned in a wide circle and was gone.

By his feet, Bertie whined. Caleb braced himself against the doorjamb once more and leaned to run his hand over the old dog's head. "It's better this way, Bert," he said. "We don't need them complicating our life."

CHAPTER THREE

"SAM, THIS IS getting really old." Laney picked up her son and stood him in the middle of the kitchen table so she could talk to him at eye level. As soon as they had arrived home, she had sent him to sit in the naughty chair while she picked up the items she'd left on the back patio and put them away. Then she had scrubbed the kitchen sink while she tried to think of what to tell him.

It had been physically exhausting, but emotionally easier when Sam was tiny. She had made all the decisions for the two of them. Now that Sam was getting older, Laney was constantly second-guessing herself. Two things she did know: she had to keep him safe whether he wanted that or not, and she had to keep him off Caleb Ransom's property.

Now she was attempting to make that clear. Whenever he tried to avoid her gaze, she turned his face back to hers and placed her hands firmly on his shoulders, holding him in place. "You are not to leave this house without my permission. Do you understand that?"

He looked at her for a second and then nodded.

"You can't go over to Mr. Ransom's house unless I'm with you. He has…things to do and he doesn't need you underfoot."

"You sure?" Sam asked. "He hurt his leg so maybe he needs help with…"

"No, he doesn't want or need us there."

"But I like Mr. Ramsun and I *love* Bertie," Sam answered in an aggrieved tone. He looked up at her, his big brown eyes swimming with tears. "He loves me, too."

Laney dropped her head forward and closed her eyes as she took a breath. This was like trying to have a conversation with a grasshopper who kept bouncing from one place to another.

"You can't go over there without permission. You can't go see Bertie—"

"But—"

"You *can't* or you'll be in big trouble with me." Her firm tone brooked no disobedience. "Sam, there are other reasons, too."

She paused, watching emotions play across his face with heartsick dismay. She couldn't let him spend his young years the way she had, never knowing where she would be or what would be happening that day or the next, who she would be with…

She frowned, trying to think of a way to make him understand without scaring him.

Taking a deep breath she said, "Sam, as your mother, I'm the one who is supposed to take care of you, so you have to do what I say."

His bottom lip quivered. "But why?"

She paused, deciding he wasn't being defiant, merely curious. "Because little boys have to have someone to take care of them, make sure they're safe. That's my job, so I have to know where you are all the time."

He hung his head, his gaze on the table-top, and she pondered whether to tell him that other people would have to take care of him if she couldn't, but then decided against it. Her mind filled with memories of being in the backseats of strange cars, all of her worldly possessions packed into a big, black trash bag, her favorite stuffed animal clutched to her chest as she stared big-eyed at the back of the driver's head, wondering who this person was and where she was being taken this time.

No, Laney decided. She would keep that information to herself. No point in scaring him unnecessarily.

"You have to do what I say," she repeated. "Now it's time for you to say, 'Yes, Mommy.'"

"Yes, Mommy," Sam responded, but she didn't know if he would obey or not.

"Thank you." She stared at him for a few seconds as she tried to decide if there was anything more she needed to say, something more convincing, compelling. Something he wouldn't "forget." Deciding that there probably wasn't, she lifted him and set him on the floor. "Now, you go stay in your room until dinner is ready and you'd better be there when I call you."

Sam shuffled off to his room. She gazed after him, hoping and praying she'd made him understand.

THE SOUND OF gravel popping beneath tires had Laney looking out the front window. She watched as her older brother, Ethan, stopped his truck and gave a wave when he saw her.

The truck doors sprang open and his twin sons, Shane and Logan, jumped out. The twins were happy, outgoing boys with dark hair that sprung out in wild curls unless it was kept cut very short, as it was now. Having recently begun to lose their baby teeth, they each greeted their aunt with gap-toothed grins. They were two years older than Sam, but the three of them got along well.

She called to Sam that his cousins were there and went outside to say hello. So much for making Sam stay in his room until dinnertime, she thought. But some fun, positive interaction with his uncle and his cousins might take his mind off Caleb and Bertie—at least for a while.

Ethan reached into the back of his truck and removed a small bicycle, which he set on the ground. He rolled it forward and propped it against a porch post so that it was the first thing Sam saw when he came barreling through the front door.

Ethan then went back to the truck and removed two more, slightly larger, bicycles.

Sam's eyes widened as he looked at the bicycles and then at his two grinning cousins.

"Sam," Ethan said, "it's time for you to learn how to ride a bike. We thought you might like this one the boys have outgrown."

"Yeah!" Sam shrieked. "Thanks, Uncle Ethan!" He raced down the steps as Laney gave her brother a worried look.

"Don't you think he's too young, Ethan?"

"No, I don't. He's got the coordination already. It'll take a little practice. I'll bet he figures it out in no time."

"Oh, great," she muttered as Logan and Shane showed Sam how to get on his new bike. "Now he'll be able to move even faster."

Ethan barely seemed to hear her as he joined the three boys. Giving Sam a few basic instructions, he then held the back of the bicycle while Sam took his first wobbly turn around the yard. Laney watched from the porch steps.

To Laney's amazement and, admittedly, pride, Sam caught on quickly, just as Ethan had predicted. Within half an hour he could go a short distance by himself before the bike began to wobble and he had to stop and regroup. Shane and Logan rode their bikes around in circles, demonstrating their skill to their younger cousin. Sam watched them for a few moments, stuck his tongue out of the corner of his mouth and tried harder.

When he felt that Sam was well on his way, Ethan joined Laney on the porch.

"Told ya," he said smugly.

Laney punched him on the arm. "I hate to admit you're right."

Ethan grinned. "He's always had good balance. That's why he walked so early. He's an active kid. He needs something to keep him busy."

Chin lifted and lips pinched together, Laney said, "*I* keep him busy."

Ethan bumped her with his shoulder. "Oh, don't get defensive. I'm not criticizing your parenting, but in town, he had other kids to play with. Jenny and the boys and I were only three blocks from your apartment. Our kids played together every day. It's different out here." He glanced at her. "But moving here was the right thing for you to do."

"Still, you've got a point. He needs something to do besides make a nuisance of himself with the neighbor."

"Who, Caleb Ransom?"

With a nod she told him about the encounters they'd had with their reclusive neighbor.

"I'm *trying* to keep Sam away from his place, but my son is enthralled with the animals, especially the dog, so it's not easy." Her shoulders slumped. "And I don't think Ransom likes people very much."

"Have you considered getting Sam his own dog?"

"Ethan, he's four. He's too young to be responsible for an animal. He can't even tie his own shoes yet."

"It would be a companion for him."

"So the two of them can run off together? So Sam can take his new dog over to make friends with Ransom's dog, Bertie? That's all I need." She gave him a helpless look. "Ransom...Ransom doesn't like people very much, so I can't imagine he'd want my son popping in to visit with his new puppy."

Ethan frowned. "There's probably more to it than him disliking people, although I understand he pretty much keeps to himself."

She turned to look at her brother fully. "Do you know him?"

"Not really. When he first came here, he was in the office to pay the property taxes and find out the exact location of the property lines on his place. I got the impression he wanted to know what his boundaries are to keep people out—although he didn't actually say that."

"What *did* he say?"

"Not a lot, as I recall," Ethan admitted. "Haven't seen much of him since." Ethan worked in the county assessor's office, but was really a jack-of-all-trades for the county, handling many tasks. "The only person who knows him is Don Parkey, the vet. He takes care of Ransom's animals and hauls those broken-down drug horses out there."

Laney stared at him. "Drug horses?"

"People find them all the time out in the desert, used, abused and abandoned by drug smugglers. They take them to Don, who patches them up the best he can and then takes them to Ransom's place to recover. The county pays him a small fee to take them in and try to get them rehabilitated."

Laney frowned. "I noticed there were some sad-looking horses in his pasture. One of them has a brand-new filly." She was pleased that she'd remembered the correct gender.

"Maybe he likes people okay, but he likes animals better. He seems like the kind of guy who takes care of things, tries to fix them. I guess once the horses are rehabilitated, they'll be sold to people who want riding horses. I doubt they'd be any good as cutting horses."

Maybe what Ethan said about her neighbor being a fixer-upper was true, Laney thought. After all, the old Camacho place, which everyone called the CR Ranch, had been pretty run-down when he'd bought it and she could see evidence of the repairs he'd made. Now she was learning that he was taking in stray, abused horses. Given the state of his old truck, she was certain he wasn't receiving much compensation from the county for their care. That kind of thing simply wasn't in the budget.

What puzzled her was that, in her mind, none of this squared with his wish to be left alone.

"He was a soldier, you know," Ethan continued. "Injured in Afghanistan. Don told me that's why he limps like he does. I guess it was pretty bad." He gave her the big-brother look. "Maybe you could be a little more understanding."

"I've done my part," she insisted, then told Ethan about their first meeting and their second.

"Hmm, that should soften him up. Nobody makes a chocolate cake as good as you do."

She smirked at him. "Thank you. And before you ask, there's none left. I gave Ransom the whole cake."

"Aaagh!" Ethan reached back and pretended to be pulling a knife from his back. She giggled.

Ethan stopped his silly pantomiming and gave her a close look, his dark eyes examining her.

"What?" she asked.

"Sam's four years old."

"I know how old my son is."

"So when do you think you'll start dating again?"

Her mouth dropped open. "Where did that question come from? We were talking about Ransom and… You're not thinking I'd be interested in Caleb Ransom, are you?"

"Stranger things have happened."

Laney thought about her encounters with him. "I don't think so."

"Give it some consideration."

Laney answered with a swift glance of annoyance, but Ethan's steady gaze held hers and she looked away. Color stained her cheeks.

"Not every man is like James Carson," he said gently.

"What's James got to do with this?"

"Only that not everyone is like him, self-ish and egotistical. Could be that you're letting your experience with that jerk color your view of Ransom."

Her mouth dropped open again. "How did this get to be *my* fault?"

"Maybe he doesn't know how to act around people anymore, been alone too long. He's got no one around here. No family or friends."

"So far, he's made it clear he doesn't *want* friends."

"Well, Laney, I'd think you'd understand better than anybody that what people *say* they want and what they *really* want are two different things," Ethan pointed out.

"Like James," Laney whispered, her gaze going automatically to Sam, who had mastered the art of turning his bike without falling off. Her ex-husband had said he'd wanted to be a father and then run off when it was about to happen. She knew she didn't need to say it out loud. The entire family—and everyone else in Sweetsilver—knew what had happened. She hadn't realized how it had affected her interaction with every new man she met in even the most casual way.

"Maybe you could cut Ransom some slack, Laney." Ethan gave her the big-brother look again and she wrinkled her nose at him.

"Dad," Shane yelled, riding up and turning his bike with a show-off skid on the gravel. "Sam can ride good now. Can we go out on the road?"

"Sure, as long as we're with you." Standing, he pulled Laney to her feet.

"You could have asked me if it was all right, you know," Laney said in annoyance.

"Why? You would've simply told them no."

She gave a disgusted click of her tongue and he laughed, throwing his arm around her shoulders and giving her a sideways hug. When he dropped his arm, Laney hooked hers with his and they walked side by side.

"You're so smug and irritating," she said with a long-suffering sigh.

"Part of my big brother charm."

They walked down her drive and onto the road, watching the boys as they wheeled along. It pleased her to see that Shane and Logan had slowed their pace to accommodate their smaller cousin.

"You've been a pretty good big brother," she admitted. "Considering I was dumped on you when you were only nine."

"Mom said I had to be nice to you and I figured I could do it for a few days until your mother came back. By the time we realized your mom wasn't coming back, it was a habit."

Laney smiled, knowing there was more to the story than that.

She barely remembered her mother who had dropped her on her older sister, Laney's aunt Vivian, when Laney was only seven. Her life up until then had been chaotic, lacking any kind of routine or stability.

Lauraine Reynolds had promised she'd be back in a few days but she'd never returned. Laney recalled how scared she had been and how Vivian and Frank Crown had welcomed her, saying they'd always wanted a daughter.

And Ethan had been great. He hadn't seemed to mind her tagging along with him until she made friends of her own.

When the family had learned a few months later that Lauraine had died from some kind of massive infection while working as a card dealer in Las Vegas, Vivian and Frank had adopted Laney. She would be forever grateful. At seven, she hadn't really understood the finality of death and asked Vivian and Frank if she could keep the name Reynolds in case her mother ever came looking for her.

"You're not like her, you know," Ethan said.

"Who?" Laney glanced up at him.

"Your mother. You would never abandon your child or put him at risk, but it's okay to let him take some *reasonable* risks."

She shook her head. "I don't know about that. He's only four."

"What if you let him risk life and limb by coming over to our house tonight? We'll probably watch a movie and play a wild and crazy game of Candyland."

Laney laughed and agreed to the plan as they continued their ambling walk down the road.

After a few more steps Ethan cleared his throat. "Laney, there's something I need to warn you about."

"Uh-oh." She looked over, concerned. "What is it?"

"Mom bought a tree."

Horrified, she stared at him. "No! They actually let her back into the nursery?"

"No, she ordered it online. Dad didn't know anything about it until he came in and found it growing in a huge pot in the living room."

"What kind of tree is it?"

"Banana."

"You've got to be kidding."

"Apparently it's the only kind she hasn't killed yet. It's even got tiny little green bananas on it." He held up his hand, thumb and forefinger a couple of inches apart.

"The poor thing," Laney said in a mournful tone. "It has no idea what it's in for."

"A slow and agonizing death from too much love, overwatering, overfertilizing."

Laney flung out her hands in a helpless gesture. "I don't understand how someone who's so kind and generous can be the angel of death to any plant she comes into contact with."

"It's a mystery," he agreed sadly.

They continued walking as they contemplated the problem. Vivian Reynolds Crown had never successfully grown a garden, a bush, a tree, or so much as a philodendron, but she never gave up trying, and many lush, living things had been sacrificed on the altar of her horticultural ambitions.

"Well," Laney finally said with a sigh, "at least it will keep her busy and involved for a while."

"Yeah, and we'll hear about every drooping leaf and dead stalk."

Laney slipped her arm through Ethan's and gave him a squeeze. "It's the burden we must bear for being her children."

Ethan gave a miserable nod and they followed their sons up the road.

WHO WAS THAT GUY? Caleb reined in Cisco behind a stand of paloverde on a rise near the road. Telling himself he was only watching because he was nearby, preparing to move Addie and her filly out of the pasture and move a few cattle in. Besides, he needed to see what was going on because he didn't want any strangers coming to his place unannounced.

He observed Laney as she walked down the lane behind Sam and two other little boys on bicycles. Her arm was entwined with that of a man whose face he couldn't quite see.

Caleb's mouth twitched in annoyance. Laney and the guy looked pretty friendly. It irritated him that he couldn't see the guy's face. If someone was around, anywhere near his place, he wanted to know who it was. He didn't like surprises and he didn't want unexpected company. He had avoided people since he'd moved to Sweetsilver and he fully intended to keep it that way.

LANEY DIDN'T KNOW what to do with herself. She had finished getting her turnouts and other gear ready for the coming fire season, worked in her yard, swept the kitchen, and showered and washed her hair, deciding to let it air dry, allowing the dark curly waves to do whatever they wanted. Sometimes she simply didn't feel like fighting them.

She ate a quiet dinner then wandered around

the house, missing Sam. She had a book to read, a suspense novel guaranteed to keep her interested and probably terrified until dawn. Or she could call her best friend, Sarah, to see if she wanted to go into Sierra Vista to see a movie, have a girl's night out—something they hadn't done in months.

None of those things appealed, though. She was too restless, too unsettled and, probably thanks to her brother's words, thinking too much about Caleb Ransom.

He did intrigue her. He was closed off, said he didn't want company or friends. He was scarred on the outside and doubtless on the inside, too, but because of the defensive wall he'd put up, she would never know the nature of his scars, never know *him*. For despite all good judgment, she sensed a need in him that drew her.

Laney couldn't have said why she even cared. He didn't want her around; not her or her son. He had his own life, his own business, and she had hers.

Thinking about him made her move to her kitchen window, which looked out onto his land. The late-afternoon sun slanted down, casting long shadows across his pasture.

So much of her mind hadn't been taken up with a man since James Carson—and she hadn't had a pleasant thought about him in years.

Laney doubted that Caleb was anything like James. No doubt he kept his promises, she thought as she gazed out the window dreamily, and carried through with anything he'd decided to do.

Taking in abused and abandoned horses was proof of his compassion, his abilities as a horse owner and—

His cattle were in her yard!

CHAPTER FOUR

LANEY'S EYES WIDENED when she realized some of the shadows she'd been watching with gooey-eyed dreaminess were moving. In fact, they had abandoned their own grama and were trampling the flowers she'd planted and devouring the small area of lawn she was trying to coax back to life. She was determined that her plants would avoid the fate of her mom's.

She turned to dash out the kitchen door, then remembered she was barefoot. She had put on a tank top and shorts after her shower, and now she yanked on the boots she'd left by the back door.

Allowing the screen door to slam behind her, she ran out waving her arms. "Get out! Get out!" How did you get in here?

The four cows didn't even bother to lift their heads, since they were too busy feasting on her lawn. She tried slapping one on the rump. It took a couple of steps away from her then glanced back as if to thank her for directing it to a fresh patch of grass.

"Stupid, smug beasts!" she huffed, fuming.

Looking around, she saw that the gate between her property and Ransom's was open. The animals had probably pressed against it as they were grazing on his land, and the latch had popped open. Never ones to waste an opportunity to find food, they'd simply invited themselves in.

She would have to call Caleb to come get his cattle. She reached into her shorts' pocket for her cell phone, then realized she had no idea what his number was, and if she had and her name came up on his Caller ID, he might not even answer.

"This isn't how it's supposed to be with neighbors. Neighbors help each other, welcome each other, share phone numbers, keep an eye on their own darned cattle." In her righteous indignation, she was building up a healthy head of steam. This time when she swatted one of the cows on the rump, it moved in the right direction, back toward the gate where it had made its unwelcome entrance. Satisfied with that outcome, she whistled at the next one, slapped it, too, and got it headed the way she wanted. The last two animals seemed to realize she meant business, so they followed along, as well.

When she had them back on their own side of the fence, she locked the gate securely and strode across the pasture to talk to Caleb about his cattle and to set him straight about exactly how neighbors were supposed to act toward each other. The fact that she had to dodge cow and horse manure as she went didn't improve her mood at all. Glancing around, she looked for the mare and filly, but they were nowhere to be seen.

She could have driven, but she was too mad. She hoped the fifteen-minute walk would take the edge off her annoyance, but by the time she stomped up his front steps and rapped on his door, she was still as annoyed as she'd been when she'd found the cows trampling her flowers and eating her grass.

CALEB THREW OPEN the door and gaped at the woman on his doorstep. He was pretty sure it was Delaney Reynolds, but in their three previous encounters, she hadn't looked like this. She was dressed in a skimpy tank top and shorts that left about twelve miles of legs for him to appreciate. It didn't matter that her feet were tucked into an old pair of boots—made an interesting contrast, if he were interested. Which he wasn't.

His gaze made a quick sweep upward once again and he saw that she was breathing rapidly, obviously from exertion. Her scent, amplified by her agitation, swept over him, bringing a hint of citrus—sharp and tangy.

Her hair was loose and wild around her shoulders, with every lock doing business for itself. Her cheeks were flushed and her eyes were full of fire.

She looked like an Amazon on the hunt.

"Mr. Ransom," she said, biting off the words.

"Yes?"

"Your cattle…" She had to stop to catch her breath.

"What about them?"

"They somehow got the gate open and were on my property, trampling the flowers I planted only days ago and eating my grass."

"Oh." He stepped outside. "I'll go get them and…"

"Never mind." She held up her hand to stop him. "I took care of it. They're back in your pasture."

"Well, thank you, I—"

"This isn't what neighbors do, you know."

He didn't know exactly what she meant. "It isn't?"

"No, it isn't." She paused as if to ready the next salvo in her argument.

"I can't watch them every second and…"

"That's not what I meant." She waved her hand as if his words were dandelion fluff. "I mean neighbors give each other their phone numbers so they can call if there's a problem. I've got the Bartletts' phone number and they've got mine."

"You're mad because I didn't give you my phone number?"

"I realize you don't want anything to do with us," she said, lifting her chin and fixing him with a steady glare.

He backed up and leaned against the door frame, his arms crossed over his chest as she went on. "True," he said.

"But since we're each other's only neighbors—only us and the Bartletts out here on this dead-end road—we have to keep each other's best interests in mind."

"And you think having my phone number would be in your best interest?" he asked, studying the intensity in her face.

"It would also be in *your* best interest," she continued. "What if I saw that your cattle got out on the road next time and went clear out to the highway? I could call you and tell you before they caused an accident, and…"

"It's nearly a mile out to the highway and I guarantee you my cows are too lazy to walk that far." It occurred to him that this was the most ridiculous argument he'd ever been involved in. "That was only an example of why it's important to be able to keep in touch." She clammed up, obviously preparing more arguments. He couldn't wait to hear what they were.

"I see," he responded. "You may be right and— Aaagh!" He scooted past her and made for the hose attached to a water pipe at the front of the house.

"What are you doing?" She followed him down the steps.

Caleb picked up the hose, turned the faucet on full-blast and aimed it across the yard. "I'm trying to keep a worthless tomcat away from my barn cats. The mama has had two litters since I've been here."

"You mean she hasn't been spayed?"

"No. Apparently, along with being a lousy cattleman, I'm a lousy cat owner."

"Yes, you are. That's completely irresponsible. The feral cat population in this county is already out of control. If she's had two litters and each of them is responsible for a litter, that could end up being hundreds more cats. Why haven't you taken care of this?"

His lips tightened and his eyebrows pulled together in a ferocious frown. The argument became too personal. "Don Parkey took the kittens to his clinic, spayed and neutered them, brought two back to me and put the rest up for adoption, but he couldn't catch the mother because, first of all, she *is* feral, and second, she and the other two know there's a pack of coyotes roaming the area, so they all pretty much stay up in the rafters. And, no, I don't know how the tomcat has stayed alive to keep coming to pay her conjugal visits." He stopped and pointed to his bad leg. "And, obviously, I can't catch her, either."

In a flash Laney's expression went from annoyance to embarrassment. "Oh, I'm sorry. I wasn't thinking."

When he saw pity drench her eyes, he looked away. That was what he hated— someone feeling sorry for him. And worse, someone wanting to do things for him that he used to be able to do without a second thought.

Laney cleared her throat. "I could catch her for you and take her in to Don's clinic. In fact, I could do it right now. Do you have some kind of cage?"

"No."

"Well, I think my dad has one. I'll get it from him and catch her for you."

"No." This time he gave her a look that invited no argument.

She argued anyway. "Now you're just being stubborn."

"Yeah, I'm good at that. I'll figure out some way to catch her myself."

"You're being ridiculous *and* stubborn."

He knew that, but it was better to be stubborn and ridiculous than to have her feel sorry for him.

Laney turned suddenly. "I'm going home. Good night."

"I'll drive you."

"I'd rather walk."

"It's getting dark, and you don't want to run into those coyotes," he answered. "I'll drive you."

"I haven't seen any coyotes." Her tone was so snippy it could have cut off his nose if he'd been standing closer.

"Maybe not, but I'll bet you've heard them."

She gave him a look that could have curdled milk. Good. Let her be mad at him. It was better than being the object of her pity. She walked to his truck and tugged the door open, not waiting for him to do the gentlemanly thing—which he did actually know how to do.

Caleb climbed behind the wheel and started the engine before glancing over at her. In spite of those crazy boots, the expanse of bare leg and the revealing tank top, she sat as primly as if she was dressed in a neck-to-heels wool dress from the 1800s. Her chin was in the air and her eyes bore holes through his windshield.

He put the truck in gear and started down the drive before it occurred to him to ask, "Where's Sam? Not home alone?"

She didn't even spare him a glance. "Of course not. He's spending the night at my brother Ethan's. He and his sons brought a bike over for Sam and then took him home with them." She clapped her mouth shut and gave him a sideways glance. Did she think she'd said too much?

Her brother. The guy she'd been so cozy with was her brother. Caleb decided he wasn't even going to think about the reason he felt a little kick of happiness.

A flash of movement beside the road had him leaning forward and peering into the gathering darkness.

"What is it?" Laney asked. "The friendly neighborhood coyotes?"

"Maybe," he answered. "And don't think they're not out there. They are. Probably be better if you didn't walk across the pasture at night."

"Probably be better if your cows stayed out of my yard," she answered sweetly.

Caleb twisted his mouth to the side. She always had a smart answer. He thought it funny that she seemed to be working so hard to control every aspect of her life but her son and his cows threw the plan to the winds.

As she and her son had done to him, he thought, sobering. But he wouldn't think about that right now. He wrestled his thoughts back to what they'd been discussing.

"The coyotes are a real threat, but there's something else out there. I heard it and when I went out into the yard, I saw…an animal, but couldn't tell what it was." He didn't mention the flashback he'd had, thinking he was back in a war zone, holding a stick the way he held a rifle, looking for a phantom enemy.

"What do you think it was?"

"I don't know. The sound it made wasn't one I'd heard before." He glanced over. In the dim radiance of the dashboard lights, he saw her chew her bottom lip. "Probably a bobcat," he concluded, though he honestly didn't know.

"I'll call the sheriff's office," she said solemnly. "Ask if there have been any reports of any predators besides coyotes."

"Be a good idea."

He had her back at her place within minutes. When he pulled into her drive, the headlights swept over the damage his cattle had caused to her property.

"The next time I'm in town for supplies, I'll get some sod, then come over here and fix this," he said. "What kind of flowers did my cattle trample?"

She turned in the seat and swept him with a look. "Petunias. Purple ones. But you can only repair the damage to my yard if you'll let me catch your cat and take her in to Don's clinic."

"Now who's being stubborn?"

She tilted her head and gave him an angelic smile. "It takes two."

He wanted to laugh, but that meant he'd be stepping over a boundary he'd set for himself. "All right. You can catch the cat."

"Good. Don't feed her tomorrow. And I want your phone number." She took her cell phone out of her pocket and waited expectantly to punch it into the memory.

Still reluctant, he gave it to her.

"I'm going to give you mine," she said.

"I don't have my cell phone."

"Then memorize it," she said. Then she rattled off the number and made him repeat it back to her. He deliberately transposed a couple of numbers just so he could see her exasperation grow, but she patiently repeated it until he had it right.

When at last she was satisfied, she opened the door and climbed out of the truck.

"I'll come take care of that cat tomorrow," she said in a tone that invited no argument. "I have to go into town, anyway, to pick up Sam, so I'll get the trap from my dad and bring it over."

"Okay."

The glow of the cab's dome light allowed him to see the suspicious look on her face—as if she was expecting more argument—but he was ready to give it a rest. His leg was starting to throb and he knew he had to get home and elevate it or pay the consequences with a night of muscle spasms and leg cramps.

"Well, then, good night." Laney closed the door.

He hit the button to lower the window. "I'll wait until you get safely inside."

Laney nodded. He watched as she reached

the door and opened it, and then drove home thinking that he would see her again tomorrow. He didn't mind that as much as he should.

FROM HER DOORWAY, Laney watched Caleb drive away. She wasn't sure that they'd made much progress, but she knew she felt energized and jumpy and it would take her a while to get to sleep tonight.

Before she went inside and closed the door, she stood for a few minutes looking into the darkness, trying to see if there was anything lurking out there, anything that might be a threat to Sam or to her.

LANEY RECONSIDERED HER plan to take Sam along on the cat-catching expedition. He would be too curious and too anxious to "help" and would probably only get in the way or, worse, put himself in danger.

She called Jenny, who was home with the boys today, and told her what was going on. She then swung by her mom and dad's house for the small-animal trap her dad used to catch pack rats and gophers before hauling them far out into the desert.

"Sorry, Laney," Frank said when she reached the house. "I loaned that out to someone a few months ago and never got it back. Can't remember who borrowed it."

She looked at him with fond exasperation. "Dad, this happens all the time. You need to write things down."

He was the most accommodating and easygoing man she'd ever known. He'd managed a local bank, but when Vivian had retired, he had, too, so they'd have more time to spend together. He would do anything for anyone and people often took advantage of him. He didn't mind at all, though, somehow convincing himself that people always had the best intentions. Ethan was the same way. Laney had realized years ago that knowing these two men had left her woefully unprepared for a self-centered jerk like James Carson.

Frank grinned at her. "I enjoy the mystery and when something is returned, it's like getting a surprise gift and it gives me a chance to visit with the person who returned it."

Laney shook her head, gave him a kiss on the cheek and started to head for the Jeep, but turned back.

"Dad, Ethan tells me Mom bought a banana tree."

Frank's smile fell. "Yes. Apparently her reputation hasn't reached the internet."

"Is it dead yet?"

He shook his head, looking puzzled. "Hasn't even started turning brown and the bananas on it are actually growing. Did you know they grow sticking up in the air? Kinda cute, but I guess it's only a matter of time before it starts to droop and die."

Laney nodded in sad agreement, gave him another kiss and headed home. She should have called first to see if he had the trap. Don Parkey probably had one she could borrow, but then she remembered a report one of her students had given about trapping a stray cat in an ordinary cat carrier and thought she could make it work. She often assigned her students research papers and speeches on a variety of topics, so she'd learned random information on a host of topics over the years.

Remembering she needed groceries, she stopped at Sweetsilver's one and only supermarket. She was wheeling her cart through the produce section wondering how she could disguise fresh vegetables so her son would eat them, when she heard someone call her name.

Glancing around, she saw Monette Berkley bearing down on her. Stifling a groan, she attempted a friendly smile that she knew probably fell short.

"Did you find your son?" Monette demanded as her shopping cart came to a stop inches from Laney's.

Laney frowned. Any conversation with Monette always put her on the defensive, and one that started out this way would probably go downhill quickly.

"You mean the other day when I saw you on the lane by my place? Yes, he was at the neighbor's, exactly as I thought. What were you doing out there, anyway?" Good, she thought, put Monette on the defensive for once.

Monette opened her mouth and closed it a couple of times. Color washed into her face, which Laney thought actually improved her drab appearance. "I…I was taking a drive in the country, and…happened to be there."

"You won't see much countryside on Bartlett Road. It's a dead end."

Monette sniffed. "I found that out." Then

she quickly asked, "So, how are you?" Monette was obviously uncomfortable being on the defensive. Laney knew she much preferred putting other people in that position.

Monette's close-set brown eyes surveyed Laney from head to toe. Her expression dripped with disapproval, which Laney found ironic since Monette was dressed in a baggy brown suit with a drooping hem and was wearing a pair of loafers that had long since seen better days. She had thick, black hair that would have been beautiful with a decent cut, but she wore it scraped back from her face in a loose bun, or in a severe ponytail held in place by a clip that Laney thought resembled a Ninja weapon. Monette would have been attractive if she took a little time for herself, but she was too busy sticking her nose into other people's business and trying to tell them how to handle it.

"Are you fighting fires this summer?" she asked, her eyes darting around. "And where's your little boy, Sean, this time?"

"His name's Sam. And he's with his cousins," Laney explained and then could have kicked herself for doing so. The less Monette knew about her life the better. Monette had been their neighbor in the small apartment complex in town, so she already knew too much about Laney's life. To make matters worse, she was a social worker with the state and felt that gave her license to interfere.

"You need to give up that firefighting job. You could get hurt." Monette clapped her hands on her skinny hips and stuck out her chin.

Laney gritted her teeth, trying to hang on to the good manners she'd been taught. Monette never seemed to be able to talk about any other subject with her than her firefighting job.

"I'm afraid I don't have time to chat right now. Have a good day, Monette." Whipping around, Laney hurried away, grabbing the things she needed, swooping through the checkout and rushing from the store. As she drove home, she took a deep breath and shoved thoughts of her former neighbor from her mind.

MONETTE WATCHED LANEY hurry away, hoping that she was doing a better job of watching her little boy than she had when they'd been neighbors. She didn't like to think about the dangers that child could be subjected to if his mother didn't look after him. During their time as neighbors, she had given advice and information freely, but Laney hadn't been interested in hearing any of it.

Pushing her cart toward the produce aisle, Monette thought about all the times she'd seen little Sean put at risk—going down the stairs without his mother holding his hand or carrying him, riding his three-wheeled toy on the landing outside their apartment. Sean was lucky to be alive.

In fact, if it hadn't been for her keeping an eye on him and reminding his mother to watch him more closely, he might not be alive at all. She nodded to herself, glad that she'd been there to secure the little boy's safety. She didn't know who would watch out for him now that his mother had moved with him out of town.

Monette congratulated herself for going out there to take a look around, but hadn't been able to see much from the road. State and department rules said she couldn't investigate or file a report without due cause, so she'd had to be careful when checking on little Sean's welfare.

Monette stopped, frowning as she slipped a head of lettuce into a plastic bag, then moved aside as a harried mother with three kids crowded past.

Not Sean, she thought as she placed more items in her cart. Where had that come from? She knew his name was Sam. Of course she knew that. Alarm zippered up her spine. She'd better check all her notes on this case to make sure everything was in order, and certainly, she had better check the file she was keeping and make sure she had his name correct. If it became necessary for him to be removed from his mother's care, she wanted to be sure she had everything in perfect order. No child would ever be put at risk because of sloppy paperwork. Not on her watch.

Monette headed toward the checkout at the front of the store then stopped short, staring into her shopping cart. There were three plastic clamshell packages of strawberries in her basket. She had picked up lettuce, tomatoes and apples, not strawberries. Her heart fluttered in her throat. She never ate strawberries. They made her deathly ill.

Glancing around, she saw the woman who'd passed her a minute ago. No doubt it was those kids, Monette thought, picking up the strawberries and returning them to the produce section, then hurriedly scrubbing her hands on the front of her skirt. They thought they were being cute or funny. In their young minds it was a harmless prank, and it probably was, but why didn't people watch their children?

Critically, she eyed the woman and tried to remember if she'd ever written a report on her. No, she didn't look familiar. Her kids might be naughty, but they seemed well cared for. Monette breathed a deep sigh. No cause for alarm. She didn't have to be concerned about these children. It was the Sean Reynoldses of the world she needed to keep an eye on.

She gave a quick shake of her head as she started once more for the checkout lane. No, not Sean. Sam. Sam Reynolds. That was his name.

CHAPTER FIVE

In spite of the heat, Laney dressed in jeans and a long-sleeved shirt in case things got too up close and personal with the cat. She'd found the carrier she'd saved from the time when she'd had a cat of her own—and then had had to give it away because of James's allergies.

"I should've kept Peterkin and dumped James right then," she muttered as she loaded all the supplies into her Jeep.

She felt a spark of excitement as she mentally rehearsed how she would coax the cat into the carrier. Of course, there were unknown factors to be considered, but she loved a challenge and was convinced she could do this.

And, really, trapping a cat? How hard could it be?

When she reached Caleb's ranch, she saw that his truck was there. As she drove up and stopped the Jeep, he appeared in the door of the barn. He was wiping his hands on a rag, which he stuffed into his back pocket before walking over to her.

"You're really going to do this?" he asked, bending slightly to peer into the back of the Jeep.

"Absolutely," she assured him, hopping out. She slammed the door shut and hurried around to the back to pull out the cat carrier. Her face brimming with excitement, she said, "There's no reason this won't work."

He raised an eyebrow at her. Even though she knew he doubted her, just as she doubted her students when they came up with outrageous ideas, she simply gave him a confident nod and told him about the trap her dad had loaned out.

She showed him the carrier. "But I think we can make this work. All we have to do is coax her into it."

He gave her a skeptical look. "How? By calling 'kitty kitty' until she comes down?"

"Down? Where is she?"

"I told you. Up in the barn rafters. She's a cat. She likes to climb." He took the carrier from her and turned toward the barn.

"Well, where do you usually feed her?"

"Right here, by the door," he said, nodding toward an empty food dish and a bowl of water. "As ordered by you, I didn't put out any food today, so all three cats are hungry. When there's food, the mama comes down and eats when she's good and ready."

Laney gave him an exasperated look. "You're not making this any easier."

He made a rumbling sound in his throat that sounded suspiciously like a laugh. "Me? It's not like I can tell that cat what to do. She's got a mind of her own and she's feral, after all."

"Then we'll have to coax her down with cat food." Laney looked up at the rafters, which were about twelve feet from the barn floor. She could see a cat observing them from a perch under the eaves.

"Is that her?"

Caleb tilted his head back and squinted. "Yup."

"First I'll try coaxing her down by calling her. Does she have a name?"

"Yeah. Cat."

"And the other two are called…?"

"Cat and Cat."

This time Laney was the one who raised an eyebrow. "Imaginative," she said.

He cleared his throat in a way that made her think he was trying to hide a laugh, but she didn't think he actually *knew* how to laugh, so she dismissed that thought.

Laney went back to studying the animal. Her tail waved lazily back and forth as she watched the two humans below. "It's really high, isn't it? Good thing I'm not afraid of heights."

"You're not going up there!"

Laney threw her hands out to her sides. "How do you suggest we get her down, then? I've got to put a tiny amount of cat food up there to lure her out, then I'll place some more every few feet until we get her down to the carrier. And I can see that you've got bales of hay and a few boxes stacked up. They'll make perfect steps for me. I suspect that's how she gets up and down, too."

"Yeah, it is."

Caleb frowned. Laney could tell he wasn't liking this plan at all, but there was nothing he could do about it.

"Do you have a better idea?" she asked.

"We could leave her alone and…"

"And you can come running out whenever a stray tomcat—or a coyote—appears. How's that been working for you?"

When he didn't answer, she was satisfied that she'd won this particular argument. She looked up to check out the rafters again. "Where are the other cats?"

"They're around somewhere."

"But that's the one we want, right?" She pointed to the one under the eaves.

"Yes." He looked at her, his frown deepening. "Laney, have you ever actually caught a feral cat before?"

"No," she said, giving him a confident grin. "This will be my first."

She heard him groan, but she ignored him. Opening the carrier, she placed it on one of the hay bales within Caleb's reach, then set an open can of cat food inside. "When she goes in, slam the door and lock it."

"Since she doesn't like people, do you really think she's going to come close if I'm here?"

"Did you ever think that maybe it's only *you* she doesn't like?" Laney asked in a tone sweet enough to cause tooth decay.

Caleb scowled in response and she chuckled then said, "It's going to work perfectly."

"You've got a lot of faith in our ability to outsmart this animal," he said dryly.

She gave him a steady look. "I hope we're smarter than a feline."

"I bet we are, but she's quicker."

"We'll see." She waved a dismissive hand at him. "You do your part and I'll do mine and we'll have this problem solved in a flash."

"*Something's* going to happen in a flash," he mumbled as he took up his post by the hay bales, ready to shut the carrier door as soon as the cat was inside.

"In spite of your belief that this plan is fraught with disaster, I happen to think it will work exactly as planned." She waved a second can of cat food at him and then tucked it into her back pocket so her hands would be free for climbing. "I bought the best, stinkiest cat food I could find. It will attract her and she'll want more and more."

Caleb shook his head, but Laney again thought that he was stifling a laugh.

She waded through a pile of loose hay and began the climb. When she reached a bale high enough to let her stretch up to the rafter near where the cat was perched, she took the can of food from one pocket and a small plastic spoon from another, popped off the lid and placed a tiny bit on the rafter.

"What's happening?" Caleb whispered.

Laney wrapped her arm around a post, leaned back and peeked at the animal. "Nothing. She's not interested."

"I suggest you try to act nonchalant. Maybe she'll change her mind."

"Nonchalant? How? By leaning against a post and smoking a cigarette?"

Caleb made a strangled sound then cleared his throat. "You don't smoke."

"How do you know that?" she asked, looking down at him.

"Because you smell like citrus and flowers, not cigarettes."

Laney noticed he hadn't met her gaze when he'd said that. A big smile curved her lips as she began stepping down to the next hay bale. "I'll move away. I'm probably spooking her."

"If by spooked, you mean she hasn't moved a muscle and has drifted off to sleep, then, yeah, she's spooked."

"Sarcasm doesn't help."

Laney spooned out some more cat food and looked up hopefully. The mama cat yawned.

"Oh. I guess she's not hungry."

"Look out," Caleb warned, pointing to a spot past her head. "Someone else is."

"What? Oh!" She looked up in time to see two furry shapes bouncing from the rafter beam to the hay bale in front of her. Her hands shot out to ward them off. The can of food flew from her grip and the two felines soared after it, clipping Laney's shoulder as they went.

Arms wind-milling, she fought for balance, bending her body forward to keep from falling. She managed to catch her balance, but her left foot slipped from the hay bale and landed hard on the next one down, leaving her right foot still on the top one. Caught in this crazy split, she couldn't stay upright and found herself tumbling down the last two bales to land on her back in the pile of hay at the bottom.

"Laney! Are you all right?" Caleb hurried over and hunkered down beside her, wincing with the effort.

The fall had knocked the wind out of her and she couldn't inhale much-needed air. She couldn't make a sound, either. Her eyes, wide with fright, fixed on his face, begging silently for help.

"Take it easy, Laney. Relax. You can breathe."

She shook her head in terror. Was he crazy? Couldn't he see?

"Look at me," he commanded, taking her chin in his hand and turning her face to his. His eyes, dark and steady with purpose, looked into hers. "Take a breath, Laney. Now," he ordered.

He slipped his hand beneath her shirt and settled it on her diaphragm, then pressed firmly to force air out. Somehow, that reminded her body what breathing was like, and at last Laney sucked air into her starved lungs. She coughed and wheezed a few times, but finally her breathing began to ease. Gulping, she tried to clear her head.

"Thank…thank you," she said, looking up at him. His eyes were full of concern as he slipped his arm around to support her back. She took another breath. She was going to stand any minute now, as soon as her body recovered from the impact with the floor.

Thank heaven for the pile of hay that had cushioned her fall.

"I didn't do anything," he said. "You only had to relax and let your body remember how to breathe." He eased down beside her, lying on his left side.

"By pushing…on my stomach."

"Your diaphragm. There's always some air left in your lungs. That's why the Heimlich maneuver works. If I push that air out, your lungs will automatically try to bring more in." He illustrated his words by gently pressing high on her belly again. "That's their job."

Her breath jerked in.

"See? It works."

His hand slid across her skin, leaving heat behind, but she was too stunned to object. Even though she could breathe now, she hardly dared.

Caleb Ransom had let down his guard. His eyes were looking into hers, not defensive or angry as they'd been every other time she had seen him, but appreciative. He seemed to like looking at her and she was glad he did. He was even smiling at her, slightly, and the scar on his cheek gave his smile an endearing crookedness.

Cautiously, because she didn't want him to scuttle back into his shell, Laney lifted her hand and touched her fingers gently to the left side of his face, the side untouched by whatever trauma had scarred the rest of him. To her stunned surprise, he turned his head and placed a kiss in the palm of her hand.

Emotion clogged her throat at the sweet gesture. "Caleb," she whispered, "what are you doing?"

"Darned if I know." Then he lowered his head and settled his lips over hers. It was tender, gentle, loving.

It had been so long since anyone had kissed her this way that Laney was delighted and scared at the same time. But truly, it was wonderful.

When at last he took his lips from hers, she lifted her head to kiss his right cheek. Her lips skimmed across the scar, following it down to the corner of his mouth.

He froze then turned his face away. His hands came up to set her away from him.

"Caleb?" she asked, blinking in confusion. "What is it?"

"I'm sorry. I took advantage of you. That was wrong." He moved away from her. Balancing on the nearest hay bale, he struggled to his feet then reached down a hand to help her up.

Laney's eyes flew to his face, closed off now, shuttered, as if that briefest of tender moments had never happened. Confused and embarrassed, she stood and dusted herself off, then avoided his gaze as she plucked hay from her hair.

"Are you all right?" he asked gruffly. "You're not hurt?"

Only her pride, she thought. Or was it her heart? She shook her head. Looking around, trying to get past the awkward moment, she said, "I'll have to try this again, but next time I'll go to Don Parkey's office and borrow a cat trap."

"Yeah, sure." Caleb took off his cowboy hat, tapped it against his leg to get the dust off and resettled it on his head as if readying his armor.

She turned to get the cat carrier, removing the opened can of cat food from inside and setting it beside the door. The two felines who had startled her were nowhere to be seen, and the mama cat was still in her place in the eaves, placidly watching the goings-on below.

Laney cleared her throat self-consciously. "I'll be on my way, then, and I'll, uh, let you know when I can…come and catch that cat."

He nodded and didn't meet her eyes.

Without another word, Laney turned and hurried to her Jeep. She put the carrier in the back, jumped into her seat and started the engine. Turning in a wide circle, she left Caleb behind and headed for town to pick up her son. It was time to get back to normal, to forget what happened and didn't happen between her and Caleb.

Her phone rang before she reached the highway and she pulled over to the side of the road to answer it. It was Kebra Wade, her fire team crew chief.

"We've been called out to a fire in Idaho, Laney. Can you meet us in Tucson by eight o'clock tonight?"

"I'll be there."

Laney knew her family would take care of Sam. She pulled back onto the road and immediately began planning what needed to be done before she left for Tucson. She would pick up her son, take him home to get ready to spend several days either with her mom and dad or with Ethan and Jenny, pack her gear and head out of town to fight a fire. She would be much too busy to give a moment's thought to Caleb Ransom. And that was exactly how she wanted it.

CALEB STARED AT himself in the bathroom mirror, turning his jaw right and left to check the closeness of his shave—something he hadn't done very much since an IED had blown up next to the Bradley fighting vehicle in which he'd been riding the last month of his last tour of duty in Afghanistan.

At first, he'd been too injured to shave. Then he'd been too repulsed by what he'd seen in the mirror. Now he could see that the scars had faded. They were red, some even diminishing to pink, no longer the puckered purple he'd seen when the bandages were first removed. Best of all, they didn't hurt— unlike his leg, which felt as bad as it looked.

Caleb touched the pattern of scars once again then met his gaze in the mirror.

He was annoyed with himself. He'd never

intended to get that close to Laney. When he'd seen her fall onto her back, his heart had nearly stopped, and watching her struggle for breath had alarmed him, but it hadn't brought flashbacks of helping his wounded men in Afghanistan. He'd been focused only on her. When she'd caught her breath and looked up at him, so vulnerable and scared, when a minute before she'd been sassy and sure of herself, he'd done what he'd told himself he wouldn't do and kissed her.

She had tasted so good, reacted so sweetly, that he had forgotten for a minute that he had no business touching her, much less kissing her.

Then she'd kissed his scar. His numb scar. The fact that he couldn't feel her lips there had jolted him, made him instantly recall how repulsive his face was.

He'd felt at odds with his own body ever since he'd been wounded, and he had tried to overcome that discomfort. Obviously he hadn't succeeded completely. In addition to his scarred face, he still cursed the weakness and pain in his right leg. He knew his discomfort showed and was the reason no one had touched him the way Laney had.

He wouldn't let anyone get that close, and he hadn't—at least not until Laney had come along.

Moving with the care he'd cultivated and still hated having to do, he went into his bedroom and dressed in clean jeans, shirt and his slip-on shoes. He couldn't wear cowboy boots because they were so hard to pull on and almost impossible to get off, even if he used a bootjack. Most days he wore a pair of his old combat boots.

At the door, his hand hovered over the hat rack as he wondered whether or not he should wear his cowboy hat. Oh, why not? Sam would expect it. He clapped it on his head and looked down at Bertie, who gazed back with a mournful expression.

"No, you're not going. You'll have plenty of time to play with Sam later on, because I don't think there's any chance his mom will be able to keep him from coming over here."

Oh, man, he was having a conversation with his dog. But then, why not? At least Bertie didn't talk back. "Right now," he went on, "I've got to go plant sod and petunias, not to mention apologize to his mom—even if I do feel like a fool. And there's no need to remind me it was crazy to shower and shave when I'm only going to get dirty again."

Bertie made a snuffling sound that Caleb took as agreement that his human was, indeed, crazy. He shut the door and headed out to his truck, which he had parked in the shade of the barn to shield the sod and flowers from the sun. He tossed the tools he thought he'd need into the back of the truck and climbed behind the wheel.

As he started the engine and turned in a big arc to head down his drive, he tried to think of what he was going to say to her. He'd been stewing over it practically every minute since she'd left yesterday and he still didn't know what brilliant thing was going to come out of his mouth.

He'd been off-kilter since he'd met Sam and Laney. That was the only explanation. His carefully constructed isolation, his defensive barriers, had been breached. Any well-trained soldier would have known to retreat, to establish a new perimeter of defense. Instead he was rushing out to meet the threat to his aloneness like a green recruit bent on self-destruction.

Tired of trying to figure out what was

going on in his own head, he was determined to plant those stupid flowers, replace the sod and get out of there.

"In other words, Ransom, try not to make a complete fool of yourself," he muttered as he slowed to turn into Laney's yard. His gaze darted around, noticing that her Jeep wasn't parked anywhere that he could see.

Stopping the truck, he climbed out and knocked on the front door and then walked around the house, but could find no one home.

Where were they? Had she gone to find the humane cat trap she was so convinced would snare the mama cat? Darn! He'd worked himself up to the point where he could face her and get out of there, even though he didn't know exactly what he was going to say. Now it would have to wait.

But replacing the plants and the grass destroyed by his cattle couldn't wait. He got quickly to work, planting the petunias, digging up the area of destroyed grass, pressing the squares of sod into place, then watering everything.

When he was done, Caleb loaded his tools into his truck and started to climb inside, but then paused. Leaving the truck door open, he walked around her house again, this time noticing what kind of house it was, how the upkeep had been done. It was almost identical to his, built long before either of them were born, built to last long after they were gone. Both places had been meant for a family, but his house would never have a family—at least, not while he owned it.

Caleb shook his head, banishing that unhappy thought. He reminded himself that he'd made his choice in life and that choice was being alone.

Shadows were lengthening and the temperature was dropping. Once again, he heard the coyotes in the distance, but not the high scream he'd heard a few nights before. Everything seemed peaceful.

Caleb headed for his truck. There was no reason to stay any longer. Laney and Sam would be home soon. Once they got the matter of the barn cat settled, he would keep his distance and she would keep hers. That was the way it was going to be.

Or at least the way it should have been. For Caleb was back the next day and then the next, riding Cisco over to the Reynolds' place. He'd even let Bertie come along, knowing it would delight Sam. But there was no sign of his neighbor. He watered the flowers and the new sod as he grew more anxious and annoyed.

"What was the point of giving her my number if she's not going to call me and tell me where she is?" he complained to Cisco and Bertie as he swung back into the saddle after his third trip to Laney's house.

He was ticked off that she hadn't let him know where she was, and even more ticked off that he cared.

"It's official, Cisco," he said as he turned the horse toward home. "I've lost my mind."

LANEY USED HER shovel to turn over a pile of scorched debris, searching for hot spots that could erupt into new flames if left alone. She sifted the leaves and pine needles, scattering them as she looked for glowing embers. Finding none, she moved ahead, crisscrossing the area she'd been assigned then signaling to Kebra that her area was clear.

Stopping to catch her breath, she took off her helmet then unhooked her water bottle from her belt and took a long drink. Next she dampened a bandanna to wipe the grime from her face. Leaning her head back, she scanned the ridge where they'd been working in shifts for three days, digging trenches, creating firebreaks, trying to deprive the eager fire of its fuel. Finally they were ahead of it. It was always a satisfying feeling when they turned a corner on a fire and began to gain control.

The crackle of dry twigs behind her had her turning to see Kebra trudging up the hill to join her. Together, they scanned the area for smoke or embers.

Kebra pointed to a spot near the top of the hill. "After you catch your breath, can you go up there and help Rita and Katie with their section?"

"Sure."

They paused and sipped water as they contemplated the work still remaining.

"It'll be a long time before this wildland recovers," Laney said, shaking her head.

"The scars will last for decades." Kebra removed her helmet, too, and blotted sweat from her face.

"Crazy, isn't it, that fire is actually necessary for new growth? But the scars are always there." For some reason Caleb's marked face popped into her mind. "They never fade," she finished quietly.

Kebra glanced at her and was silent for several seconds as if waiting for Laney to go on. When nothing was forthcoming, she said, "We'll be finished up here by tomorrow and we can go home. I guess you're anxious to get back to that little boy of yours."

"Yes. When I talked to him yesterday, he said he's been riding his new bike every day and he can do tricks now."

Kebra grinned. "Those are words guaranteed to strike terror in a mother's heart." She moved off to check on the other crew members.

Laney contemplated the burned hillside again before going up to help Rita and Katie. Here, the scars were obvious, she thought, but Caleb Ransom's were on the inside, as well. Then she wondered why her troubling neighbor had popped into her mind. She'd been very conscientious about keeping him out.

She still felt bothered by the way Caleb had pulled away from her. She'd thought he was enjoying kissing her as much as she was enjoying being kissed, but something had stopped him and she didn't know what. If only she could get past his defenses, pull him out of that shell where he spent so much time closing everyone out and— Darn! Once again she was spending way too much time thinking about him. She clapped her helmet back onto her head and, grabbing her shovel, climbed the hill.

CHAPTER SIX

CALEB EMERGED FROM Don Parkey's veterinary clinic with a small paper bag in his hand. Some of the horses Don had brought out to his ranch had probably never had inoculations of any kind, so Caleb had to take care of it. He didn't mind, especially if it meant the horses would be ready for adoption sooner. He was glad to see their progress, but they needed to move on to permanent homes, for Don intended to bring him more. And it would be best if he didn't get too attached to them.

He'd also told Don about Laney's plan to capture the mama cat in his barn and asked for the loan of a humane cat trap, which he'd already placed in the bed of his truck.

He was about to climb into the truck when a high-pitched voice shouted his name.

"Mr. Ransom! Mr. Ransom! Wait for me!"

He turned to see Sam Reynolds racing

up the sidewalk toward him, arms and legs pumping while an older man and woman hurried along behind him. Familiar with Sam's enthusiasm, Caleb quickly moved to brace himself against the cab of the truck before the boy reached him.

True to form, Sam barreled into him and wrapped himself around Caleb's good leg. Caleb leaned back and grinned, touched that this little boy was so accepting of him. He reached down and lightly chucked Sam under the chin, making the little boy giggle.

"Hi, buddy."

"Hi, Mr. Ransom. Where's Bertie?"

"Hey, you got my name right," said Caleb. "Well done."

"I been practicing," Sam said proudly. "Where's Bertie?" he asked again.

"He's home." Caleb indicated the paper bag in his hand. "I had to come in to town to get some medicine for some of the horses."

"Are they sick?"

"Ah, no." Caleb frowned. How did he explain inoculations to a four-year-old? "No, but this will keep them from getting sick."

Before Sam could ask any more questions, the woman with him stepped forward and held out her hand. "Hello, I'm Vivian Crown, Delaney's mom, and this is my husband, Frank."

The two men shook hands as Vivian went on. "Sam has been filling our ears with stories about the wonders of Bertie."

"He can be on his back and put *all four* feet up," Sam told his grandparents.

Probably not for the first time, Caleb thought, observing their indulgent looks.

"Amazing," they agreed, smiling at Caleb, who returned an awkward smile of his own.

While Sam entertained them with more stories about Bertie, Caleb studied them. He didn't see much family resemblance between these two and their daughter. They were both fair-skinned and blond, where Laney and Sam had dark hair and eyes. They weren't very tall, either. Frank couldn't have stood much over five-six and Vivian was shorter still. Laney must tower over them.

As he pondered the discrepancy, Caleb's eye was caught by someone who'd stepped out of the same office building that housed the vet and was standing there about twenty feet away, staring at them. She was a skinny woman in a severe blue suit. She seemed to show avid interest in Sam, who prattled on about Bertie, oblivious to the newcomer. The woman moved closer.

Sam's grandparents, however, when they saw her, seemed to draw in on themselves. Frank reached down and caught one of Sam's gesturing hands, holding it protectively. Curious about this new dynamic, Caleb barely heard what Sam was saying.

When the boy's stories about Bertie finally ran down, Vivian managed to get a word in. "Laney should be back in a day or two," she said to Caleb.

"Back? Where is she?"

"My mom fights fires," Sam said, wiggling his hand out of his grandfather's grip and holding up his fists like a pint-size prizefighter.

Caleb's gaze darted between the two adults. "Fires?"

"Oh, I guess she didn't tell you," Vivian said. "During the summer, she's a wildland firefighter. They get called out several times each season. Sometimes they go straight from one fire to another." She smiled down at her grandson. "So Sam stays with us or his aunt and uncle."

The newcomer cleared her throat, demanding acknowledgment.

"Hello, Monette. How are you?" Vivian said coolly, her sudden change in demeanor surprising Caleb. In a crisp tone she introduced the woman as Monette Berkley and told her that Caleb was Laney's neighbor.

"So she's still fighting fires, is she?" the newcomer said. "It's dangerous—"

"Monette!" Vivian snapped. "Laney knows what she's doing."

The skinny woman's mouth shut and her lips almost disappeared into a thin line as she frowned. Her eyes narrowed into angry slits.

Caleb's gut was burning. He'd been in firefights, the kind where bullets and rocket-propelled grenades flew instead of sparks. Now Laney was in danger and he had a mental picture of flames and explosions. Sweat popped out on his forehead and he couldn't trust his voice, so he nodded in apparent agreement with Vivian. He could see the woman named Monette gazing at him with speculation in her eyes, but he turned away.

The Crowns looked at him oddly as if he'd suddenly been struck mute—which he had.

Then they each took one of Sam's hands, said goodbye and hurried down the sidewalk.

Sam called back over his shoulder. "Mr. Ransom, give Bertie a hug for me."

Ignoring Monette, who still stood there, Caleb climbed into his truck, but had to sit for several minutes to let his hands stop shaking. Laney was in danger and it made him sick. She was a mother, for crying out loud. How could she take chances like that? Possibly leaving her son an orphan?

Didn't she know what that was like for a kid? To have a parent snatched away? And in this case, she was apparently Sam's only parent. If something happened to her now, Sam probably wouldn't even be able to remember her. Family photos wouldn't cut it, wouldn't make up for the loss of his mother.

What was she thinking?

Gripping the steering wheel, he took a deep breath, held it, released it and breathed in again. By sheer force of will, he pushed the panicky rage down. After a few more seconds he reached out to start the engine.

"Not your business, Ransom," he said through his teeth, shoving the key into the ignition and cranking the engine. As he drove away, he looked in his rearview and saw Monette Whoever-she-was staring after him.

LANEY ARRIVED HOME at midnight the next night, but didn't stop to pick up Sam even though she had a new book about cowboys that one of her team members had bought for him. The thoughtful gift was carefully wrapped in her last clean T-shirt and stored in her duffel, awaiting her son's surprised delight.

She always preferred to get cleaned up and rested before she saw him. As a four-year-old, he had a vision of her firefighting job that didn't quite fit with reality and she was content to leave it that way for now. He had never seen her grimy from soot or red-eyed from smoke and exhaustion. It was all she could do to make the hour's drive home from Tucson, shower and fall into bed.

When she awoke the next morning she felt groggy and out of step. It took her much longer than usual to comb the tangles out of her hair, since she'd gone to bed with it wet.

She finally managed to tame it into submission and into a loose braid.

After four days in her heavy, protective turnouts, she wanted to wear as little as decently possible. Pulling on shorts and a tank top, she dug a pair of sandals from the bottom of the closet.

Since she had been fighting fires for three years, she knew that when returning from a fire, it took her a day or so to decompress and return to her usual routine, and it always seemed as though she was moving in slow motion.

In the kitchen, she considered what to eat for breakfast while coffee seemed to drip into the carafe with agonizing sluggishness, its tantalizing aroma torturing her. As she waited, she called Vivian to say she'd be there to pick up Sam in a couple of hours, reassuring her mother that no one on her team had been injured in the fire. Then she sat, sipped her coffee and tried to think about what needed to be done.

First, she had to get her equipment ready in case she was called out again soon. It wasn't unusual for her to go to back-to-back fires across the West during the summer.

Getting her equipment ready was part of her process of winding down from the last fire. After she completed that task, she would go get Sam.

In between, she had to stop by to talk to Caleb Ransom about that darned cat. She had managed to entirely avoid thinking about Caleb for six days—well, almost entirely. Recalling what had happened the last time she'd seen him made her squirm.

She hardly knew the man and yet she'd kissed him desperately. "Desperately" being the operative word. She had never reacted to a man that way, not even her husband, James. It was confusing and embarrassing, but remembering how Caleb had felt and tasted was also exhilarating.

The embarrassing part was the way he'd pulled away from her, as if her touch had been distasteful.

They certainly hadn't done anything wrong. They were both adults and a few kisses didn't amount to much.

She frowned. It wasn't the kisses; it was the emotion behind them. It was her need, her attraction to him and the hungry way he had responded to her—at least until he had pulled away.

He was her neighbor, though, and out here neighbors depended on each other, so she had to pretend that nothing out of the ordinary had happened. Besides, Sam liked him and he seemed to like her son. She would get past this awkwardness for Sam's sake. She simply had to remember that being neighborly didn't mean being overly friendly or begging for kisses. And it especially didn't mean she had the right to pry into his personal demons or into whatever it was that made him so withdrawn.

After she finished her tasks, she locked the house and climbed into her Jeep. As she turned toward the road, she saw that her grass had been replaced and some petunias had been planted to replace the ones Caleb's cattle had destroyed. These were pink, though, instead of purple. Maybe the nursery had been out of purple ones. She had to smile at the thought of Caleb wheeling a cartful of pink petunias around the store. She would thank him for replacing the ruined plants. It would give her something to talk to him about as she tried to establish some kind of neighborly rapport with him.

When she reached the ranch, she saw that Caleb's truck was parked in its usual place in front of the house. So, unless he'd gone out on his horse, she knew he was home.

Bertie didn't greet her arrival with his usual single bark. She thought maybe he was accustomed to the sound of her Jeep coming up the drive. Her knock went unanswered, so she decided to check the barn.

When she stepped inside, she waited for her eyes to adjust to the dim light then scanned the rafters for the cats. They weren't to be seen. By the door, she saw that their food and water dishes were in the same place and her cat carrier had been set to one side. Next to it sat a humane cat trap, which Caleb must have borrowed from Don Parkey.

She considered that for a moment and decided it was a positive sign. He had expected her to come back. That's why he'd gotten the trap. He had kept his promise by replacing her ruined plants and he depended on her to do what she'd promised: catch the mama cat and take her in to be spayed.

A faint smile touched her lips. In spite of

his prickly nature and his desire to be left alone, Caleb knew he could depend on her.

That gave her confidence to continue her search for him.

"Caleb," she called out as she walked farther into the barn. There was no answer.

Laney became aware of a high-pitched whining noise coming from a room at the back of the barn, which she hadn't noticed in her misguided attempt to lure the cat into the carrier a few days ago. It was a tack room and the sound she was hearing was a drill.

The noise stopped as she approached the door, which was open part way, then started up again when she pushed the door wide.

Caleb stood with his back to the door. Shafts of sunlight streamed in around him and specks of dust floated in the still air, bathing him in a warm glow.

Laney's heart did a slow roll in her chest when she saw that he was shirtless against the heat. He was bent over a couple of sawhorses where he had redwood fence slats balanced. He was drilling holes in them.

His movements were sure, easy, as if he'd done this many times before and could do it as long as he wanted. The muscles in his arms and back flexed and stretched in turn.

She knew she really shouldn't be watching him when he didn't know she was there. But she was enjoying this too much.

The drill went silent as Caleb shut it off. He turned slightly, stretching out his right arm to grab another drill bit from a box balanced on one of the slats. When Laney saw that the skin on his right side was red and puckered, she gasped audibly.

Caleb whirled around, the drill held out in front of him like a weapon. Eyes narrowed, he took a quick step forward as if to defend himself. When he saw that it was Laney, he raised the tip of the drill into the air and said, "What are you doing? Sneaking up on me like that? I could have hurt you."

She held out her hands as if to soothe him. "I...I didn't mean to startle you. You didn't hear me when I called and..." She couldn't take her eyes from the scars on his chest. They were like the ones on his face. No doubt, the ones on his leg were even worse.

Seeing where her attention was focused, Caleb placed the drill on top of the wood he was working with and grabbed his shirt from a nearby hook. He pulled it on and quickly buttoned it. All the while, he kept his eyes downcast.

For some reason Laney thought of a knight buckling on his armor, making sure he was invulnerable to injury.

He didn't say anything, only waited for her to speak. She finally managed. "I came to tell you thanks for the work you've done in my yard," she said. "And I'll come back to catch that cat. I see you got the trap. Did you get it from Don?"

He nodded—one abrupt movement of his head—but still didn't say anything. He only watched her, as if waiting for some kind of reaction. Did he think she was going to run away screaming because she'd seen his scars?

She pressed her palms together in front of her, smiled awkwardly and gave a little nod. "That should work fine, then. The trap, I mean."

He still just watched her.

This was like trying to have a conversation with a chunk of granite, she thought in despair.

She felt as if her forced smile was plastered onto her face in the most fake manner possible. "Okay, well, then… I'll be on my way.

Gotta pick up Sam and get some groceries. I'm completely out of milk and breakfast cereal, Sam's main sources of nutrition and—"

"Was it bad?"

She blinked at him. "What?"

"The fire. Was it bad?"

He was asking a question, one that almost seemed personal. She answered cautiously, not wanting to send him scuttling back into his shell. "Not as bad as some I've seen. No danger to homes."

He looked at her for several seconds. "That's not what neighbors do, you know."

"What?" she asked in complete bewilderment. Was there something wrong with him that he couldn't stick to a topic?

He tilted his head in the direction of her place. "You insisted that I give you my number so we could keep in touch if necessary. Going off to fight a fire isn't on your list of things to tell your neighbor?"

Heat rushed into her face. "Oh, I didn't think about it," she said, flustered. "When I lived in the apartment in town, my neighbors all knew when I was called out because the walls were paper thin and I had one who broadcast it all over—"

"Doesn't matter." He held up a hand. "But don't lecture me on keeping in touch if you don't plan to do it."

"Yes, of course." She felt stupid. He was right.

"I took those flowers over there and you weren't home."

She studied his expression. Was he mad? Sulky? What? She felt as though she was walking on eggshells.

"Again, thank you for that," she said quickly, afraid he would interrupt again, though she didn't know why that bothered her. At least he was talking.

Frowning, he turned, picked up the drill again, inspected the bit, set it back down, turned and looked at her once again. "I didn't know where you were until I saw Sam in town with your mom and dad."

She smiled at the mention of her son. "Oh, I haven't had a chance to talk to Sam yet and so he didn't tell me—"

His gaze met hers. "Firefighting, Laney? That's what you were doing?"

"Um, yes. That's my summer job."

"It's dangerous." He gave her a fierce look,

his dark eyes boring into her. "You've got a little boy."

Her jaw dropped. She could hardly think of what to say. Anger began to spark. "I'm well aware of that."

"He needs you."

"And I'm attempting to provide for—"

"What if something happened to you?"

She clapped her hands on her hips and stuck out her chin. "My family would take care of him. I have a will, life insurance…"

"It's dangerous," he repeated. "Fire, sparks, falling trees, wind, flashover fires."

"I've been very well trained and I've had three years of experience," she answered tersely, taking a step forward. She didn't like being on the defensive, and she *really* didn't like it when someone tried to tell her what to do. "I've been on the same team the whole time. They're excellent and we always look out for each other."

Not seeming to even hear her, he ran his hand through his hair in a jerky movement. As if restless, he turned and walked away a few steps, then turned back to her. "You never know what's around the corner or five clicks down the road." His hand shot out, punching the air for emphasis. "You don't know what's going to happen, what might blow up, where or when things might go wrong."

Through a fog of mystification and anger, Laney realized that he was worried about her and didn't want to be. But there was more than worry behind it.

"My team and I—we always look out for each other," she repeated, her voice taking on a gentler tone.

"They can't see everything. They can't be everywhere even if they want to be."

With a flash of insight, she understood his concern. Her annoyance vanished and her lips curved into a smile. She took a step closer to him and held out her hands, palm up. "Caleb, no one was shooting at us."

She heard his breath hitch in his chest. His gaze shifted away from hers.

For a moment Laney didn't know what to say for fear he would shut himself off. He probably felt embarrassed because he'd overreacted, but that was what made it so touching. He was trying his best to be tough, uncaring, inaccessible, but it was getting harder for him. He probably hated that, but she saw it as a good sign. She wanted to drive a wedge into the cracks forming in his wall.

Laney reached out and placed a hand on his arm. The muscles jumped beneath her fingers. "Thank you for caring about Sam. About us."

He didn't meet her eyes, didn't answer. He shook his head.

"Don't deny it, Caleb. It's good that you care about us."

"No. No, it isn't." His voice was gruff.

Her hand tightened on his arm, turning him to face her.

"Don't, Laney."

The pace of her heart picked up. "Don't what, Caleb? Care about you? Too late. I do, and so does Sam."

"Don't care about me. Don't touch me," he answered, though he didn't try to shake her off or to move away.

Forget about a fire being dangerous, she thought. *This* was dangerous. Excitement began to build as she faced the challenge of breaching his defenses. She tilted her head and gave him a steady look. Her smile was meant to provoke him and her tone held the barest hint of mockery. "Why not, Caleb? What do you think might happen?"

This time he really looked at her, meeting her gaze, touching on the way strands of the dark hair that had escaped her braid and curled around her face. His eyes grew dark with purpose. When he spoke, his voice was low. "Haven't you played with enough fire this week?"

Her smile widened. "Apparently not."

"Don't do something you'll regret."

"Stop telling me *don't*."

He pulled her to him, locking one arm around her shoulders and the other around her waist. She couldn't have moved away if she'd wanted to, and she certainly didn't want to. To let him know that, she slipped her arms up around his neck and smiled into his eyes.

"Don't—"

"I told you, stop telling me *don't*."

His mouth tilted into one of his rare smiles, as if he was pleased with her answer, and then his lips touched hers.

In spite of her absorption with Caleb, Laney became aware of a faint noise outside. It took her a moment to realize it was the sound of a vehicle coming up the drive and parking.

Wherever Bertie was on the property, he gave one of his characteristic barks in greeting, alerting them that someone was coming.

She turned her face from Caleb and tried to catch her breath. He chased her lips with his own, but she held him off.

"Caleb," she said shakily, "we have to stop. There's someone here."

His head came up, looked around and then back at her. "I didn't hear…"

She grinned. "You were otherwise occupied."

He shook his head as if coming out of a fog. "I always hear. You distract me."

And he obviously didn't think that was a good thing. The warmth she'd been feeling cooled and dismay took its place. What had she been thinking? That a few kisses from her would suddenly turn him into a warm, social human being who would want to be around other people?

Her heart sank. It would take more than that, much more, but she didn't know what. She hated that he was brushing her aside this way. As it had the last time they'd kissed, it embarrassed her and made her angry.

"You distracted me, too," she said. "I only came to say I'll take care of that cat tomorrow."

"You don't have to…"

She gave him a warning look. "I'll take care of the cat tomorrow, Caleb. And in the meantime, maybe you should go see who's invading your privacy out there."

His jaw tightened as if he was biting back his words. He turned away from her and left the tack room.

Laney wrapped her arms over her stomach and stood for a minute, waiting for her heart rate to slow down and her sense of annoyance and betrayal to ease. She had to stay away from him. She admitted that she was attracted to him, and only heaven knew why. He was solemn, often surly, distant and puzzling.

But he was a puzzle she seemed bent on solving, a confusing jumble of standoffishness, need, prickly independence and vulnerability. He made her want to know more about him and never see him again. He was endlessly challenging.

And he kissed like a dream.

"You're a pathetic, love-starved woman, Laney," she muttered, smoothing her clothes and hair and stomping out behind Caleb.

To her complete shock, she found Monette Berkley standing in the yard talking to Caleb as her gaze darted around, taking in the barn, the house and especially the man.

Monette was dressed in another of her drab suits, this one a muddy green. Laney didn't know how she could wear an outfit like that in the Arizona summer heat, especially since it was obvious she was suffering. Her face was red and sweaty, huge half-moons of perspiration spread down the sides of her jacket, and the thick, black hair that was falling out of a clip was plastered to her face and neck.

When Laney emerged from the barn, Monette rounded on her. "I came over to see your new place, but when I drove by, I saw your Jeep so I knew you were here." Her attention focused on Laney's flushed face. Immediately her eyes narrowed. She looked quickly from Laney to Caleb and back again.

Caleb met the woman's gaze steadily while Laney could feel heat rising in her face. Annoyed with herself for her reaction, she looked at Monette squarely and said, "It's best to call before you come in case I'm not home."

"I don't have your number."

Laney didn't offer to give it to her.

Monette raised her chin haughtily as her gaze traveled over Laney, finally landing accusingly on her face. "And you've probably been off fighting fires."

"That's really none of your business." Laney hated the defensive note in her voice.

"It is if you're neglecting your son." Monette grasped the lanyard that hung around her neck and waved the badge that identified her as a social worker with the Department of Child Safety. She considered it proof of her right to interfere.

"Is that why you've been hanging around out here, Monette? To see if I'm neglecting my son?"

"The welfare of the children in this county is my responsibility. I can't shirk my duty," Monette responded without actually answering the question. "The people of Arizona are depending on me to make sure children are properly cared for by their parents."

"I certainly don't neglect my son!"

Monette sniffed. "It's my job to make sure that you don't."

Fury choked Laney and she fought for control as Caleb stepped forward. Before he could say anything, the three of them were distracted by a truck and horse trailer that turned off the road and rumbled up the drive. Laney recognized Don Parkey behind the wheel.

Monette stared at the rig as it pulled in, then flinched in alarm when a loud whinny split the air. The crash of hooves against the inside of the horse trailer had her turning once again to Laney.

"Mr. Ransom, are those horses coming here?" Monette's already pale face had whitened even further.

"Probably. Why?"

"They're dangerous." Monette's mouth worked as if she was trying to form words but no more came out.

"That's why the vet is bringing them out here, so they won't be around too many people."

Monette barely seemed to hear what he was saying. "You be sure you keep Sean away from those wild horses," she warned, lifting a shaking finger to point at the trailer.

"Sam," Laney said through gritted teeth. "His name is Sam."

Monette didn't respond. Another loud squeal from one of the animals had her scuttling toward her car. Laney wondered if Monette had realized she'd overstayed her welcome, but she doubted it. The woman never noticed or cared what other people thought.

"What was that about?" Caleb asked as Monette sped away and Don came to a stop. "I saw her in town when I saw Sam with your parents. She was asking about you then."

Laney saw red. "She was my neighbor in town. She's always sticking her nose in my business. One time when Sam was about two and a half, I was taking him and his tricycle to the park. While I was locking my door, he climbed on his trike and headed for the stairs. Monette let out a shriek and I grabbed him. While I was glad she let me know he was in danger, she seems to have seen that episode as her license to tell me how to raise my son. She's a social worker, so she thinks she has the right to tell everyone else—well, mostly me—what to do. She considers herself an expert in child welfare." Laney took a breath, trying to calm herself. "The only good thing is that I hardly ever see her now."

"She doesn't look you in the eye when she talks to you."

"No, she doesn't," Laney acknowledged, wondering where this was going.

Before either of them could say anything else, Don hopped out of the truck. Eager to forget about Monette, she turned to greet him. The vet had grown up in Sweetsilver, as she had, but he was several years older than she was. He was married and had four children under the age of ten. One of them usually accompanied him when he took a trip away from the office in the summer, but he was alone today.

Even though he wasn't yet forty years old, was a licensed veterinarian and had graduated summa cum laude from the university, he appeared to be the ultimate Arizona cattleman. He had cattle of his own, drove a truck wherever he went, wore a cowboy hat, pressed jeans and rattlesnake-skin boots. Seeing him always made Laney smile.

"Hello, Laney."

When she returned the greeting he turned to Caleb. "You catch that cat yet, Ransom? You want me to try again? I don't have time right now, but…"

"I should go," Laney said. "Have to pick up my son. I'm running a bit late." She couldn't wait to get back to her normal life. She headed for her Jeep.

"No, haven't caught the cat yet, Don," Caleb answered in a lazy tone, "but Laney offered to help."

She swung around and gave him a look that asked why he wanted to involve her in this conversation. His face was unreadable.

"Oh?" Don looked at her and then his gaze swiftly traveled between the two of them.

Oh, no, she thought. He sensed something. His big, happy grin confirmed it. He actually put his hands together gleefully.

"That's good. That's really good," he said. "Laney, when you catch old mama cat, bring her in and I'll take care of her. No point in adding to the feline population any more than we have to."

Don looked from one to the other of them again, and his grin grew even bigger. "That's good," he said again. "That's really good."

Laney knew he was seeing something that wasn't actually happening, but she didn't know what to say. The three of them stood looking at each other, Don grinning like a father whose child had done something brilliant, Caleb and her looking like two kids who'd been caught with their hands in the cookie jar.

Finally, Caleb said, "Don, did you bring me some more horses?"

"What? Oh, oh, yes. A couple of geldings, both of them lame, which is why they were abandoned in the desert. Idiot smugglers can't be bothered to learn how to pack an animal— put on a sawbuck or a decker, distribute the load, make it easier on the animals so they last longer."

"Don," Caleb asked mildly, "you planning to coach drug smugglers on how to load a pack animal?"

Don ignored him, caught up in his diatribe. "That's probably why these two pulled up lame and the criminals turned 'em loose... won't even spare a bullet and put them out of their misery. But these two didn't need to be put down. They'll heal if they're given enough time and attention."

"I thought I'd put them in the east pasture," Caleb said, heading toward the horse trailer.

Taking that as her chance to leave, Laney waved a hand at the two men and hurried to her Jeep. Obviously, it was past time for her to go.

CHAPTER SEVEN

THE TWO MEN watched Laney's Jeep make a wide turn and head toward the road.

Caleb could feel Don's gaze on him and he returned it, giving the inscrutable sergeant's stare he'd perfected for the benefit of his soldiers.

Don only grinned. "Glad to see you're getting to know your neighbors, Ransom."

"Don't have much choice. Her little boy is in love with my dog. He makes tracks over here whenever he can." Caleb paused, reaching into his jeans' pocket for his cell phone. "Speaking of tracks…" He thumbed through the photos on his phone and held one up. "Do you recognize these?"

Don took the phone, shielded the screen from the sun with his hand and, for several seconds, studied the image of an animal track with an open pocketknife placed beside it to indicate its relative size. He glanced up, eyes narrowed in concern. "Looks like a mountain lion."

"I was hoping it was a bobcat."

"You got the pocketknife you used for comparison?"

Caleb pulled it from his pocket, flipped it open and handed it over.

The vet looked at it and then at the picture. "Definitely mountain lion. A big one, too."

Caleb grimaced. "That's what I was afraid of." He took the phone and put it back in his pocket.

"Where did you see these?"

"By my stream." Caleb jerked his thumb to the west. "Or what there is of it before the monsoons start. There's always a little seepage, but usually I see only coyote and rabbit tracks." He paused, remembering the scream he had heard a couple of times now. He described it to Don then said, "I thought I saw something out here in the brush one night, but it was dark, not enough moonlight to see by."

"That's definitely lion. It's unusual to have one in this area, but we've been in a drought for years, more than a decade, so their usual food and water sources have dried up." Don lifted his head and looked across to the corral where Addie and her filly were standing, apparently asleep in the shade of a cottonwood tree. "Better keep an eye on that filly. It's easy for a lion to take down a foal, and if this one is desperate enough, he won't hesitate."

"I will." Caleb gazed at the long-legged, big-eyed filly. But he was thinking of Sam innocently running through the pasture or down the road without a clue that he might be in danger.

In spite of his stated goal to be left alone, Caleb knew he would feel responsible if something happened to Sam.

"I will," he repeated. "I'll keep him safe."

Don's crack of laughter brought him back to reality. "You've got a lot to learn about horses if you think that filly is a *he*."

Caleb grinned, recalling how he'd corrected both Laney and Sam about the foal's gender. "Come on. Let's unload these two geldings."

MONETTE PULLED OVER when she was several miles down the road and sat with the engine idling and air conditioner blasting in her face as she gulped for air. She tried to still her pounding heart and quell the terror that sent chaotic thoughts skittering through her brain.

Horses. She hated them because they were unpredictable, determined to go wherever they wanted to, jump any fence and come pounding down with their huge, fearsome hooves.

Memories of such an occurrence flashed through her mind, causing sweat to pop out on her forehead in spite of the cold air. They were memories she didn't want. She'd shoved them down for years, never letting them linger, driving them relentlessly away whenever they surfaced.

Nausea welled up in her, filling her throat with burning acid. Hands shaking, she fumbled in her briefcase and pulled out a bottle of water. After taking a long gulp, and then another, she felt calmer, able to think rationally.

"They were in a trailer," she whispered to herself. "They couldn't get out."

She practiced slow breathing as she worked to calm herself. "They weren't a danger to… to me."

"But what about that little boy?" She took

another gulp of water. "What about Sean—
I mean Sam?"

She hadn't seen him, but that didn't mean
he wasn't there. He could have come running
up at any second, right under the hooves…
Monette's mind scurried away from that
thought. She tossed down more water. Sean
could have been hurt.

She sat for a few more minutes, staring
through the windshield at the blindingly
bright day. That little boy could get hurt
around those horses. It was her job to protect him.

Okay, then. She would keep an eye on
Caleb Ransom's ranch, as well as on Laney's
place.

Monette straightened in her seat as purpose and determination filled her. Nothing
was going to happen to little Sean. Not on
her watch.

THE NEXT DAY Sam and Laney were both
happy to be home and together, but Sam
missed his cousins and was looking for
something to do.

"Can I go visit Bertie?" he asked that morning. He had scooted out of bed and come to

find her in the kitchen where she was enjoying a cup of coffee and the online news. He had made a stop at the bathroom. His pajama bottoms were twisted around to the side and every hair on his head was on a mission of its own.

She gave him a kiss and said, "No. Not today. Some new horses were delivered to Mr. Ransom's house, and he'll be busy with them."

"New horses?" Sam's eyes lit up like Christmas morning. "You mean babies?"

Laney could have kicked herself for mentioning that, but she knew Sam would have found out soon, anyway. "No. They're older horses, but they've been injured, so he has to take care of them."

Sam tilted his head. "What's gingered?"

Laney stifled a laugh. "Injured means they've been hurt, like the time you fell and hurt your knee. Remember when you had to wear a big bandage?"

Sam nodded and Laney knew he was probably imagining horses with bandaged knees, but he soon changed the subject and began telling her about his bike-riding adventures with his cousins.

After they ate breakfast and he was dressed, they went outside so she could watch him demonstrate his new skills. When Sam grew tired and they returned to the house, he began looking around for something to do.

Laney knew that boredom and Sam were not a good combination. A plan formed in her mind. The high school student council was raising money for a group of students to go on a trip to Mexico where they would help rebuild a school that had been damaged in a flood. Laney had agreed to help with a bake sale to be held on Saturday in front of Wilson's Emporium in town. She wanted to get her cookies made ahead of time in case she was called out on another fire. Her mother could keep them frozen until time for the bake sale.

That was the day after tomorrow, she realized, looking at the kitchen calendar. She'd been so busy she hadn't noticed the date.

"I need to get something over to your grandma today, Sam." Vivian had retired from her job as the high school's guidance counselor and social worker, but still remained involved with volunteer projects at the high school. "So, how about you help me bake cookies?" she asked.

His face lit up again. "Sure. How many can I eat?"

"Two."

"How many are we gonna make?"

"Several dozen."

"Is that more than two?" he asked, wrinkling his nose.

"Lots more. But you can still only eat two."

Laney began looking around the kitchen trying to remember where she'd stored everything when they'd moved in. She'd put some of her things away hurriedly, thinking she would straighten things out when she had to. Obviously that moment had come.

"Can other people eat two?"

"Measuring cups," she muttered, opening the cabinet where she thought she'd put them after baking the cake for Caleb.

"Mommy," Sam asked again, "can other people eat two?"

She looked at him. Blinked. "What? Oh, yes, honey. Other people can eat two."

"Are we making chocolate cookies?"

"Aha. Here they are." She snagged the measuring cups from the back of the cabinet and took down her biggest mixing bowl. "Chocolate? No, butterscotch."

"Can we share them with other peoples?"

"Sure." Now she was on the hunt for her favorite cookbook. She glanced around, recalling that she'd put all her cookbooks in one place and then moved them. The bookcase in the living room, she recalled, hurrying to grab the one she wanted. When she came back into the kitchen, Sam was perched on the tall kitchen stool, swinging his feet against the cross braces.

"It's good to share, right?"

Laney liked where this was going, so she turned and smiled at him. "Yes, it sure is."

"Okay, then," Sam said in a satisfied way. He looked up and smiled his happy, little-boy smile. "I'm ready to help."

"Go wash your hands."

Sam bounced away and she knew he was washing his hands by the volume of the song he was singing. He was back in a few minutes, dragging the tall stool over and climbing onto it, ready to assist.

Laney helped him measure the ingredients, which he added carefully while she mixed them.

"You're doing a good job, Sammy," Laney said, watching him grip the measuring cup of flour with both hands.

"Yup, this is my job." Sam's brow wrinkled. "Mom, what's a job?"

Accustomed to the way his mind worked, jumping from one topic to another, Laney answered. "A job is something you do for money, or something you do to help someone else. The job you're doing right now helps me, and when we give the cookies to Grandma, the high school kids will sell them and their job will be to go to Mexico and use the money to rebuild a school…"

Her voice trailed off when she saw the puzzled look on Sam's face. Once again, she had given him much more information than he needed. She didn't know if that was because she was a mom or because she was a teacher.

"So," Sam said slowly, "helping can be a job?"

"Yes."

He seemed satisfied with that answer and they finished their task.

When she was ready to place the dough

on the cookie sheets, Sam stood by with the spoons she would need.

"Thanks, buddy. You're very handy to have around."

"That's 'cause I got two hands," he answered solemnly.

Laney swallowed a laugh. Whenever Sam made one of his funny observations, she wished she had someone to share them with, someone to talk to about how wonderful he was without it seeming as though she was bragging about her son. His father had chosen not to be part of Sam's life, except to send the child support payments. Even those came directly from his bank to hers. James didn't even have to write a check. It was a painful reality she had long since accepted, though she didn't think she would ever understand how Sam's father could have walked out on him.

When the cookies were baked and cooled, Sam helped Laney separate them into packages of one dozen each, which they sealed in plastic wrap. Sam made sure she put some in the cookie jar for the two of them. With a cookie in each hand, Sam headed for his room.

After she finished cleaning up the kitchen,

Laney looked down at the smear of flour across her blouse. "Sam, I'm going to change clothes before we take these to Grandma and Grandpa's." She hurried to her room.

It took her only minutes to change into another shirt and a pair of shorts and to brush her hair into a ponytail. But when she emerged from her room she discovered that Sam had disappeared once again.

"NOT AGAIN," CALEB MUTTERED, his heart sinking. Bertie's happy woof of greeting had alerted him, and he'd scooted out from under his truck to see Sam coming up the drive.

Caleb had hoped that Sam's time away from home would have made him forget his obsession with Caleb's animals. He'd hoped that Laney had finally gotten through to her adventurous little boy. But it seemed she hadn't. And this time Sam was on his bicycle. His face looked very determined.

Moving gingerly, Caleb pulled himself to his feet. By the time he was upright, Sam was only a few feet away. The little boy held something in one hand, which made hanging on to the handlebars of his bicycle a challenge. Still, he was managing.

Sam came to a wobbling stop and put his feet down on each side of the bike. "Hi, Mr. Ransom," he called out as he tried to step off his bike and hang on to whatever was clutched in his fist.

Bertie was a little quicker on the uptake than his owner. He ran up to the boy and made a swiping grab for whatever Sam was holding with such determination.

"No, Bertie!" Sam shouted, stretching his little arm as high as he could while trying to disengage himself from the bicycle. "You have to share!"

Bertie, of course, didn't listen. He had Sam's hands empty in no time. As the little boy made a flailing gesture at Bertie's head, his bike fell over, taking him with it. He landed, face-first in the dust.

Caleb felt as if he'd taken a knife to the heart. His first instinct was to crouch and pull the boy into his arms, but he knew his weak leg wouldn't allow that. Instead he braced himself against the truck and leaned over, gesturing for Sam to come close as he said, "It's okay, Sam. Get up and come over here."

Crying, Sam pulled away from his fallen bike and got to his feet. Slowly, he approached and buried his face against the dusty leg of Caleb's jeans.

"Hey, it's okay, sport," Caleb said, awkwardly patting Sam's head. The trusting way the little boy leaned against him put Caleb's heart in his throat. He wanted to pick him up and hug him, but knew they would both end up in the dirt. Besides, he wanted this kid to keep his distance, didn't he?

"I brung cookies," Sam wailed. "I was gonna share, but Bertie ate 'em."

"Well, he's a dog and dogs aren't used to sharing." Caleb looked down at his own rough, grease-stained hand as it rested on Sam's shiny brown hair. He hadn't expected this and he didn't want it.

He *didn't*, he thought with a fierce kick of emotion. But it was hard not to offer comfort to this kid. "It…it was nice of you to want to share with us."

After a minute Sam pulled away and knuckled the tears from his eyes. "I helped my mom make 'em and they were butterscotch."

"Mmm, that's good—" Caleb stiffened as a thought occurred to him. Fear prickled along his nerves. "Sam, you didn't come through the pasture, did you?"

"Nuh-uh." Sam shook his head and rubbed his face against Caleb's jeans, no doubt sharing his tears and snot, Caleb thought. "I rode my bike on the road. I ride good now 'cause Shane and Logan teached me."

Caleb sighed in relief. "Sam, you know you shouldn't have come over here by yourself, but I'm really glad you didn't come through the pasture."

Sam looked up. Apparently ready for a change of topic, he glanced around and noticed the tools scattered by the truck. His own troubles forgotten, he asked, "What are you doing?"

Glad to talk about something that didn't involve too much emotion, Caleb said, "The truck's making a noise. I ran over something out in the pasture. I'm trying to find out what it was."

Sam gave him a suspicious look. "Did you runned over that pony?"

"Pony? Oh, you mean Addie's filly? No." He turned and pointed toward the corral. "See, I moved the mommy horse and her baby so they can both start liking people more." Caleb paused, unable to believe he'd said "mommy horse."

Sam gave one of his little hops of excitement. "Can I pet the pony?"

"Uh, no, not yet."

"But she wants to be my friend. She wants me to ride her like a cowboy does."

"She's too little. Nobody can ride her yet."

Determined to have the last word, Sam said, "I could."

Realizing he was getting nowhere, Caleb changed tactics. "We can go over by the corral later so the, uh, mommy horse can see that you won't hurt her baby."

"I won't hurt no baby," Sam promised solemnly. "Cowboys don't hurt babies."

"I know."

"What's her name?" Sam asked abruptly.

"Who? The baby horse? I haven't given her a name."

Sam stared at him. "Then how does she know when you're talkin' to her?"

"I don't really talk to her…"

"How's she gonna know you like her if you don't?"

Caleb had no answer for that. "Would you like to name her?"

Sam gave another of his hops of delight. "Yeah!"

Caleb watched in amusement as the little boy squished up his face in thought and gazed at the filly.

"Awesome," he announced after a minute.

That surprised a chuckle out of Caleb. "You want to name her Awesome? Why?"

Sam stared at him. "'Cause she's so awesome. Can I pet her since she's got a name?"

"No, you still can't pet her," Caleb answered, amazed at this kid's persistence.

Sam stuck out his bottom lip in a pout but it only lasted a few seconds because his attention turned to the tools on the ground. His gaze swooped back to the truck. "Can I help fix it?" In his eagerness, he bounced up and down.

"Well, I don't know..." Caleb heard a noise on the drive and looked up to see Laney's Jeep approaching. "Here comes your mom."

Sam turned and saw her, too. "Uh-oh," he said, scooting behind Caleb.

Caleb suppressed a laugh as Sam wrapped his arms around his leg—at least it was the good one—and hung on. The kid had more strength than Caleb would have suspected.

"Don't let her get me," Sam begged, hiding his head in the back of Caleb's thigh and, no doubt, squeezing his eyes shut.

As Laney stopped the Jeep and jumped out, Caleb reached down and attempted to peel the boy off his leg. "Sam, you did something wrong and you have to face up to it."

"Nuh-uh," Sam responded, holding on tight.

Laney approached with the sharp, quick steps of an angry mom. She had a look on her face that Caleb remembered receiving from his own mother. Hoping to head her off, he held up his hand and said, "He's all right."

"Temporarily!" she said, rocking to a stop in front of him. Her anger brought high color to her cheeks and a spark to her eyes.

"Take a breath," he recommended, then, leaning against the truck, he braced himself again so that he could bend over to pry Sam's arms away from his leg. "Come on, sport," he said in a soothing voice he didn't even know he possessed. "You have to come out and face the music."

"Don't like music," Sam answered.

"You still have to listen to your mom."

Reluctantly, Sam let Caleb peel him away,

though he still had one arm wrapped around his leg. The little boy stood with his head down, sliding one foot back and forth in the dirt.

"What did you do that you weren't supposed to do?" Laney demanded, crouching in front of her son. Placing her hand under his chin, she raised his head until he was looking into her eyes.

Caleb could see that she was really angry. Obviously, Sam could see it, too.

"You said we could share our cookies with other people."

"Sa-am," she warned, stretching his name out. "What did *you* do that you weren't supposed to do?"

He peeked up at her and then looked down at the dirt again. "I brung Bertie and Mr. Ransom some cookies, 'cept Bertie ate all of 'em."

"No. What you did that you weren't supposed to do was to come over here *at all*. You didn't have permission."

"I'm sorry, Mommy." Sam hung his head, the very picture of abject apology.

Caleb watched her expression, seeing the play of emotions as she tried to decide what to do about this defiant son of hers. He hoped she never decided to take up playing poker. She'd lose on the first hand, Caleb thought with wry amusement.

Dismay and frustration chased exasperation across her face. The brown of her eyes deepened to almost black. She stood with her hands on her hips, her head thrust forward, her dark hair drifting around her shoulders as she looked at her son. She took in a mighty breath then exhaled slowly.

Caleb could tell she was weighing the various forms of punishment, trying to find one that would convince Sam he needed to obey. She was so distressed and stymied that he felt a pang of pity for her—an emotion he didn't want to feel. Between her and this boy of hers, he felt like he was drowning—and he'd only known them for a couple of weeks.

This was way out of hand and he didn't know what to do. He'd tried to make it clear that he didn't want company, didn't want other people around at all. Things had been fine, wonderful in fact, until the two of them had moved in next door. He'd kept to himself and nobody had bothered him. But Sam was having none of that. And every time Sam showed up, his attractive mother showed up, too. He could deal with the boy much easier than he could deal with the mom.

"Sam," Laney finally said, "you can't come over here. Mr. Ransom has work to do. Jobs that need to be finished every day."

Eyes bright, Sam looked up. "Jobs? You mean like helping? Helping is a job. You said."

"Um, well, yes, but…"

"I could help Mr. Ransom."

"No, Sammy. You can't."

Caleb watched her shoulders slump. Laney's struggle to make her son understand was defeating her. Being a single mom wasn't easy, he knew, especially with a lively boy like this one.

"I could! I could!" Sam insisted. "It's my job." He whirled around, his gaze scanning the ground. Spying Caleb's tools, he dashed over and lifted a wrench, though it took two hands to do so. Moving back to them, he said proudly, "See, Mom. I can give Mr. Ransom his tools." He looked up at the two adults, tears swimming in his eyes. "And I can play with Bertie."

Laney's face creased with compassion as

she crouched in front of him again. "No, Sammy. You can't."

Caleb stared at the little boy in dismay. He opened his mouth to tell Sam in no uncertain terms that he had to stay away, and then couldn't believe the words that actually came out.

"Sure, Sam. I could use a little help around here."

Sam's head snapped up and Laney let out a squawk of surprise as she rose. "What?" she said. "What do you mean?"

His gaze shot to meet hers. She was staring at him in horrified wonder, asking what on earth he'd been thinking.

Darned if he knew. For some crazy reason, though, he thought the idea had merit, so he blundered on.

"Bertie could use the company." He glanced around, trying to find the place where his good sense had gone to hide out. "And…and Sam's right. I could use some help. Like when I was working on the truck right now. If you'd been there to hand me tools, it would have been easier."

He looked from Laney's dazed expression to Sam's overjoyed one. Well, he'd started this now and he couldn't back out of it. He carefully avoided making eye contact with Laney as he pointed a finger at Sam. "But you are never, ever, to go under or around or on top of any animal or piece of equipment on this place unless I'm there. And you don't ever come over here unless your mom brings you or I come pick you up. Agreed? And you don't ever go into the pasture, and especially not near the spring." He held out his hand.

Sam looked at him, obviously trying to process all the words that had come pouring out of this man who up until now had been relatively silent. The boy broke into a grin and reached out his hand to shake.

That was when Laney found her voice, thready and squeaky though it was. "Sam, why don't you play with Bertie for a minute while I talk to Mr. Ransom?"

Seeing the fire in her eyes, Caleb wondered if he should be wearing body armor. He didn't think he was going to like this "talk" at all.

"Okay," Sam said, trotting over to where Bertie, ever ready for a nap, had made himself comfortable in a little patch of grass beneath a mulberry tree. "Bertie, guess what! I get to come work here and see you all the time." He fell down beside the dog to pet him and whisper in his ear.

Caleb heard Laney's quiet moan of distress and his attention swung back to her stricken face.

She stepped closer to him and whispered, low and fierce, "*What* were you thinking?"

He lifted his hands and then let them fall to his sides. "Give it some thought. This might be a good idea."

Her eyes widened and she shook her head as she advanced on him. "A good idea. Are you completely crazy? You didn't even ask me and you offered my four-year-old a *job*?"

When all else fails, he thought, bluster. "You're right, I should have talked to you about it, but you looked a little frustrated with him, and if he's going to be coming over here, anyway, it might as well be to do something worthwhile—planned—not something he'll get in trouble for. Isn't it better than having him come through the pasture or ride down the road?"

Color washed into her face. Boy, she really was mad. "It's better if he learns to *obey*."

"As I see it, we're zero for three in trying to keep him from coming over here."

"*We?* You mean me." She clapped a hand to her chest and thrust out her jaw. "You think I can't control my son, keep him safe? Do you plan to report me to Monette?"

"Who? Oh, you mean that woman who was here. No, of course not." Caleb wished he'd never started this. "I thought I could help."

Laney threw a hand out in a wide arc. "Two weeks ago you were telling us to stay off your property and now you're trying to help."

Caleb stepped closer and lowered his voice into a fierce whisper. His dark eyes bored into hers. "I think we're past the point of either of you staying off my property. I seem to recall we were in my barn yesterday kissing and—"

"That's got nothing to do with this!"

"Of course it does, even if it's something neither one of us wants. There is no possibility that Sam will stay away—or you, either, for that matter—so it might as well benefit both of us."

Red stained her already flushed cheeks and her eyes shot angry daggers at him. "You're undermining my authority."

"Baloney."

So furious at the way he dismissed her concerns, she couldn't even form a sentence.

Taking advantage of that, he said, "Besides, if he's here, we'll know he's safe. At least this way I can control the situation."

"Since I obviously can't."

"I didn't say that."

"You didn't have to." Spinning around, she called Sam, who jumped to his feet and scampered to join her. The tone in her voice brooked no disobedience. She hustled him into the Jeep and strapped him in, then boosted his bicycle into the back and quickly got behind the wheel and sped away.

Caleb watched them go, a tangle of emotions twisting his gut. He hadn't meant to make her so mad. Every step he took with her seemed to be wrong.

CHAPTER EIGHT

IT TOOK LANEY a good half hour to calm down. As soon as they got home, Sam took one look at her face, ran into his room and shut the door. She spent the time sweeping the kitchen and washing up the cookie-baking dishes.

"Now all of a sudden this man that I didn't even know a few weeks ago is trying to tell me how to raise my son?" she seethed aloud. "When did this happen? *How* did this happen? He made it obvious from the very beginning that he didn't want us around. There were moments when it seemed like he could barely bring himself to even look at Sam. And now he wants to *hire* him?"

Even though it made her squirm with embarrassment, she couldn't deny that Caleb had been right about their kissing yesterday. She didn't want to admit it, but she felt an undeniable attraction to him. Did he feel attracted to her or was it only a matter of proximity? She was the only woman around so he'd felt free to kiss her?

No, she didn't think that was it, but it only added to the snarl of emotions in this situation.

"I'm not going to allow this," she went on, stomping around the kitchen. "I'm not going to let Sam spend time over there, get involved with Caleb, come to depend on him, want his company…"

She sank onto a kitchen stool. "Oh, who am I trying to kid? *I'm* the one who wants those things, but he had no right to offer Sam a job!"

She wasn't going over there. She wasn't going to try being neighborly or to get involved with him at all. Whatever he did was his own business and none of hers, just as what she did with her son was her business.

She was doing her best with Sam. She was! Raising a four-year-old on her own was hard, but she knew what she was doing. There was no reason for Caleb to interfere.

Laney would keep Sam away if it killed her—as soon as she caught that darned mama cat.

WHEN SHE FELT that she wouldn't be a danger to herself, her son and every other driver on the road, she put Sam and the baked goods into the Jeep and headed for her parents' house.

As soon as she lifted Sam down from the Jeep, he dashed up to the front door and into the house. Laney followed him with her containers of cookies. Inside the living room, she found Vivian fussing over her banana tree. Laney had seen it yesterday when she'd picked up Sam, and had been pleased to see it hadn't yet started to droop. In fact, it seemed to be thriving.

Vivian turned to give hugs to Sam and Laney and then indicated her new plant and the tiny green spears of fruit that were sprouting. "Isn't it beautiful? And it's producing a bumper crop of bananas. I think I'll order another one or two. Can't you simply imagine all the healthy, delicious fruit we can all have? We'll never have to buy bananas again."

"That's good, Grandma," Sam said before dashing off to the hall closet to find the box of toys Vivian kept there for her grandchildren.

Laney smiled at her mother, imagining the crates of bananas that were about to invade their lives. "Why don't you wait to see how well this one does, Mom, before you buy more?"

Vivian looked astounded at her daughter's suggestion. "It's doing beautifully! Why would I wait to buy more?"

Laney thought of all the plants that had been sacrificed to serve her mother's enthusiasms, but decided not to dampen Vivian's happiness over this one. Besides, it was her own money she was spending.

Instead she indicated the containers in her hands. "I brought cookies for the bake sale."

"Oh, wonderful!"

Vivian whisked them out of her hands and into the kitchen. She scrubbed her hands and then began separating the cookies into groups of one dozen, placing them on attractive paper plates, which Laney then wrapped securely in plastic wrap. The entire time, Vivian continued to talk about her banana plant, thrilled with the idea of succeeding in growing something.

Laney listened, smiling in acknowledgment of Vivian's passion and thinking how much she admired her mom's perseverance in trying to get something green to grow. Vivian never gave up, convinced that if she could only find the right combination of plant, soil, water, fertilizer and light, she could be a master grower of houseplants, if not a master gardener.

Vivian was petite and plump, appearing much younger than her sixty-two years, her hair dyed blond in her attempt to fight aging. She was what Laney wanted to be—content, sure of herself and her convictions. She had always worked with an economy of motion that Laney envied, never seeming to hurry but accomplishing a great amount of work in a short time. She had loved her career as a high-school counselor and had, in fact, been the one to inspire Laney to become a teacher.

Vivian was so engrossed in what she was saying now, that she didn't hear a truck stopping out front. Laney did, though, and glanced out to see Ethan and his family approaching. Sam heard them, too, and ran out to meet them.

Once her monologue had wound down and she had her mind off her new love affair with the banana tree, Vivian glanced up with a smile, took one look at Laney's face and said, "What's wrong? Are you okay? Is Sam okay?"

Laney finished wrapping the last of the cookies, then waved her hand dismissively. "We're fine."

"Then what is it? I can tell something's wrong." Vivian searched her expression, her motherly instincts rushing forward.

Laney knew she would have to tell her. Vivian wouldn't let it go until she did. Before she could begin, though, Ethan sauntered into the kitchen with Sam on his shoulders. Jenny followed with Shane and Logan. Ethan wasn't a tall man—none of the men in the Crown family were—but he'd made a big show of dipping his knees as he came through the doorway, warning Sam to watch his head. Sam had laughed and ducked his head, but reached up to slap his hand on the top of the door frame.

"Laney," Ethan said, "your son tells us he's got a job. Isn't there a law against putting four-year-olds to work?" He reached up and hooked an arm around Sam, easily flipping him to the floor.

"*That's* what I'm upset about," Laney said, looking at her mom. While Ethan and Jenny pulled out chairs and sat at the kitchen table, she went on to tell them about her encounters with her neighbor, ending in his crazy offer to give Sam a job. She didn't mention the kisses. "I don't understand how he could have come up with such an idea and why he didn't discuss it with me first. Does he think he has to step in and take over because I can't take care of my son?"

The three boys lost interest in the adults' conversation and went to play with the toys.

"I doubt that's what was on his mind, Laney," Ethan said.

Laney looked at her brother. "The problem is that I don't *know* what's on his mind or why he's going along with the idea."

"Maybe he likes having Sam around the place, so he's not so lonely," Jenny suggested. "Ethan told me about him. That he's single and lives alone with his dog."

Frowning, Laney looked at her sister-in-law and considered that. Jenny was from a large family and couldn't imagine having no one around.

"I didn't think he minded being alone.

From the beginning, he said he didn't want us at his place, but…"

"That's changed?" her mother suggested.

Laney nodded as she thought *how* it had changed, what she had done to make it change, although that hadn't been her intention.

"Remember what I said before." Ethan crossed to her and gave her a one-armed hug. "That you know better than anybody that what people say they want and what they really want are often two very different things. Maybe Ransom didn't know what he was missing until you and Sam started showing up around his place."

"Maybe," she admitted. "I'll have to think about this before I decide what to do."

Ethan gave her a hard look and started to say something more, but the boys came running into the room, begging for cookies, and the conversation broke up.

It was just as well, Laney decided. Her emotions were in such a snarl that she didn't know which one to untangle first. Uppermost was her anger with Caleb for suggesting she couldn't keep her son safe even though that very thing was the driving force in her life. Next was the push-pull of her attraction to him, something she hadn't asked for and didn't want.

When she'd kissed him, she'd been operating from pure need. Her attraction to him was growing, but she felt constantly off-kilter and out of step. He seemed to want to push her away, but he kissed like a dream and she couldn't get it or him off her mind. This was getting complicated.

"So are you going to let Sam do this?" Ethan asked, coming back into the room.

"I don't know. I'll have to talk to Caleb about it. I've got to go back over to his place tomorrow, anyway." She looked up in time to see Vivian and Ethan exchange a look. "To catch a cat for him," she said quickly. "It needs to be spayed and Caleb can't catch it on his own."

"Oh." Ethan nodded knowingly. "Catching a cat. Sounds neighborly."

"Since you already have plans with him, you might as well talk to him about Sam working for him. Can't hurt," Vivian added.

Oh, yes, it could. Catching that silly cat was neighborly, not personal. Talking to him about Sam was personal.

"GET THE CAT, LANEY," she muttered to herself the next day. "Talk to Caleb about this crazy idea of hiring Sam. Get the cat. Take it to Don and leave everything else—including Caleb Ransom—alone."

"Huh, Mommy?" Sam looked up from the bowl of his favorite crunchy cereal. "You gonna leave Mr. Ransom alone?"

"I wish I could," she answered with a sigh, buttering a piece of toast and taking a bite. She had spent hours last night trying to fathom why he wanted Sam to work for him. Jenny was probably right, that Caleb was lonely and wanted to have someone around without actually coming out and saying it. She wasn't sure about that, though. Caleb certainly hadn't shown any reluctance to express his desire to be by himself. Things had changed, though.

One way or another she and Sam had wormed their way into his life—and she and Caleb had kissed, more than once, and she had completely enjoyed it. She didn't know what she'd been thinking when she had come on to him so strongly, touching his arm, turning him to face her, teasing him. Only that Caleb had awakened a neediness in her that she'd been ignoring since her husband left. Why did it have to be her moody, difficult neighbor, though? Why couldn't it be someone who was nice, easy to understand...? "Boring," she muttered.

"Good morning, Mom," Sam said dutifully, having misheard her. "Are we going to go say good morning to Bertie and Mr. Ransom? Can I show them my new cowboy book?"

"Yes, Sammy, we are, and yes, you can." And that was all. She would trap the cat and they would leave. "As soon as we finish breakfast and you've brushed your teeth and washed your face."

"Okay," he answered, surprising her. He loved running water, but didn't like washing his face in the morning, or brushing his teeth at any time. But the certainty of visiting his favorite dog and cowboy had made his usual objections evaporate.

Cheered that they were avoiding their customary morning confrontation, Laney dressed in khaki Bermuda shorts and a sleeveless navy blue shirt. Sam dressed in red shorts and a cowboy shirt. Clapping his hat on his head, he announced he was ready then dashed to the Jeep.

When they arrived at Caleb's, Sam's feet had no more than hit the ground than he spun around, his face frantic. "I forgot my new book, Mom! I want to show Bertie and Mr. Ransom my new book." Tears filled his eyes.

"Oh, Sammy. I'm sorry, but…"

"If you want to go back for it, he can stay with me," Caleb offered, stepping out of the barn. He held a bridle in one hand and a cleaning rag in the other.

Sam gave a little hop of joy. "Please, Mom?"

Laney looked from her son's hopeful face to Caleb's watchful one. She didn't know why she hesitated. She knew Sam would be safe with him.

"Oh, all right," she said. "I'll only be gone for a minute." Sam ran to stand beside Caleb while she jumped back in the Jeep and hurried home.

As soon as she was gone, Sam looked eagerly at Caleb. "Can I say hi to Addie and Awesome?"

"Sure. Let me put these away," he answered, indicating the bridle and rag in his hand.

"Can I pet Awesome? She wants me to. I *know* she wants me to."

Sam's pleading face got to him. He mulled the request over for a second then said, "Sure, why not?"

With a whoop of joy, Sam ran for the corral as Caleb muttered, "I'm already in deep manure with your mom, anyway."

As Caleb headed back into the barn, Sam reached the corral fence, which he quickly clambered up. "Hey, Awesome," he called out. "What are you doing?"

Caleb smiled as he put the bridle away. Sam loved everything about the ranch and the horses were second only to Bertie on the little boy's list of things he loved.

Since his leg was a little stiffer than usual, Caleb moved slowly toward the corral. He glanced up to see Sam teetering on the top rail, his extended hand within inches of the filly's velvety nose.

With an effort Caleb kept himself from calling out and startling the boy, but he moved more quickly, wanting to reach Sam before he fell.

Then everything seemed to happen at once—Sam reaching out for the filly, Addie turning and seeing the little boy, Bertie's sudden, furious barking, and a big, tawny-colored shape emerging from the shadows beside the horse trough.

It was a mountain lion.

Addie whinnied, high and furious, the sound splitting the air and startling Sam who immediately tumbled into the corral, landing with a thump and not moving. Awesome danced away skittishly, close to her mother.

"Sam!" Caleb broke into an awkward run, his attention fixed on the new threat to the corral. The mountain lion was long and lean, too lean. It was obviously hungry and therefore desperate.

Caleb watched in horror as the cat turned its attention from the filly and began to stalk the prone figure of the little boy.

"Sam!" Caleb called again, desperate for him to stand, to move, anything to escape the danger, knowing that the wild animal could move much faster than he could, especially with his bum leg.

He reached the corral fence at the same moment Addie apparently saw the danger to the little boy. Whirling around with another sky-splitting scream, she lunged toward the cat, then, Awesome close to her side, moved to Sam and stood protectively over him. Sam sat up shakily and looked around in confusion.

Caleb, who was climbing over the fence and dropping down to the other side, cursed as his bad leg crumpled beneath him and agonizing pain shot through him. He clapped a hand around a fence slat, fighting the blackness that threatened to overcome him.

"Not now, not now," he whispered fiercely from between gritted teeth, trying to focus on what was happening.

Addie, oblivious to Caleb's plight, was still taking care of business. She stood over Sam, who'd begun to whimper. Her head was down, her screams of fear and warning, one after another, splitting the air. When the mountain lion took a step toward her, Addie reared up on her hind legs and the cat backed off.

Caleb stepped toward Addie and Sam, hoping to pull Sam to safety, but his knee buckled and he went down. As he fell, he banged his head hard against the fence, but still, he managed to snag Sam's shirt and drag him close.

Addie reared again and again, driving the mountain lion to the other side of the corral, until the desperate animal leaped over the rails and lit out for the Mule Mountains. The mare stood, chest heaving, breath huffing from her nose, then turned to examine her filly, ignoring the two humans huddled by the fence.

Caleb felt unconsciousness closing in and tried to fight it, but finally had to surrender. "Stay here, Sam," he murmured as everything went black.

WHEN LANEY RETURNED, she could see right away that something was very wrong. Bertie ran straight for her, planted his feet and began barking. It wasn't the single bark of greeting, though. This time he went on and on, then began turning in circles.

"What's the matter, boy?" Laney asked, her gaze sweeping the yard for Caleb and Sam.

In response, Bertie turned and ran around the end of the barn with Laney close behind.

Bertie loped to the fence and continued

barking. Laney rushed up behind him and saw Caleb and Sam in the corral. Caleb lay crumpled on the ground, apparently unconscious, his bad leg twisted beneath him. Sam was on his knees by Caleb's head. He looked up at her with frightened eyes.

"Sam, what happened?" she asked as she scaled the fence and dropped down beside him.

He nodded, his face caked with dirt and streaked with muddy tears. "I was gonna pet Awesome. Caleb said I could. Then I falled in and then Caleb falled in. Then Addie was screaming and the cat runned away."

Deciding now wasn't the time to sort out all that, Laney quickly examined her son; saw that, except for scrapes on his hands, he was unhurt. She hugged him and then fell to her knees beside Caleb.

"Oh, Caleb, what happened?" she asked. She checked his pulse, which seemed normal, then ran her hands over his head, examining it for an injury. When her hand came away bloody, she stifled a horrified gasp and looked at her son, whose eyes were huge in his face.

Jumping up, she dashed for the gate. "We've

got to call 9-1-1. I want you to wait here with Caleb while I get my phone, okay? You stay right here." She swung through the gate and Bertie ran in to check on his humans, sniffing and whining. Then she quickly closed it.

Sam nodded, looped his arm around Bertie's neck and stared at Caleb's white, still face.

Laney hurried to the Jeep to get her phone, dialed quickly and soon had paramedics on the way. She grabbed a blanket she always kept in the back and returned to the corral. By the time she was at Caleb's side again, he had begun to stir and was trying to sit up.

Groggily, he asked, "Sam, are you okay? What happened to the…?" He tried to struggle to his feet.

"No, Mr. Ransom. We have to stay right here," Sam said, putting a small hand on Caleb's shoulder to push him back. "Or my mom will get mad."

"She sure will," Laney said, dropping down beside Caleb once again and grasping him by both shoulders. "Stay still," she commanded.

Caleb's dark eyes were full of pain, but he muttered, "I'm okay. I can get up."

"Maybe so, cowboy," she said in her firmest mom-and-teacher voice. "But you're not going to. You're staying right where you are until the paramedics get here. They'll move you."

He started to argue, but a wave of pain hit him and he sucked in a sharp breath between his teeth. He passed out again.

Caleb was still unconscious when the paramedics arrived fifteen minutes later, loaded him into their vehicle and left for the hospital in Sierra Vista. Laney made sure Caleb's corral gate was closed and the house was locked up, gave Bertie food and water, and then followed the ambulance. On the way, she dropped Sam off at her parents' house, promising him she'd call to tell him how Caleb was doing.

By the time she arrived at the hospital, Caleb was awake and being examined in the emergency room.

In spite of his obvious pain, he was glowering at the doctor. "I've got to get back to my place, Doc," he said as Laney walked up.

"No, he doesn't," she said. "Don't listen to him, Doctor."

"Are you his wife?"

For some reason Laney's gaze shot to Caleb's face. He scowled, obviously not liking that suggestion.

"No." Her answer came out squeaky and she cleared her throat. "No. I'm his neighbor. He can stay here as long as you think he should. Other people can take care of his place and his animals."

"Don't start thinking you're going to march in and take over," Caleb barked.

Laney tilted her head and smiled. "I already have, and don't tell me don't."

The doctor looked from one to the other as if trying to decipher the dynamic between them. "The cut on your head doesn't look too bad, but we'll know more after we do some X-rays." He left, pulling the curtain closed behind him.

"Caleb, what were you doing when this happened?" she asked.

To her surprise, he answered. "Chasing off a mountain lion."

Laney gave a horrified gasp.

"Don't worry, Addie did the job for me. She saved her filly, and Sam, and me. I need to tell the sheriff and the Game and Fish Department."

"That's what Sam meant when he said the cat ran away. I thought he meant one of the barn cats." She started to shake as she thought about how close her son had come to being killed by the wild animal.

"To him," Caleb said, "I guess it looked like a really big cat, and I'd never seen one before, but it was definitely a mountain lion. I could see he was starving—he's so thin!—so there's no telling where he'll try again. Thanks for all you did today, Laney, but I can't stay here."

"We don't know that yet," she answered calmly, sitting in the chair next to the bed. "But I suspect the unthinkable is about to happen to you."

He gave her a wary look. "What might that be?"

"You're going to have to accept help."

He glowered at her and then looked away. When he didn't respond, she went on. "Is there anyone you want me to call? Your family?"

"No. I'll call them if there's anything I want them to know."

Laney's eyes sparked with interest. So he *did* have a family. A dozen questions sprang to her lips but she held her tongue. "You realize, don't you, that you're ridiculously stubborn?"

"So I've been told." He leaned his head back on the pillow and closed his eyes.

Laney watched as his face relaxed and he appeared to doze off. She knew she should probably leave, and she didn't doubt that's what he wanted. This time, though, he wasn't going to be able to go down that avenue of avoidance. He'd shoved people away long enough, including his family, from what she could tell.

The emergency room and imaging department weren't busy, so Caleb was taken to X-ray within minutes. He would also undergo a complete examination.

Laney took the opportunity to call the sheriff about the mountain lion and was promised that a deputy and officers from Game and Fish would be out to Caleb's place right away. She then called her dad to tell him what had happened and to ask him to bring Sam in for a more thorough examination than the one she'd given him in the corral. Besides, she wanted to hug her little boy again and reassure herself that he was all right.

"Your head looks okay, no concussion," the doctor was saying to Caleb as she re-entered the exam room. "Probably that cut won't need stitches."

Laney bit her lip against a comment about the hardness of his head. Caleb gave her a look that said he knew precisely what she was thinking.

The doctor then held up the film and Laney stared when she saw the amount of metal in his leg. For a moment she thought the shiny objects were fragments of shrapnel, but then realized they were strategically placed pins. Surgeons had fastened the pieces of his leg back together.

"IED?" the doctor asked tonelessly.

"Yeah. Afghanistan," Caleb responded, giving Laney a look she couldn't decipher. Was it a challenge? Daring her to say something? Puzzled, she looked at him, but he turned his gaze back to the X-ray.

The doctor pointed to a line that slanted across his shin bone. "Hairline fracture here, but it's a clean break. You'll need to be in a cast for six weeks, as well as physical therapy. This may have been the best thing that could have happened to you."

"How?" Caleb asked, frowning.

"You'll have to give it time to heal. I don't think you did before. If you take care of it this time, though, it shouldn't cause you so much pain. Of course, with that much metal in you, you'll feel it every time the weather changes." The doctor turned to leave. "After we get the cast on, we'll get you to a room. You should be able to go home in a couple of days."

He was gone before Caleb could open his mouth to argue.

Laney reached over and took his hand. "Give it up," she said. "You have to rest in order to heal. You don't have to do this alone."

Caleb looked at her then away. "I'm not good at accepting help," he said in a gruff tone.

"Then it's time for you to change, isn't it?" She paused, her eyes searching his face. As she looked at him, thoughts of what might have happened that day suddenly hit her with the force of a Mack truck. Tears filled her eyes.

"Sam c-could've…b-b-been killed and…

and you, too," she said between sobs, leaning forward, her arms crossed over her stomach. "Y-you s-sa…saved his life." Boneless in her grief, she dropped her head onto the bed and sobbed in earnest.

Caleb placed a comforting hand on her head, letting her fright and worry pour out.

She felt his hand and reached for it, gripping it hard and turning her head so that his palm rested on her cheek. The steadiness of him calmed her and, after a few minutes, she sat up, embarrassed.

Caleb handed her a box of tissues. "It wasn't me," he said. "Once my leg went out from under me, I was pretty much useless. Addie saved Sam. Her protective-mother instincts included Sam, as well as her filly. I've never seen anything like it. She was incredible."

Laney gave him a wobbly smile. "Then she's getting a lifetime supply of sugar cubes from me."

"She'll like that."

Caleb's color was coming back, though he still looked exhausted. She saw how his mouth tightened whenever he fought a wave of pain.

Laney was glad to think about something besides her terror over what might have happened to Sam. "You'll have to take the pain pills, you know."

"How did you get so bossy?"

"I teach high school. I spend my life with adolescent boys. Had to learn how to handle them."

The corner of his mouth kicked up, but another wave of pain hit him and his breath hissed out from between his teeth. "Hate those pills."

She reached for his hand. "Why?"

His rough fingers gripped hers. "They knock me out and I have...nightmares."

Fresh tears filled her eyes. With her free hand, she reached up to smooth his hair back from his face. His forehead felt clammy. "Take the pills, please, Caleb? As soon as we get Sammy checked out, I'll be back and I'll stay with you tonight. I'll be there to wake you up if you have a nightmare."

"But my animals..."

"They'll be fine. I'll get my mom and dad to go get Bertie and I know other people who will go out and look after the horses and cattle. I'll call Chet Bartlett. I need to tell him about the mountain lion. He's right on our lane and he and his son, Ryder, owe me big time. I tutored that kid every day after school so he could pass the writing portion of the state standardized test."

Caleb's eyes fixed on hers. She saw a battle going on behind his before he sighed and said, "Okay. Thanks for the help."

She beamed at him and was going to reward him with a kiss when the doctor returned with a nurse and all the equipment necessary to set his leg. With a wiggle of her fingers, she scooted out of the way and went outside to make some phone calls. And to wait for her parents and her son to arrive.

CHAPTER NINE

"THERE'S SOMETHING TO be said for pain medicine," Laney whispered as she gazed down at Caleb's sleeping form. "It makes you too groggy to kick me out."

As promised, after Sam had been checked out at the emergency room and pronounced unharmed, she had organized care for Caleb's animals. There was nothing for him to worry about, she thought smugly as she settled herself into the recliner beside the bed. The nurses had brought her a pillow and blanket even though they'd assured her she didn't have to stay the night because they would be checking on him regularly.

No doubt, they thought she was overreacting since it was only a broken leg, but they didn't know about his nightmares. She closed her eyes, though her mind kept replaying the day's events. If Caleb had been alone in that situation, he would have eventually made his way back to the house and tried to deal with the pain on his own, for a while at least. She knew being idle wouldn't be easy for him, but it was the best thing. And he could forget about being a recluse, at least for the next few weeks.

Too restless to sleep, she got up and wandered aimlessly around the room. She picked up Caleb's clothes, folded them and started to put them in the small closet. Unable to resist, she lifted his shirt to her nose and sniffed the combination of laundry soap, dust and Caleb that clung to the fabric. Even though she knew no one had seen her, she quickly put the shirt away and closed the closet door.

Glancing down, she saw his boots and picked one up. He had big feet and these boots were heavy, probably reinforced, she thought. They weren't cowboy boots. Tipping it up, she looked for the manufacturer's name and was surprised to see something handwritten on the back in bold, black ink. It was the letter O and a plus sign. She stared at it for several seconds before understanding clicked into place.

"His blood type," she whispered. "O positive."

Shakily, she set the boot down and then stood staring at Caleb's sleeping face. She hadn't known that soldiers wrote their blood type on the backs of their boots. Humbled, she turned away, marveling at the men and women who were willing to die for people they didn't even know and used such a simple gesture to try to preserve their own lives.

IN SPITE OF the painkillers, or maybe because of them, Caleb slept fitfully, dreaming of mountain lions and horses and little boys, and waking several times to find Laney curled up in the chair near his bed, her head resting on a pillow she'd balled up and stuffed beneath her neck so that her head lolled over the arm of the chair. He'd never seen anyone do that before and he wondered groggily how she avoided getting a stiff neck. He hadn't wanted help from her, but here she was, sleeping a few feet away—and he found it…comforting. He drifted off to sleep again, expecting his usual nightmares to invade, but oddly, they didn't.

When he woke again, sun was coming in

the window and Laney was gone, the blanket she'd been using neatly folded on the chair. He wondered if she would be back.

To his frustration, except for the times when the nurses got him up and moving around, he spent the morning in forced inactivity, something he hated, mostly because it gave him too much time to think.

Right now, he was thinking about how his life had gone off the rails, off the course he'd been so sure was the right one, of coming to Arizona, buying his place, keeping to himself. First it had been Don Parkey, showing up with those pitiful drug horses, then Laney and Sam. He was still trying to figure out how he'd given in to the idea of having Sam work for him.

Shudders rattled him whenever he thought about Sam, so small and defenseless, lying in the corral dust being stalked by a hungry mountain lion.

LANEY SWEPT IN right after lunch, whirling into the room and letting the door whoosh shut behind her as she dug in her shoulder bag for something. She was wearing a yellow sundress that showed off her toned arms. Her hair was down, swirling around and bouncing on her shoulders. She was gorgeous. Caleb felt as if he'd been socked in the gut.

She looked up and gave him a distracted smile. "Hi, how are you? Ah, here it is." She pulled a small object out and handed it to him. "Your phone," she said as if he wouldn't recognize it. "Your mom wants you to call her. I assured her that you're all right, but she seemed worried. She said she'd be here in a few days."

His mouth dropped open. "You called my mother?"

"Of course not. Even *I'm* not that nosy. You dropped your cell phone in the corral when you fell. I found it this morning when I went to see about Cisco. It rang. I answered it."

"But you're not nosy?"

"Certainly not, but I can't resist a ringing phone and when I looked at the Caller ID and saw the last name was Ransom, I knew it had to be a relative. Luckily, it was your mom."

"Luckily," he said dryly. "You know, you really don't have any right to…"

"To what?" she asked sassily. "Save your life? See that your animals are looked after?"

Caleb gave her a disgruntled look to make sure she understood that this discussion wasn't over.

"Did the sheriff or Game and Fish come out to my place?"

"Everyone came, found the tracks, followed them back toward the mountains, but couldn't find the cat." She chewed her bottom lip anxiously.

"Probably long gone. Don't worry," he said gruffly and then asked about Sam.

"He's okay." Laney sat abruptly as if her knees had gone rubbery on her. "He thought it was just a big kitty cat in the corral with you guys."

"It was big, but it was no kitty cat."

"I didn't tell him any different because I don't want him to worry. I talked to my parents about it this morning. We're going to keep it quiet, not make a big deal of it." Shakily, Laney lifted her hand to her face. "If you hadn't been there…"

"I tell you, it was Addie. She drove the cat away." Caleb wasn't trying to make light of what had happened, only to ease her mind.

She gave him a grateful smile and nodded as she inhaled a deep breath.

Before he could say anything else, the physical therapist, a matronly woman with iron-gray hair and a no-nonsense attitude, came in. Within minutes she and Laney had him in a wheelchair and into the physical therapy room.

Caleb looked around grimly. He'd hoped to never visit one of these places again. The therapist explained what they'd be doing over the next few weeks to strengthen his leg.

"Yeah, I know the drill."

She placed her hands on her hips and gazed down at him. "Good, because you'll be here two or three times a week."

"I don't think so. I've got a ranch to run, and—" he started to say, but Laney cut him off.

"Tell us when he needs to be here," she said, ignoring his glare and whipping out her cell phone. "I'll put it on my calendar. When I can't bring him, someone else will. We'll set up all of his appointments right now. Don't you worry, he'll be here. Aa-aa-nd," she added pointedly, "he'll be your best, most cooperative patient ever."

The therapist grinned her approval and picked up a large paper calendar from a nearby desk. They discussed the best times and dates for his appointments while he sat and fumed.

When he was back in his room and settled in bed once again, he turned to Laney and gave her his best army sergeant's glower— which was actually hard to do when she was tweaking a pillow under his head.

"Laney, I don't need you to take me to physical therapy."

"How are you planning on getting here? Obviously you can't drive. Ride Cisco? Hitchhike? If you give people that look you're giving me right now, no one will pick you up and give you a ride."

"I'd find a way."

"No need. I already did." She settled into the chair where she'd spent the night. Even though he knew she probably hadn't slept well, she looked fresh, impertinent and, hang it, beautiful, sitting there. Her smile was self-assured and challenging, daring him to contradict her.

Since he couldn't, he folded his arms over his chest and stared at the ceiling. *Real mature, Ransom.*

Laney sighed happily. "I love it when a man knows he's lost an argument. Now, here's what's happening." She launched into a recitation of the arrangements she'd made for his animals and his place.

"Sam couldn't stand the thought of being separated from Bertie, so both of them are at my mom and dad's house. I'll pick them up later and if I'm called out to a fire, I'll take them back to my mom and dad's."

Caleb lifted himself onto one elbow and stared at her. "You might be going out on a firefighting job when…" His words fumbled to a stop. What had he been going to ask? "When I need you?" Which would make him feel like more of a fool than he already was?

Laney blinked at him. "I'll have to go if I'm called. I'm part of a team."

"Yes, of course." He lay back against his pillow. *Shut up, Ransom.*

"Chet and Ryder Bartlett are keeping an eye on your cattle and horses. They'll help you out until you're fully recovered if you need them to. I programmed Chet's phone number into your cell so you can call and thank him."

"But I could need help for six weeks."

Laney's eyes rounded. "Imagine having to accept help for six weeks." She reached over and squeezed his hand. "You can do this," she said as if she was giving him a pep talk.

"Looks like I have no choice."

Laney tossed his hand away from her and stood. "And as soon as you're well, you can crawl back into your little crab shell and stay there." She turned to leave. "I'll be back tomorrow to take you home. Call your mother," she said over her shoulder.

Glumly, Caleb watched her go. He supposed there was no chance of her spending the night with him again.

CALEB WOKE TO the late-night hospital sounds of doors quietly whooshing shut and a low call over the intercom. He knew these sounds, these smells, and they gave him a sense of familiarity—far better than the moments of terror he'd been experiencing in the nightmare he'd just had.

He sat up, rubbed his hands over his face

and reached for the water pitcher and glass that had been left at his bedside. He took a big drink and tried to recall what the nightmare had been about. He couldn't pull it into focus, but it didn't matter. It would be back. It always came back.

He'd been having the same nightmare, fighting the same battle, for nearly two years. Now, along with the smoke of combat, the blood, the shouting and screaming, the explosions and the *thunk-thunk-thunk* of ammo rounds, were a mountain lion and an injured little boy, as if the craziness that went on in his head whenever he took painkillers wasn't enough. The ironic part was that the nightmare was a battle that had never happened, or rather, an amalgamation of every battle he'd been involved in, every one he'd witnessed or had heard about. The addition of an innocent little boy and a hungry wild animal only ramped up the terror level.

He'd had to ask for a painkiller, with the result he'd expected, and now his brain was foggy and unfocused, full of demons he fought but couldn't seem to drive away. Reaching out, he tried to set the glass back in place, but it slipped from his grasp and clattered to the floor.

Glancing down, he saw that it had rolled under the bed.

"I'll get it for you," a voice said from the doorway.

Groggily, Caleb looked around to see a woman he vaguely recognized come into the room, kneel down and retrieve the plastic cup from beneath the bed. She made a point of taking it into the bathroom and washing it before returning it to his tray table.

"Thank you," he said, trying to recall where he'd seen the woman with the untidy black hair and ill-fitting jacket.

"Monette Berkley," she offered as her gaze darted around the room.

"Oh, right. Laney's old neighbor." There was something else Laney had mentioned about this woman, but he couldn't remember what it was.

"Do you need more water?" she asked, her hands hovering over the pitcher and glass.

"Nah. Thanks, but I'm good."

Silence fell and Caleb felt himself begin to drift.

"Did you have an accident?" Monette asked, pulling him toward wakefulness.

Though he thought the answer to that was obvious, he mumbled, "Yeah, fell into the... corral... Sam..." His voice trailed off, along with his thoughts.

"Sam? You mean Sam Reynolds was there? Around that wild horse I saw?"

"Yeah, wild horse," he muttered, repeating her words as he tried to focus.

"That horse was dangerous. That boy was in danger?"

Caleb heard the urgency in her voice but couldn't focus on the reason. He knew she wanted some kind of response so he muttered, "Yeah. Mountain lion," as he slipped back into a deep sleep.

MONETTE GLANCED AROUND FURTIVELY, then reached out to shake the sleeping man. "What did you say? Hey, wake up."

He didn't wake or respond and, knowing a nurse might come in at any second and ask what she was doing there, Monette turned and hurried away, muttering to herself as she rushed down the corridor and out to the parking lot. "I knew something was going to happen. That Laney is completely irresponsible. She shouldn't have put Sean in danger. What did he mean about a mountain lion? I can ask around. Somebody will know."

Sitting in her car, she gazed into the night. It was a good thing she'd come to check on one of her cases, a little girl in a foster home who'd developed appendicitis. There was no need for alarm there, for the girl was being well cared for by her foster parents and the hospital staff. She was going to be all right.

"But what about Sean?" Monette asked. His irresponsible mother wasn't looking after him if he was being allowed around wild horses and mountain lions. She paused, shook her head. That couldn't be right, though. She'd never heard of a mountain lion in the vicinity of Sweetsilver. She would have to check everything out very carefully. It wouldn't do for her to make a slipup now, to jeopardize the case she was building against Laney Reynolds. It was the best thing for the little boy. She had no doubt about that, but she had to make sure everything was done correctly.

She relaxed against the headrest while she planned. Lingering heat from the day permeated the car, causing sweat to pop out on her face, but she barely noticed. Her mind was focused on what she needed to do to save Sean Reynolds. She wasn't going to let him get hurt. Not again. She remembered when it had happened before in another corral, on another ranch where nobody had been watching him.

He had wandered away from them. Nobody was watching, his mother too busy flirting with yet another man to see that her little boy was in danger.

There wouldn't be a repeat of that. Not on her watch.

THE NEXT DAY Laney picked Caleb up from the hospital and now they were on the way home. He hadn't said much to her, but he'd seemed happy to see Sam and Bertie, who were in the backseat. Sam had a running commentary going about everything they passed, educating both man and dog about every building, ranch, animal or fence post along the way. Some of his stories were amazingly far-fetched, but Caleb listened and commented, asked questions and complimented Sam on his recall of the facts.

She was happy to let her son prattle on because it eased the tension between Caleb and her. Caleb had to respond every once in a while to something Sam said and that gave her a chance to judge his mood.

He still wasn't very happy with her, she could tell, but she was beginning to think it was out of habit rather than real annoyance. She gave him a sidelong glance. Well, habits could be changed. She was dying to ask if he'd called his mother. She wanted to know about his mother—in fact, every member of his family—but maybe she should wait.

When they pulled into his place, there was a blue pickup parked out front, next to Caleb's truck.

Caleb sat forward. "Is that Bartlett's truck?"

"Looks like it. This'll give you the chance to thank Chet in person," she said brightly. "You were going to do that, right?"

"Of course." He gave her a steady glare.

She waved a dismissive hand. "Give it up, Ransom. I'm a high school teacher, remember? Those nasty looks won't work on me."

"Worse luck," he muttered, but she saw the corner of his mouth curve upward.

Laney took the crutches out of the back

of the Jeep while Sam and Bertie scrambled out and ran off to play. At the hospital, she hadn't been surprised to see that Caleb was an expert at using crutches. He'd probably had a great deal of practice when he was first wounded. She held the crutches while he stood and moved them into position. They were starting into the house when Chet and Ryder Bartlett rounded the end of the barn.

They stopped to stay hello. Caleb immediately held out his hand to father and then son, thanking them for their help.

"We'll be over every day until you're back on your feet," Chet said. "But call if you need anything else."

Laney watched Caleb, who nodded and said, "Thanks. I'll do that."

The pair started to turn away but then Chet looked back. "We went out to check on those two geldings in the pasture. They're really skittish, aren't they? And so is that mare in the corral. She wouldn't let me near her foal."

Caleb explained about them and the other horses he'd taken in for Don Parkey and the county. "Don's hoping to find good homes for them."

"I've got news for you, Ransom," Chet said with a grin. "He's already done that. They seem to like it fine right here."

"That's what I'm afraid of. Still, there's plenty of grass and they'll be okay in the pasture, unless..." He shot a quick glance at Laney, then another at Sam, playing nearby with Bertie.

When he paused, Chet nodded. "Yeah, I heard about what happened, and I saw the tracks, too, but not recent ones."

Ryder also nodded. "So did I."

He didn't go on.

Laney looked from one to the other of them. "What? What did you see?"

Caleb gave Chet and Ryder an infinitesimal shake of his head, but Laney wasn't letting him get away with that. The look he and Chet shared made her heart leap into her throat. "What?"

"I was going to tell you," Caleb said. "Before this happened," he said, indicating his crutches and cast, "I was out in the pasture near the spring and I saw some coyote tracks..."

"There are coyotes all around here."

"...and what looked like mountain lion tracks."

She stared at him. "You knew there was a mountain lion around and didn't tell me?"

"I had no idea how close he was. I told Don about it and he reported it to the sheriff, but—"

"They obviously didn't catch it since it ended up in your corral!"

"No, no they didn't." Caleb looked away, unable to meet her horrified gaze.

Instead, he looked at Chet, who nodded toward where Addie and her filly were placidly standing in the shade by the barn. "I saw the tracks he left the other day, but he's probably moved on."

"Yeah, yeah," Caleb said a little too heartily.

Laney gave the two of them a skeptical look. "Moved on? When there's a coyote buffet in the neighborhood?"

"Not to mention a new filly," Ryder added, clamping his mouth shut when his dad touched his arm and shook his head.

Dismayed, Laney looked from one to the other of them, then at Addie and her filly, and then at her son. She could feel the color drain from her face. "Sam…?" was all she could manage, her mind filling with images of her heedless little boy being in danger again. "You don't think the lion'll come back?"

"We'll keep an eye on Sam, Laney. We won't let him go in the pasture by himself."

Because she could feel all three men watching her closely, she nodded numbly. It was several seconds before she felt as if she could breathe normally again.

Once the men saw that color was returning to her face, Chet and Ryder headed for their truck with Caleb calling out thanks after them.

When the Bartletts were gone, Laney turned to Caleb and managed a shaky smile. "I think you're making progress in the friendliness department."

His dark gaze searched her face as if looking for reassurance that she wasn't going to faint. "Don't count on it," he answered. He didn't sound as gruff as he used to.

Smiling, Laney hurried ahead to get the door.

CHAPTER TEN

"HERE SHE COMES AGAIN, BERTIE," Caleb said to his companion, who had hefted himself to his feet to greet the approaching Jeep with his customary single woof. "Laney's determined to be in charge of things around here."

Caleb frowned, knowing that her intentions were good. But matters had moved too fast since the beginning of summer. He'd been relieved when she'd been called away to a couple of fires, for a few days each time, and he'd had to depend on the Bartletts for help.

He'd come to know his neighbors. The Bartletts and some other neighbors had searched for the mountain lion, and had seen evidence of him miles away. The Game and Fish Department had finally found the cat, sedated, and relocated him high in a protected area of the White Mountains. He wouldn't be back. One or the other of the

Bartletts had been over every day to help out and had stuck around to chat.

Ryder was especially interested in anything Caleb could tell him about the army, about his tours of duty, what it had been like over there. Caleb's heart sank a little whenever the kid brought it up. He didn't want to be rude, but he also didn't want to think about it, to remember. He'd answered briefly, which was more than he would have done a few weeks ago, then changed the subject each time to Ryder's plans after he graduated from high school, or to the horse his parents had recently given him.

And Ryder's mom, Karen, had brought him food several times, bustling into his kitchen with pies and casseroles, salads and loaves of homemade bread. He had seven of her salad bowls and casserole dishes washed and sitting on the kitchen counter waiting to be returned. With enforced idleness and too much food around, he'd gained weight, which had thrilled his mother and Laney. What was it about women that they felt they had to fatten up their men? Not that he was Laney's man, he amended quickly.

Caleb knew everything had begun to change

from the moment he'd met Laney and Sam. He hadn't been ready for change then and he still wasn't. Now he was five weeks into his recovery. His leg felt stronger than it had since before he was first wounded. His mother had arrived from Las Cruces the day after he'd been released from the hospital. She'd noticed the changes in him right away. Caleb didn't know if he was or not, but he no longer felt so much of the restless anger that had been clawing at his guts for almost two years.

Strangely, he missed it. If he didn't have that anger to hold on to, then he was going to have to fill that hole with another emotion. Like most men he knew, he didn't spend a lot of time thinking about his emotions, so he didn't know which one to plug into the gaping chasm. He refused to think that the hole was exactly the right size and shape for Delaney and Sam Reynolds—in fact, he fought against it.

There was something about the situation—not being able to exhaust himself with work, not being able to ride Cisco around his property, but instead having other people nearby, interacting with them, talking and carrying on more conversations than he'd had in months, and seeing Laney and Sam almost every day. Yes, there was something about this—in fact, everything about this had thrown him completely off-kilter.

But there was one really good thing about the situation. His nightmares almost never ripped through his sleep anymore, breaking him out in a sweat, torturing him. When they did, they usually started benignly with him and his men riding along in an up-armored Bradley, looking out at the endless vistas of Afghanistan. The dreams always ended the same way, though. With an explosion. But it was happening less and less and for that he was grateful.

It was ironic to him that he was better physically than he'd been in two years, but he still felt shaky, both mentally and emotionally. And yet, may God forgive him, he'd taken his fears out on Laney.

Two days ago, after an exhausting session in physical therapy, then a stop to get his full cast removed and a walking brace put on, Laney had driven him home. As he sat in her vehicle, turned sideways to rest his leg—and to watch her drive—it struck him yet again that he was coming to depend on her way too much.

She'd been dressed in a bright red sundress with matching sandals, her hair twisted up into one of those knots that drove him crazy because there were always tendrils sliding down her neck, curling around her throat, teasing him. And her scent, some combination of honeysuckle and rose, got to him in ways he couldn't even define.

He'd frowned at that thought and picked a fight. "I won't need you to take me to physical therapy anymore."

"I don't mind, Caleb." She'd nodded toward the backseat. "I always take work with me. Your therapy sessions have given me a great opportunity to sit and do nothing but plan and prepare for next school year." She'd grinned. "At least on the days I don't have Sam with me."

"I've got the walking brace now, Laney. I can drive. I can take care of everything by myself now."

As she had turned into his driveway, she'd given him a puzzled look. "Shouldn't you give yourself time to get used to it?"

"I've been in a walking brace before."

He'd known his voice was way too harsh, but he'd forged ahead. This had to stop. "I can handle everything myself now. I did before."

He'd seen the hurt in her eyes before she lifted her chin and given him an icy glare. "I was right there at the doctor's with you, remember? He said for you to avoid driving for another week. So that's what you're going to do."

As she'd swung the Jeep in a circle in front of his steps, he'd opened the door and stepped out, then pulled his crutches from the backseat, grateful he could put them away. "You don't have to drive me, though. In fact, don't—"

"I keep telling you, don't tell me don't. And I still have to catch that mama cat. I'll be back in two days." Then she'd driven away without so much as a backward glance.

Watching her approach now he wondered, Why did it always have to be her? Always the one he lashed out at. Well, that was easy to answer. She was always here.

"Bertie, do me a favor," he said. "If I say anything mean and stupid, bite me in the leg, will you? You can even bite me in my bad leg."

But Bertie wasn't interested in helping him out. He only wanted to be close to Sam, who leaped from the car at a full run and embraced his canine soul mate.

Sam spied an old tennis ball, which he scooped up and threw for Bertie. The ball only flew a few feet, but that was okay with Bertie, who wasn't fond of running all that far, anyway. He picked up the ball and brought it back to Sam, who crowed with delight.

"Look, Mr. Ransom. Bertie brought me the ball!"

"I can see that. Throw it again."

Sam complied and, seeing that boy and dog were safely occupied for the moment, Caleb turned to look at Laney, who was emerging from her vehicle at a much slower pace than her son.

Caleb knew she was mad at him, and rightly so, but that didn't stop him from enjoying the sight of those long, bare legs of hers stepping down and the swing of her hips as she bumped the door closed. He loved it when she wore shorts, and when she paired them with a tank top, he liked it even better.

But what kind of sick bastard did that make him, to stand there lusting after her when he'd been so rude to her, and with her son playing not ten feet away?

Fortunately she didn't give him the chance to find an answer to that. She merely gave him a cool look and said, "I came to catch the mama cat and take her to Don's office. What with one thing and another, I've left it way too long."

"What's the plan this time?" He didn't really care what the plan was. He only wanted her to start talking to him. The last time they'd tried to catch the cat, her eyes had been lit with enthusiasm because she was convinced her idea would work without a hitch. When she'd fallen and he'd helped her catch her breath, her eyes had been full of fear, which had struck terror into him. And when he'd kissed her, her eyes had flooded with warmth. He'd liked the enthusiastic and warm expressions. The cool look she was giving him now, not so much.

"Same as the last time," she answered in a no-nonsense tone that she probably used to great effect with her high school students. It didn't work with him.

"Does it involve you falling off hay bales?"

She gave him a look that should have frozen him on the spot. It only made him fight a grin.

Laney reached into the backseat of her Jeep and pulled out a grocery bag. The heavy *thunk* of metal on metal told him it contained cans of cat food. Carrying the bag, she marched into the barn, calling out to Sam to either stay where he was, playing with Bertie, or to come into the barn.

When Sam looked up, Caleb caught his attention, winked and nodded toward the barn. Eager to see what might happen there, Sam hurried after his mother and Bertie followed.

"This may take a while," Laney said.

"I've got nothing but time," Caleb answered as he entered. He sat on a hay bale and Sam scrambled up beside him. The little boy looked at how Caleb was sitting, with his injured leg stretched out straight, and attempted the same pose. But since his legs were too short to even reach the floor, he had to be content with crossing his arms over his chest exactly as Caleb had, even making sure he had his right arm on top of the left. Bertie padded over and collapsed at their feet.

"My plan," Laney said, "is to bait the humane trap with food, wait around for a while and then see which cat we catch. If we catch the two we don't want, we'll take them out and put them in the cat carrier. If we catch the mama cat, I'll take her straight to Don's."

"Brilliant," Caleb complimented her. "I've known battalion commanders who couldn't come up with a plan that good. Right, Sam?"

"Right!" her son said, though Caleb knew the little boy didn't have the foggiest clue what he was talking about.

"But that means," Caleb pointed out, "we have to get out of here as soon as you get it baited. Or the cats will never come near it."

"I know that," she said, giving him a frosty glance. If he could bottle that look, Caleb figured he wouldn't have to pay for air-conditioning in his house.

"She knows that, Mr. Ransom," Sam said solemnly.

He liked this, Caleb decided. He liked sitting in his barn watching her ready the trap, trading barbs with her while Sam made innocent observations. It made him feel like part of a...family, he thought. And for once, the thought didn't put him on the defensive, make him lash out.

"There, all done." Laney straightened and picked up the grocery sack. "Sam, let's go home. Mr. Ransom can call us when one of the cats goes into the trap."

"Might as well stay," Caleb said quickly, scrambling for a reason for them to do so. "This could happen pretty fast. I didn't feed them today because I knew you'd be back."

"Pretty sure of yourself," she said, strolling past him and gesturing for Sam to come with her.

"No. Sure of you." Caleb stood to follow and Bertie trotted along in the little parade. "I knew you'd keep your promise."

They walked away from the barn and stopped beneath the mulberry tree. Sam dashed off to find the ball he'd been throwing for Bertie. Laney carefully avoided Caleb's gaze.

"It's almost dinnertime," Caleb found himself blurting out. "You and Sam want to join me? I didn't make chili."

Her eyes flashed to his face and he saw a flicker of a smile. "What did you make?"

"Nothing yet, but Ryder Bartlett went to the grocery store for me. I've got ground beef, hamburger buns, ears of corn. I'm not much of a cook, but I can grill."

Laney looked at him, then over at her son, who was happily romping with Bertie. He could see the war of indecision going on in her face and stayed very still. No question she had doubts about his ability to remain civil, not shut Sam and her out. He was determined to be on his best behavior.

"Sounds good," she said. "I'll fix the corn."

Turning, she called out to Sam who scampered after her, bringing Bertie with him. She strode confidently ahead, opening his front door, shooing her son and his dog inside, and generally making herself at home.

Caleb liked the fact that she didn't coddle him, didn't shorten her steps to match his limp or make any concessions to his handicap. What he didn't like was knowing that she didn't make concessions because she was still mad at him. He wondered what he'd have to do to get on her good side again.

Apologize, no doubt. A mere invitation for dinner wasn't going to be enough.

SHE WOULD HAVE to be the one to bring it up, Laney knew. She would have to tell him exactly what she'd thought of the harsh way he'd spoken to her when she was only trying to help. Oddly, it would be a whole lot easier if he wasn't being so accommodating, so… Mr. Nice Guy Host with the Most.

He had everything together in the kitchen, as if he'd planned all along to invite her and Sam to dinner. She helped him take it all out back where the gas grill was waiting, while Sam, who'd brought Bertie's tennis ball along, was busy throwing it. Half the time, he threw it and then ran to grab it before Bertie could get it, but Bertie didn't seem to mind. He trotted along and waited for Sam to throw it again. Being incredibly lazy, sometimes he even sat to wait, his wagging tail sweeping an arc in the dust.

Since the house faced west, the back was shaded, giving them a cool spot away from the long, hot rays of the setting sun. There was even an old picnic table that looked as though it had been freshly painted. Laney stood looking around as she wondered where Caleb's good manners had been hiding all of this time. Then it dawned on her that he was making amends.

While he formed the hamburger patties— including an especially small one for Sam— she pulled down the husks, stripped the silks off the ears of corn, then took some of the outermost husks, split them into threes and braided them to make ties to hold the husks back in place. She laid them on the grill and turned to see Caleb watching her.

"Wish I'd known that trick in Afghanistan," he said, putting the patties he'd made beside the corn. There was an old laundry sink beside the back door, and Caleb scrubbed his hands there while he spoke. "We actually managed to get our hands on some corn one time, but we boiled it. It was okay." One corner of his mouth lifted in a smile that tugged at her heart. "The real star of the meal was a hunk of roast beef that one of my soldiers, Berman, came up with."

Laney listened carefully as she sat at the picnic table, barely daring to breathe for fear he would stop talking, clam up again. He had never, ever, said anything personal before, and rarely anything about having been a soldier—or about Afghanistan.

"We never did ask where he got it." Caleb returned to the grill, closed the lid and stepped back. He lifted his head and stared out at the horizon.

Laney knew he wasn't thinking about this meal, but one he'd shared with his men in another time and place.

"Usually it was better not to ask where Berman got some of the things he came up with. He could always convince people to trade with him even if they didn't speak the same language. He could have conned an Eskimo into trading his last pair of long underwear for some tighty whiteys—in the middle of winter."

She laughed, but then he paused for so long, Laney thought he wasn't going to say any more. But, finally, he did.

"Roast beef," he said, shaking his head. "We were out in a convoy…knew we'd be gone all day and into the night. There was no way we could cook that beef, at least not before it spoiled. With the heat over there, fresh meat doesn't stay fresh very long. We had MREs…"

"MREs?"

Caleb glanced over at her as if he'd forgotten she was there, and Laney almost regretted breaking into his thoughts. "Meals Ready to Eat. Packaged meals we used when we were away from base. Some of them aren't too bad."

She nodded, signaling for him to go ahead with his story.

"We could have eaten those, but Berman wanted that beef. He was from Montana and from the way he talked, his family ate beef at every meal. He'd heard about a way to wrap up a piece of meat, tie it to the manifold of a truck and let the engine heat cook it, so that's what he did."

"Wow. Did it work?"

Caleb moved to the table and sat opposite her. Then he placed his hands on top of the table and laced his fingers together. She saw scars there, some probably from ranch work, but one that ran from his wrist to the knuckle of his little finger as if he'd been cut with something long, thin and deadly. If he'd realized she was looking at it, he probably would have put his hands under the table, but he wasn't focused on her. His thoughts were far away.

Indulging herself, she studied his face and felt her heart give an unaccustomed little flutter. He was a young man, only thirty, but his eyes held an experience of life that made him seem much older, which fascinated her. He wasn't wearing the hat that usually shaded his face and Laney could see his facial scars clearly. But, again, it didn't seem to bother him. She realized it was the most relaxed she'd seen him since the night they'd spent together at the hospital—and that tranquility had been drug-induced.

"Yeah, it did," he said in response to her question. "We smelled that meat cooking all day. Every time we stopped, he'd jerk up the hood of the truck to turn it over and see how it was doing, but of course it was wrapped up tight, so he couldn't see anything. Attracted a lot of flies, though."

Laney chuckled. "I've heard of people cooking meat like that. So how'd it taste? Good?"

"We finally got back to our FOB—um, forward operating base—cooked our corn, unwrapped that meat and got ready to dig in. The roast beef was perfectly cooked—and tasted exactly like engine exhaust with a delightful hint of crank case oil."

Laney burst out laughing. "What a disappointment!"

"Not to Berman. He was convinced it was delicious and started coming up with other things we could cook that way. He thought goat's meat cooked by that method would be absolutely delicious. It was easy to obtain there."

"Sounds awful. Where's Berman now? Still in the army?"

Caleb went very still. The softness in his expression hardened and his hands tensed. Then he stood and returned to the grill, grabbing a pair of tongs to turn the corn and nudge the hamburger patties to test for doneness.

He didn't have to answer. She knew something bad had happened to Berman and she wondered how many others of Caleb's soldiers had been wounded or killed. He didn't need to tell her that he still carried the pain—and, probably, guilt.

They didn't speak again until the food was ready. She hustled Sam inside to use the bathroom and wash his hands. When they returned, she saw that Caleb had lit candles on the table.

He met her surprised gaze with a shrug. "Citronella. To ward off the mosquitoes."

She smiled, wondering if she would ever understand this man. He had to struggle to accept help or even company—especially hers—but made accommodations for them, anyway.

As they ate together, the talk flowed easily. Sam was delighted with the little hamburger she handed him. After he checked to make sure she hadn't slipped in any pickles or onions, he showed it to Bertie, who was definitely interested. "Look, Bertie, it's a little hangkupper," he said.

She looked over at Caleb. "How did you know to do that?"

He shrugged. "He's got small hands."

She laughed and realized she was over being annoyed with him. As soon as Sam finished eating, he made to run off to play with Bertie once again. But he paused and turned back. "You amember you said I can work for you, Mr. Ransom?"

"I remember."

"My mom said I have to wait'll your leg gets better. Is it better?"

"Yes, it is. Are you ready to start work?"

"Yeah!"

Laney noticed that Caleb carefully avoided looking at her when he said, "Okay. I'll talk to your mom about it."

"Okay!" Sam rushed off with Bertie on his heels and the two of them darted around in the quickly falling dusk.

When Laney was finished with her food, she said to Caleb, "He can't actually work for you. You know that, right?"

"Why not?" Caleb shifted on the bench, easing his leg out. "If nothing else, he can keep Bertie occupied, make him get some exercise."

"Won't that interfere with Bertie's busy napping schedule?"

He grinned. "The hound will have to make the best of things."

She spread her hands wide. "What else would he be doing around here?"

"I don't know. Whatever I can think of."

She looked at him. He obviously didn't know any more than she did, but maybe he was ready to have people around. Only two days ago he'd made it clear he didn't want her here, but apparently that was no longer the case. She remembered what her brother had said—that she should be the one to understand that what people say they want and what they really want can be two very different things.

Over the summer she'd asked herself many times why she was so drawn to Caleb. He'd been rude more than once, yet she'd convinced herself it was because of his circumstances, not his nature. She hoped she was right because she was drawn to him in a way she couldn't understand and couldn't explain. For some reason her feelings for him made her think of the morning glory vines that grew up and around her porch posts. Even though the vines had been ruthlessly cut back to control their growth, they always came back, their sturdy tendrils ever climbing, encircling the posts, around and around, holding on firmly and producing their beautiful flowers—not that she expected any relationship she had with Caleb would produce something of beauty. Still…

Bertie returned and flopped down beneath the table. Sam followed, lying on his stomach on the bench so he could pet Bertie. She reached over and rubbed her son's back while she thought about Caleb's idea. As far as she could tell, before he'd reinjured his leg, Caleb had been busy all the time, either with his cattle or his horses. And while it was true that he could use help, even the help of a four-year-old, and he probably would keep Sam with him every minute, he didn't know how fast Sam could move when he became interested or distracted by something—like the filly named Awesome.

And she kept remembering that mountain lion. It had been captured and relocated to another area, but she knew there were always other dangers lurking, waiting for her curious little boy.

As if he'd read her thoughts, Caleb said, "You're welcome to come, too—make sure he's okay. And you're here every couple of days, anyway, taking me to therapy."

She met his gaze. Darkness was falling and she couldn't read his expression very well, but he seemed to be… Content, she decided. It wasn't something she'd seen in him in all the weeks she'd known him, and it was probably very fleeting. That she'd played a big part in this contentment filled her with pleasure.

"All right, then. A couple of mornings a week, he can come over and help you out, after we get back from town."

He nodded agreement and suggested they go check on the cat trap.

"Let's get the dishes cleaned up first," Laney said.

He shook his head. "I'll take care of them later."

Laney stood. As she looked down, she saw that Sam had fallen asleep on the bench while petting Bertie.

Caleb came around the table to see her son sprawled bonelessly, deeply asleep.

"Should we wake him?" Caleb asked.

"Don't even bother trying. Once he's asleep, he's down for the night. Nothing could wake him up." She started to reach for Sam, but Caleb stopped her.

"I've got this," he said, lifting Sam easily and holding him against his shoulder.

"But your leg…"

"Don't worry. I'm pretty steady."

Her little boy sighed and snuggled his face against Caleb's neck.

A look flashed across Caleb's face that Laney couldn't quite decipher. It was a combination of surprise and tenderness and something else she'd never seen there before. Quiet joy, maybe?

Eyes downcast, Caleb raised his big, work-toughened hand and rested it on her son's vulnerable back.

A lump lodged in her throat and a warm feeling flowed through her at the picture they made. Carrying Sam, Caleb turned away, heading for the barn. She followed slowly, watching the way Caleb adjusted his gait to compensate for the additional thirty-five pounds he was carrying. He held Sam tightly, though, and she knew that if he was in danger of stumbling, he would fall on his wounded leg before he would let Sam hit the ground.

"He takes care of things," she murmured to herself. "And he tries to make them right. But he's been hurt while doing that and that's why he's wary."

Laney realized that if she wasn't very careful, she could fall in love with this man.

Inside the barn they saw that luck was finally on their side. The cat trap held a very angry mama cat, which hissed at them and clawed at the wire mesh that kept her captive.

"Success," Laney said happily. She then looked at her sleeping son and frowned. "I had planned to take the cat to Don's office tonight, and I have to stop by my mom and dad's house for something Mom's being very mysterious about, but says will change my life. I don't want to take Sam all the way to town and back." She looked doubtfully at the cat trap. "But I don't really want to keep her in this thing overnight."

"If you want, I'll go with you to your place first, and you can drop me there with Sam. I'll put him to bed. Meanwhile, you can take the cat to Don's office and stop by your parents'. When you get back, I can walk home, so you don't have to leave Sam alone. It's not far if I stick to the road, and it won't be too hard even with the brace."

"Well," she said hesitantly, "if you don't think it'll be too much trouble."

"I guarantee you it'll be a lot less trouble than that cat's going to be."

Laney laughed. "Okay, then. It'll take me about forty minutes," she said hesitantly. She could only hope that the stop at her mom and dad's would be a short one.

"We'll be all right." Caleb carried Sam to her Jeep and strapped him in while Laney placed the cat carrier in the back.

When she pulled into her drive, she stopped and said, "I won't be long."

"I've got your cell number, Laney. We'll be all right," Caleb answered.

She knew that was true so she unhooked her house key from her key ring and handed it to him. Within a few minutes Sam and Caleb were inside her home and she hurried off to town.

CHAPTER ELEVEN

HE HADN'T BEEN in her house before. It didn't take Caleb long to carry a sleeping Sam into his room and put him to bed. He decided it wouldn't hurt the kid to sleep in the shorts and T-shirt he'd worn all evening. He put him on his bed, pulled the sheet and a light blanket up over him, and then stood to watch him as he slept.

There was perfect trust and innocence in the way Sam lay with his dark head against the pillow, its case emblazoned with his favorite superhero. Caleb couldn't help wishing that superheroes were real, that they could protect little boys from harm, from the villains and monsters that roamed the earth.

Because he'd been trained to check out his environment for potential threats as well as assets, Caleb looked around the room. The kid really was crazy about cowboys. Cowboy items were everywhere—hats, boots, ropes, even a branding iron, which hung on the wall.

"Funny kid," he said quietly. Most boys his age were into video games, space aliens, dinosaurs, but this one liked cowboys, even though his sheets were printed with superheroes. There probably hadn't been any sheets with cowboys on them. Caleb saw that there was a cowboy boot-style nightlight plugged into a socket, so he switched it on, pulled the bedroom door closed most of the way, and went into the living room.

He wandered around, looking at the books on Laney's shelves, mostly biographies and social histories with a few historical romances thrown in. Family pictures crowded the top of the bookcase and covered the walls, most of them featuring Sam. He studied them, a smile curving his mouth, and decided his favorite was one taken when Sam was about a year old. Laney stood behind him, holding both of her son's little hands as she looked up at the camera. The love and pride in her face drew Caleb to the picture, reached right in and squeezed his heart. He analyzed the feeling and decided it wasn't pain. It was longing.

Not willing to give any more thought to it, he turned and surveyed the rest of the room.

His place could only be described as Spartan, he thought. It had only the barest of furnishings, some of which had come with the house. He hadn't really cared what the furniture was like. He'd been glad to have a place of his own. A place where no one knew him, could pity him. A place where he could focus on his cattle, become a hermit.

Laney liked comfort, though. She had a sofa with big, puffy pillows to cushion the back, and a matching chair with an ottoman. He knew she'd be a little while getting back and that chair looked awfully inviting, although there was always the possibility he wouldn't be able to get out of it once he got in. He was willing to risk it, though.

He lowered himself into the chair and stretched his legs out on the ottoman, using a small pillow to support his right knee. It immediately relieved the pressure on his hip and he sank into comfort. Leaning his head back, he closed his eyes and let the silence engulf him. He drifted off to sleep thinking how peaceful Laney's house was. There were no demons here.

LANEY STRUGGLED UP the steps of her house and onto the back porch. She set the huge pot down and massaged the place on her back where she was sure she'd pulled something important.

"A banana tree," she muttered for the umpteenth time, shaking her head in amazement. "This is what's going to change my life?"

She smiled, recalling how overjoyed her mom had been when she had given it to her. Vivian was so excited about being able to grow something that she wanted to share the wealth with the entire family.

Deciding it could wait until tomorrow to change her life, Laney went inside. She didn't know why she was surprised at the gift. She'd known her mom was ordering more of the plants. Of course she'd give one to her daughter.

Crossing the kitchen, she stopped in the doorway when she saw Caleb sprawled in her chair. She approached slowly, hoping not to startle him, but his eyes flew open as soon as she stepped into the room. He watched as she approached and scooted his legs over so she could sit on the ottoman.

"Get the cat delivered okay?" he asked

around a yawn. With his hands resting on the arms of the chair, his head back and hair tousled, he looked relaxed and content. He made such an appealing picture that Laney had to glance away.

"Yes, and she has no idea what's going to happen to her tomorrow, poor thing."

"Maybe it'll improve her disposition."

"We can only hope." She looked around. "Is Sam okay?"

"Yup. Didn't even stir when I put him to bed. I left him in his shorts and T-shirt. That okay?"

She nodded, and now she allowed her gaze to rest on him. His hair was messy from contact with the chair back, his eyes were tired, but his smile was…soft, she decided, as if he didn't have to be on guard.

"I should go," he said, though he made no move to get up.

"There's no hurry."

"So what did your mother have for you that's going to change your life?" he asked.

Laney grinned. "A banana tree. It's even got little green bananas on it."

He stared at her. "A banana tree?"

"Yes. My mom has finally found a plant

she can't kill. The fact that it pays her back with fruit is a bonus." Laney told him about the unhappy results of Vivian's attempts at gardening.

"She's got banana trees for my brother, Ethan, too, but he and his family are going on vacation tomorrow, so they'll be spared this for a week or so. The lucky devils," she sighed.

When he chuckled, Laney felt a shiver skitter up her spine. She'd had similar reactions to him all evening, exactly as she'd had every time he'd kissed her—weeks ago now. But it confused her because her attraction to him was tempered by wariness and an unwillingness to become involved with someone who wouldn't let her share in his thoughts and feelings. And she had a son to consider. She couldn't let just any man who came along into her life—not that Caleb had expressed a desire to be allowed into hers and Sam's life. His attitude toward them was more one of benign tolerance than anything else, in spite of his occasional snappiness since he'd broken his leg.

This would all be so much easier, Laney

thought, if she wasn't so intrigued by him, attracted to him.

"But you've got a green thumb," Caleb said. "Your plants are doing great. Didn't inherit that from your mom, huh?"

She shook her head. "Actually, I'm adopted. They're really my aunt and uncle. My mother, Lauraine, was Vivian's sister. She kept me with her, dragging me around from place to place, job to job, man to man, until she got here to Sweetsilver. I didn't even know I *had* any family, or what family was, really, but right here in Sweetsilver was my great-uncle Calvin Reynolds, Aunt Vivian and my uncle Frank with their son Ethan…" Laney's voice trailed off as she remembered the crazy insecurity of her young life.

"Lauraine dropped me off for what was supposed to be a few days. She never came back. We found out later she'd died in Las Vegas, some kind of infection. Nobody knows for sure, but maybe she knew she was sick when she left me, and we certainly don't know why she went to Vegas. It's a nine-hour drive from here." She looked up and met his eyes. "I have no idea who my father is. My birth certificate says his name is

John Smith and he's from Los Angeles, but my uncle Calvin—the one who left me this place and the one who raised my mother and my mom, Vivian—said that Lauraine really didn't know who my father was."

It all came out in a rush and Laney released a breath she hadn't even known she'd been holding.

Caleb didn't say anything for several seconds, only watched her with those dark eyes that seemed to take in so much and reveal so little. "I'm sorry. That must have been tough on you, a little kid."

If she'd thought he was going to tell her anything about his background, about himself, in exchange, she was disappointed.

"It *was* tough," she said. "But I was lucky. I ended up with a family who loved me and provided for me. I had everything I needed or wanted, including an education." She spread her hands wide to encompass her house. "As I said, my great-uncle left me this place in his will. So I probably had a better life than I would have had if my mother had kept me with her."

She had tried to recite the history of her young life in a matter-of-fact way, as she'd done many times before when she'd come to know a friend well enough to share it. But it hadn't come out so matter-of-factly here. Though she wasn't sure why, Laney felt that she needed to make Caleb understand how grateful she was to her family for the life they'd given her.

He tilted his head, regarding her with those solemn, dark eyes. "But you've always wondered what it would be like to know your mother and to know why she left you."

Laney answered with a nod and a little shrug.

"She wanted something better for you than what she could provide," Caleb said. "And even if she didn't know how sick she was, or what was wrong with her, she wanted the best for you."

"I'd like to believe that. I guess in everyone's life there are questions that never have answers—at least not ones we can understand."

She glanced up and saw pain flicker in Caleb's eyes, but she knew it wasn't physical. Would he ever talk about it? Was she expecting far too much since they were only neighbors and sort-of, almost friends?

He regarded her silently for a minute. "I know this is none of my business, and I hope you don't mind me asking, but where's Sam's father?"

Laney's lips quirked into a sardonic smile. "Dr. James Carson is in San Francisco."

"Doctor?"

She nodded. "Of philosophy. He was one of my college professors. Young, worshipful girl and a man heading into an early midlife crisis. Bad combination." Laney pressed her palms together, trying to think of a way to say this without pain. "He thought he wanted a wife and family. Turns out he didn't. What he really wanted was an adoring fan who lived in and also cooked and cleaned. The marriage lasted less than a year and he left before Sam was born. He's never seen Sam."

Laney saw Caleb's eyes narrow and color suffuse his face, making the scar stand out in stark relief. "Bastard."

Their eyes met and held, and she saw something in his that rattled her. It was fury, she thought, on behalf of her and her son. She also glimpsed compassion, and it was coming from a man who, a few weeks ago, hadn't even wanted her on his property.

Caleb said, "I'm sorry about that. You deserve better and so does Sam. If that jerk could see what you've become, how you've taken care of yourself and your son, he'd be ashamed of himself."

Laney was so surprised by his burst of candor that it was a moment before she could think of anything to say. "I'd like to think so. I do my best for Sam, but I never realized before how hard it is to be a single mom, to make all the decisions and hope they're right."

"Believe me, you're making the right decisions. He's a great kid."

Surprised by the compliment, she smiled and nodded. "Thank you."

"Not everyone can be a good single parent. It sounds like your birth mom couldn't handle it, but it's obvious that you can."

As if he suddenly realized how out of character he was acting, Caleb's gaze skittered away from hers. "I guess I'd better get back home. Bertie'll be wondering what happened to me."

Bertie wasn't the only one, Laney thought, feeling raw with emotion at what she'd revealed and how compassionately he'd responded.

But would she ever learn anything about his life? She wondered what had happened to him, to his pinned-together leg, his chest and every other scarred part of him. How deep did those scars go and would they ever heal?

She smiled. "Are you kidding? Bertie's probably finished off every bit of food we left and fallen asleep." She turned toward the back door, ready to walk him out, being careful not to watch him as he got out of the chair, fearing he might be offended if she saw him struggle.

"Probably."

It took Caleb a few minutes, but he joined her at the kitchen door. She flipped on the porch light and indicated the banana tree. "I hope I can keep that thing alive."

"Like I said, you kept your other plants alive."

"At least until your cows ate them."

He grinned. "Do you want to bring Sam over tomorrow?"

"Sure." She wanted to see him again.

Caleb nodded then paused with his hand

on the door. His eyes were on the banana plant but he spoke in a quiet voice. "Berman died in Afghanistan, killed by the same IED that got me these scars. Tonight was the first time I've talked about him."

Caleb lifted his gaze to meet hers. "Thank you."

Tears welled into her eyes and emotion clogged her throat. "You're welcome," she whispered.

Caleb's lips curved in a smile. He lifted his hand to hold her chin for a fleeting kiss. "Good night."

"Good night."

Laney gave him a flashlight, then watched him go, holding firmly to the railing as he descended the steps. He headed out with a wave of his hand and she turned off the porch light and stood in the dark, her fingertips covering her lips.

It wasn't the most passionate kiss he'd given her, but it was certainly the sweetest.

SAM WAS READY to go as soon as his feet hit the floor the next morning. Laney hadn't even had the opportunity to tell him they would be going over to Caleb's, but he was determined that they were.

"Mr. Ransom needs my help," he told her while he ate a bowl of cereal. He was still wearing the shorts and T-shirt that Caleb had put him to bed in last night. "And Bertie will miss me. He gets only."

Laney smiled. "Lonely," she corrected.

"Yeah."

"Before we go, you have to take a bath and put on clean clothes."

He stared at her. "Mom, cowboys like dirt."

"But cowboys' moms don't."

"But, Mom…"

"And the longer you argue, the longer it will be before we get to Caleb and Bertie's."

That was a thought her son couldn't abide so he finished his cereal in record time and scooted for the bathroom.

Once he was ensconced in the tub caroling a made-up song about cows as he scrubbed, Laney fussed over what to wear. What *did* a woman wear when she was taking her four-year-old son to spend the day with a neighbor she found so captivating and yet disturbing?

She took her yellow cotton sundress from

the closet. It was simple, sleeveless, with a full skirt and a white leather belt at the waist. "It's not a date, Laney," she muttered, stuffing it back into the closet. And what if Sam decided to climb up into the rafters of the barn? She couldn't go after him in a dress.

"Jeans?" She had an expensive pair that did nice things for her behind. No, too hot for jeans.

Deciding she was being ridiculous, she pulled on a pair of tan Bermudas, a peach-colored tank top and then slipped her feet into sandals. She picked up her laptop computer and a book. She didn't know what Sam would be doing for Caleb, but she suspected the two of them wouldn't want her in the way. She would work on curriculum alignment for next year's lesson plans.

Sam didn't care that it was too hot for jeans. He insisted that was what cowboys wore, so that's what he needed to wear, too. By the time he was dressed in a shirt with his boots and his cowboy hat, he was fairly dancing with impatience to be out the door and on the job.

Before she could get out the door to join

her eager son, her phone rang. Glancing at the Caller ID, she said, "Hi, Mom. What's up?"

"We've got to go up to Alpine. Someone broke into the cabin and we need to see what's missing. There's nothing of value there, so I can't imagine what they were after."

"Stale coffee?" Laney suggested. Her parents owned a cabin in the White Mountains, where they spent time every summer, but it had only the barest of essentials in it.

"Laney, honey," Vivian went on, "I need you to come by the house and check on my banana trees. I'm about to harvest my first crop."

Wincing at the mental image of the boatloads of bananas that were about to invade their lives, Laney agreed and hung up, then hurried outside.

Sam was already at the Jeep, dancing impatiently in place for her to join him.

"Let's go, Mom. I hafta go to work."

Laughing, she scooped him up and kissed him, although he tried to fight her off. "Mom, cowboys don't kiss!"

"Wanna bet?" she said, thinking of the kisses she and Caleb had shared. As they started off, she noticed a car in the lane, moving away from her at a snail's pace, as if the driver was checking out the scenery.

Laney frowned when she recognized the car. This driver wasn't admiring the view. It was Monette Berkley, snooping around Laney's place again. What was she hoping to find? Wrongdoing on Laney's part? A dangerous situation for Sam? It didn't exist. There was nothing to find.

Still, knowing her nosy former neighbor was prowling around, looking, was enough to make knots form in Laney's stomach. She was doing everything possible to make sure that Sam was in a safe, loving environment, and there was no way Monette could prove otherwise. Laney chewed her bottom lip as she wondered if she should find out who Monette's boss was and see what the misguided social worker was hoping to find.

With an effort, she pulled her mind away from thoughts of Monette and finished the short drive to Caleb's place. Bertie came out to greet them, and Sam rushed to hug the dog with his usual enthusiasm. Caleb walked out of the barn and lifted his chin in greeting, the quick gesture she'd seen so many men do so many times, but it had never made her heart flutter like this.

She called to Sam and Bertie, and they raced over to where Caleb waited for them.

"What are we doing today, Mr. Ransom, huh?" Sam shouted as if he thought Caleb had gone deaf overnight.

"We're going to ride out to check on some of the cattle, maybe put them in another pasture."

"Okay, boss," Sam answered, startling a laugh out of the two adults. He ran toward the truck, but Caleb called him back, redirecting him to the barn.

"I can't drive, remember, buddy?" Caleb pointed to his leg. "But we can ride on Cisco. You want to help me saddle him?"

Sam rocked to a stop and his eyes grew huge as if he'd been presented with the most wonderful gift ever. "Yeah," he said, ready to dash into the barn, but Caleb stopped him.

"You're going to have to slow down, buddy. It's not a good idea to run up to a horse, especially one who doesn't know you very well."

Sam nodded and began walking toward the barn with exaggerated slowness, rocking from heel to toe in his little boots, arms bent at the elbows and swinging with each step. He had a serious expression on his face as if he was sneaking up on some unsuspecting creature.

"Do you think you'll be able to ride Cisco while wearing a cast?" Laney asked.

"Don't know," Caleb answered with a shrug. "Haven't tried it yet."

"You can't use the stirrup, and having your leg hang down could hurt your hip," Laney persisted.

"Or it might work just fine." He paused and stared at her. "How did that happen?"

"What?"

His hand made a seesawing motion between them. "We seem to have switched places. You're usually the one thinking things will work fine and I'm not so sure."

Laney shook her head. "I don't know how that happened."

They grinned at each other, a warm current of understanding flowing between them.

Laney glanced around then started in alarm when she saw that Sam had detoured to the corral fence, enthralled as usual by

Addie and her baby, Awesome. Even though she reminded herself that the mountain lion was long gone, she started to hurry after him.

Caleb reached out and snagged her hand, pulling her back. "Wait," he urged. "Let's see what Addie does. She's much calmer than she was a few weeks ago. Seeing the mountain lion really spooked her and set her back, but Ryder Bartlett has been spending time with her."

"Ryder's not a little boy," she protested.

"Still, Addie hasn't shied from him and, look, she's watching Sam but she's not panicking or trying to get her filly away."

"Petting the filly is what caused Sam to fall into the corral before, remember?"

"He's not climbing up, trying to reach her, though. This time Awesome will probably put her face down for him. She's as curious about him as he is about her. Let's see what happens."

Laney gave him a look that questioned his sanity, yet his calm assurance had her staying put and watching.

Tiny and vulnerable, Sam stood by the fence, looking in at the horses. Addie watched him, her hooves shifting in place, but she didn't rush the fence when her filly trotted over to check out this little human. Awesome put her face down close to him and Sam reached out a tentative hand.

Laney made a low sound of distress and began once again to step forward, but Caleb's grip on her hand held her back. "Let's see what happens," he repeated, his voice low and steady.

Although her heart was pounding, Laney waited and watched as her son put out his hand and touched the filly's silky face. She whinnied softly and let Sam pet her as Addie took a few steps closer, then a few more, her concern for her baby overcoming her fear of humans. She was ready to bolt, though, and drive her baby away at the first sign of a threat.

Delighted, Sam looked back at Laney and Caleb. "She likes me, Mom," he called. "She's letting me pet her."

"I can see that, Sam. Good job, honey."

"Good job, Mom," Caleb said quietly.

When Laney glanced back at him, she saw that he was looking at the mare. Still, she felt his words had been directed at her.

Sam held out his open hand for the filly to nuzzle, but when she snorted into it, he let out a shriek and stumbled backward, landing on his bottom. "Ew," he said, holding up his hand. "Awesome blew her nose on my hand!"

Laughing, Laney hurried over to pick him up. "It'll wash off. Come on, we'll go into the house."

When they returned a few minutes later Laney saw that Caleb had walked over to the corral. He was petting the filly with one hand, and his attention was on her, but his other hand rested, palm up, on the top rung of the corral fence in a gently inviting gesture. Addie took a few steps closer, sniffed his hand then seemed to lift something from it with her lips. Caleb chuckled.

"Mom," Sam said, breaking into her thoughts. "I've got to go get Cisco now. Mr. Ransom said to."

"Oh, okay. But remember to walk slowly." She smiled down at him as he again moved off at a snail's pace. Carefully, she approached the corral, too, thrilled that Addie only gave her a suspicious look before turning her attention to Caleb once again.

"Caleb, what are you giving her?"

"Sugar. Turns out she's got quite a sweet tooth."

"Hmm." She tilted her head to the side. "So it seems that you *can* be sweet when you want to."

He looked at her, the corner of his mouth hitching up in that crooked way that never failed to catch at her heart. "Let's keep that a secret, okay?"

Sam called out from the barn, snapping the two adults back to the moment.

"He's going to be more obsessed than ever with horses and cowboys. You have no idea what you've gotten yourself into," Laney said.

Caleb grinned again. "I'm a quick learner."

He made his way to Sam, seemingly un-bothered, this time, by the usual hesitation in his step. "We'll be back in a while," he said over his shoulder. "Parkey's bringing another horse out this afternoon. He said he'd bring the mama cat back, too."

Laney waited to see what would happen and a few minutes later the two of them trotted out on Cisco, Sam seated in front of Caleb, a huge, happy grin on his face. His small hands were wrapped around the saddle horn. Caleb held the reins with one hand, twitching them to the right so that the big horse would turn in that direction. His other hand rested on Sam's stomach, holding him steady. His right leg stuck out, but it didn't seem to bother him.

Something about the way Caleb protected her son brought a lump to Laney's throat. As they rode by, Sam lifted his hands in the air and flexed his muscles as he shouted, "'Bye, Mom! We're going to move cows!" She laughed, wondering if he had a mental image of himself lifting a cow up and carrying it around.

Caleb's eyes met hers and they shared a moment of silent laughter.

She watched them ride away, thinking how much things had changed since she and Sam had first met Caleb.

MONETTE LOOKED AT the stack of forms she'd unearthed from the pile on her desk. They were all forms related to the Reynolds boy's case file. She'd driven out there today to check on things. She hadn't seen anything amiss, but that didn't necessarily mean everything was all right.

Looking at the completed forms, she felt satisfied, but she didn't know where all these other papers had come from. She frowned as she looked at them and then glanced out the open door. Some of the others in the office had come in here and messed up her desk, thrown things around, stolen her calendar to make her look bad. They were jealous because she handled more cases than anyone else and did it really well. Well, she wasn't going to let them get to her. She had an important job to do. As soon as she found her calendar.

The changes in the system were good. Too many cases of child abuse, neglect or endangerment had gone uninvestigated, and the new procedures were designed to prevent that. People in her office were struggling with the new forms, the new way of doing things, but Monette knew she was doing everything right. Others in the office were jealous because she had adapted so quickly and mastered the new procedures. That's why they were trying to make her look bad. She wasn't going to let them annoy her. She could handle anything. As soon as she found her calendar.

"Good morning, Monette. Could I speak to you in my office, please?"

Monette started violently and looked up from the pile of papers on her desk to see her boss, Susan Martinez, waiting in the doorway to her office. Had she been there a second ago? Monette didn't think so.

Susan was smiling and Monette tried to smile back, her lips flickering up then down. "I have a lot to do," she mumbled, her gaze darting to Susan's crisp, tailored slacks and top to her own gray suit. Monette always tried to look neat and professional. But wait—were those spots on her skirt? Where had those come from? She'd been looking for her calendar, and...

"I know," Susan said. "You've been working so hard. This will only take a minute." She turned and moved down the short hallway to her office.

Monette stared after her in dismay. The only thing she could do was follow.

Standing, she brushed her hands down her skirt and tried to tuck in her blouse, then she did as she was told.

Once she was inside Susan's office, she took the chair indicated for her while Susan closed the door to ensure their privacy.

"Would you like a bottle of water, Monette?" Susan asked, watching her, still smiling. "It's summertime in Arizona, and we can't let you get dehydrated."

Monette shook her head; a quick, hard shake. "No, uh, no thanks. I had some water." Hadn't she? Or maybe that had been earlier. There had been a bottle of water on her desk and she'd had some with lunch. She'd eaten lunch, hadn't she? Blinking, she waited.

"Monette, when was the last time you took a day off?"

"Um, I don't know. I don't need a day off." Her fingers began picking at her skirt, trying to fold pleats over the dirty spots that had appeared from nowhere. Folding, smoothing, folding, smoothing.

Susan leaned forward and clasped her hands lightly together on top of her spotless desk. "It was last January. Now it's July and you've worked every day and most weekends."

"My job is important."

"Yes, it is and you're a valuable employee. But we can't let you get burned out."

"I'm not!" Monette sat forward urgently. "I have lots to do right now, but when I get ahead of it, I'll take a vacation. I've been thinking about going to Hawaii." That was someplace people went on vacation, wasn't it? She didn't know. She'd never taken one.

Susan smiled again, apparently relieved. "That's a great idea. Lie on the beach, relax…"

"I'm not going to get burned out," Monette said again as if her boss hadn't spoken. "I'm fine. I like working. Our clients need me." Monette forced down the panic that fluttered in her throat, threatening to choke her. She had to work. What would she do if she didn't come to work every day?

"Yes, they do, but we, as a department, have a huge responsibility to our clients, and we have to be at our best."

"And you don't think I'm doing my best?" Monette sat forward and grasped the front of Susan's desk, her fingertips whitening as her grip tightened. "I am. I do my best every day. You can't deny that I handle more cases than anyone else."

"But you don't need to, Monette. There

have been some complaints from some of our other caseworkers that you've interfered with their cases, and some calls from the public."

"Who?" Monette jumped to her feet, fury surging through her. "I work harder than anybody. Who's been complaining about me?"

"You know I can't say." Susan stood, too, and came around to place her hand gently on Monette's arm. "I need you to get your case files together before Friday the twenty-first, and we will disperse them to the other caseworkers so that you can take some time off to rest."

"But I don't need time to rest."

"It's very obvious that you do, Monette, and I'm insisting that you take at least two weeks off. You've been very stressed for the past three months."

"No more than anyone else," Monette said defensively.

"Yes, much more," Susan responded, still in her gentle tone. "Did something happen in April that caused…"

"No. I'm fine."

April, she thought. April six. Sean's birth-day. The day that little girl had been found—

She jerked her thoughts back to what Susan was saying.

"You need a complete break—take that trip to Hawaii you were just talking about. Get your case files organized by a week from Friday and—"

"I can't." The panic she'd been fighting overwhelmed her. Sweat broke out on her face. "But this is Tuesday. That only gives me…"

"A week and a half. Plenty of time to get things together." Susan put her arm around Monette's stiff shoulders. "Would you like some help?"

"No." Monette's stomach heaved. "I can do it… I don't want anyone in my…" Her words faded away as the enormity of the situation faced her. Stumbling a little, she turned around. "I've got to go. There are cases to finish and there's one…" Clutching at the door frame, she scrabbled for the knob and shuffled out the door.

CHAPTER TWELVE

CALEB HAD TOLD Laney to make herself at home, so she took her schoolbag from the Jeep and carried it inside. Bertie followed, padding into the kitchen to see if anything interesting had magically appeared in his food dish. When he saw that it hadn't he slurped some water and returned to the living room to turn a few circles, then crumple on his rug.

Laney laughed at him and began arranging the items she'd brought with her. She soon had her laptop set up on the kitchen table, and books and papers scattered over its surface. It took her a while to get down to work and focus her mind on the ninth-grade English curriculum because her thoughts kept wandering to her son and especially to Caleb. From the first time they'd met, she'd spent much more time thinking about him than was probably necessary for someone who was a neighbor. But he was more than a neighbor, and the fact that she'd let her son go off with him on horseback was proof. She trusted him and thought he trusted her, something that his initial hesitation around her and Sam told her was difficult for him— though things had certainly changed since he'd reinjured his leg.

Laney stared at the blinking cursor on her laptop screen. She had revealed much of herself to Caleb last night. She'd told him about her mother and about James, her history of abandonment. She hadn't been looking for pity, but for understanding, because Caleb was becoming important to her in a way she hadn't experienced since she'd become infatuated with James. Her incredibly bad judgment in that situation had resulted in her becoming a single mother when James had run out on her and their unborn son. She couldn't imagine Caleb doing that. When he'd told her last night that he hadn't spoken of his friend, Berman, since the man's death, she'd felt the depths of his despair. He carried Berman's memory with him, and probably others of his men, as well. He couldn't leave the memories behind, forget about those men.

Realizing she'd spent enough time thinking about Caleb, she focused on the work in front of her. Just before noon, she cleared the table, found everything she needed for sandwiches and prepared lunch. Sam and Caleb rode up a few minutes later, turned Cisco loose to graze on the small patch of grass in front of the house and came inside, their boots—and Caleb's cast—thumping on the hardwood floor.

"Mom!" Sam shouted, petting Bertie, then running to her. "We moved a *hundred* cows and they didn't like it, but we made 'em go."

Laney hunkered down to hug him and meet him at eye level, then glanced up at Caleb, who held up the fingers of both hands and mouthed the word *ten*.

She kissed Sam, who didn't seem to mind this time, and said, "I'm proud of you for showing those cows who's boss. Now go wash your hands for lunch."

He trotted away and they heard him singing at full volume while he soaped and rinsed.

Caleb crossed to Laney, reached down

and hauled her to her feet. Clamping one arm around her waist, he pulled her close. Surprised, she tilted her head back to look at him and he took the opportunity to close his mouth over hers, as if he'd been waiting all day for the moment.

The kiss was sweet and fast, and she barely had time to react before he released her and stepped away. He gave her a wink and headed to the bathroom to wash his hands as Sam came pounding back into the kitchen and climbed onto a chair. Her son launched into an excited recitation of their "big roundup," as he called it. Her lips still tingling, it took Laney a few moments to focus on what he was saying.

Caleb returned to the kitchen and they sat at the table to eat. Sam chattered on and Caleb provided clarification whenever Sam's tale became a little too far-fetched.

As they were finishing their sandwiches, Don Parkey's truck rolled into the yard, pulling a horse trailer behind it. They went out to greet him, but the three of them stopped, startled, at the thumping and banging noises coming from the trailer. It sounded as if the horse was trying to break out.

Don jumped out of his truck and hurried over to them. He was holding the cat carrier, which held a very disgruntled mama cat.

"She doesn't look very happy," Caleb said, peering into the carrier.

"Don't worry about her. Her troubles are over. She can get back to chasing mice," Don answered, handing the carrier to Laney. "It's this horse I'm worried about. I don't know about him, Caleb," he said. "Been traumatized by people and wants nothing to do with any of us, or any of his own kind, for that matter. I think we should put him in a corral or pasture by himself and then just leave him alone for a while."

With a nod, Caleb pointed to the corral at the far side of the barn, which opened onto an empty pasture. Don climbed back into his truck, turned in a wide circle, then backed up to the corral gate.

Laney told Sam to stay where he was on the porch then hurried to the barn with the carrier and released the mama cat, who immediately streaked up to the highest rafter, then looked down angrily at the interfering humans before settling down to wash her paws. Laney barely spared her a glance be-

fore rushing back outside to grab the gate
and give it a mighty opening swing.

The men had lowered the trailer ramp and
opened the trailer gate. The horse, instead
of backing out, kicked at Don, who vaulted
off the end of the ramp, out of danger. Laney
was sickened to see the long, vicious scars
on the animal's rump, as if he'd been beaten
many times. He had a reason to hate humans, she thought.

"How did you load him, Don?" Caleb asked.

"With great difficulty." The veterinarian
sighed. "It took the guy who found him, his
wife and me nearly an hour to get him into
the trailer. I hope it doesn't take us that long
to get him out. I've got other patients I need
to see."

Caleb stepped up to the end of the trailer
and began speaking to the horse in a low,
soothing tone. She could see the animal tossing his head. After several minutes Caleb
took a step closer, lifting himself onto the
ramp. The horse's hooves danced, clattering
on the floor of the trailer, the animal obviously unsure of this new human approaching him. Caleb's voice never changed as he
continued to talk in his soothing tone.

At one point Caleb reached out a hand but the horse tried to kick, causing Caleb to hobble back.

"Misjudged his fear," Caleb said easily, and started all over again.

Laney glanced over her shoulder to see that Sam and Bertie were still on the porch. Her son's eyes were wide as he watched. She tried to control her anxiety as Caleb stepped in closer. Her gaze went automatically to his injured leg, fearing the horse would panic again and kick him there. Caleb seemed to have forgotten his own injury as he worked to calm the animal.

"You've been mistreated, big fella, I get that," Caleb was saying. "I know you don't trust us. I wouldn't trust us, either. Some people suck. They didn't deserve to have a beautiful boy like you, but you're free from them now. We'll treat you better than they did."

Laney wasn't even sure he was aware of what he was saying; only stringing words together in a kind of patter to calm the horse.

As she watched Caleb, her mind flashed back to everything that had happened in the weeks she had known him, from the day they'd met and he'd rescued Sam from being trampled by a mare, to their adventures with her lively son, to the cattle trampling her flowers, the cat that needed to be spayed, the terrifying encounter with the mountain lion, and his own broken leg. She had seen this gentle side of him before; last night when he'd carried her son to the truck and put him to bed at home. He understood this wounded, scarred horse because the same thing had happened to him.

Caleb Ransom had been badly hurt and he'd survived. Slowly, he was beginning to take an interest in life again, in those around him.

And she was in love with him.

Laney stood perfectly still, holding on to the corral gate as the realization sank in. Blood rushed to her face and her heart pounded in her ears as she came to terms with it. She didn't know how this had happened. They'd only known each other for a few weeks. They'd never been on a date, spent time with each other's families, anything that couples usually did. And they certainly *weren't* a couple, she reminded herself. They were only friends—or had been until right now when she'd realized she loved him.

She didn't know if she could trust this feeling, because she'd been so wrong about James. But, somehow, the comforting things Caleb was saying to the horse eased her mind, too, making her think it was possible to have faith in him.

Still, in love with him? Hadn't she told herself that if she ever fell in love again, it would be with someone she really got to know first? Someone who shared her interests and values? She wasn't going to make the same mistake she'd made with James, was she? She couldn't do that, especially not now that she had a child to consider.

And most important was that Caleb hadn't given any significant indication that he was romantically interested in her, beyond a few kisses. Her experience with James had taught her that kisses meant something different to a man than they did to a woman.

Confused and dismayed, she went back to watching Caleb working with the horse, seeing the easy, slow movements, listening to the lulling tone of his voice. This was one of the things that confused her about him.

So many times there had seemed to be a war raging inside him, and other times, such as this one, he was as calm and peaceful as a forest meadow. She wasn't sure which was the real Caleb Ransom, so how could she be in love with a man like that?

Finally, after several long minutes of soothing talk and careful movements, Caleb was close enough to place a hand on the animal's rump. It shied away, but then steadied and Caleb was finally able to sidle to the front of the trailer, where he stood with his head against the gelding's neck, continuing to talk. Then, gently easing the horse back, step by step, it was down the ramp and in the corral.

Laney swung the gate shut and snapped the latch into place. The beautiful black gelding whinnied, reared and then trotted around the corral and out into the pasture. He kept going, as far and as fast as he could, mane flying, muscles rippling, until he reached the fence on the far side. He turned and ran along the fence, back and forth, for several minutes.

Laney signaled at Sam, who ran over, Bertie at his heels. Caleb lifted him onto the top rail of the fence and held him in place while the four of them watched the horse run, trying to find a way to freedom.

"I think he'll settle down in a while," Don said as he turned to go. "In spite of his scars, his wounds aren't physical. He's suffered mental trauma. He'll be here for a while, Caleb. He's not like the others, who can be put up for adoption after just a few weeks."

Caleb nodded. "I knew that as soon as I saw him. I'll see what I can do with him."

"Good luck." With a wave, Don closed the back of the horse trailer, climbed into his truck and drove away.

Caleb, Laney and Sam stood watching the restless gelding dance nervously around the pasture, staying as far away from the people as he could.

"What's his name, Mr. Ransom?" Sam wanted to know.

Caleb shrugged. "I don't think he's got a name. You want to give him one? Like you did with, um, Awesome?"

"Yeah! 'Buddy,' like you call me sometimes."

Laney chuckled, loving the way Caleb blinked in surprise. He glanced at the skittish animal, then back at her son. "Okay, Sam. I'm not sure that name fits him, not the way it does you, but if you want, we can call him Buddy."

"The pony needs a name, too," Sam informed them.

"You already gave her a name, Sam," Caleb responded. "You called her Awesome, remember? You think she needs another name?"

"People have two names," Sam pointed out. "I got two names, Sam and Reynolds." He looked at Caleb curiously. "You got two names, Mr. and Ransom."

Caleb chuckled and reminded Sam that his first name was Caleb.

Sam held out both hands. "Well, see? Awesome needs two names, too."

"All right, then. What's her other name?"

Sam screwed up his face. After several seconds he said, "Miss. I want to name her Miss Awesome, 'cause she's so..."

"Awesome," Caleb supplied. "Yeah, I get it. Why don't you go tell her what her new name is?" he suggested. "But don't go inside her corral." Addie and her filly's corral was adjacent to this one, and Laney could see the mare and filly watching the proceedings with the new gelding.

"Okay, boss!" Sam bounced away, but remembered to slow down and approach slowly. The filly trotted over to greet the little boy and Sam eagerly presented her with her new name.

Laney looked at Caleb. "Miss Awesome?" she said, and the two of them laughed.

After a moment Sam rushed back to tell them that Miss Awesome liked her new name. Then he climbed back onto the fence rail and Caleb put an arm around him to hold him in place.

Laney's phone rang and she saw that it was her fire-team captain.

"We're being called out to Texas," Kebra said when she answered. "Can you meet us in Tucson?"

Automatically, Laney's gaze flew up to meet Caleb's. "Sure, Kebra… Oh, wait, no, I can't. There's no one to watch Sam. My brother's on vacation and my mom and dad are out of town for a day or two."

His eyes never leaving Laney's, Caleb lifted Sam down from the fence rail. "Sam, take Bertie back to the house so, uh, Buddy doesn't scare him."

"Okay." Her son trundled off with the dog.

"Laney, I'll keep Sam." Caleb met her eyes in a steady gaze.

"I'll call you right back, Kebra," she said into the phone. "What did you say, Caleb?"

"Sam can stay with me until you get back, or until your mom and dad come and get him."

"I can't ask you to do that."

"You didn't. I offered." He waited for her response.

A flurry of thoughts whirled through her mind. Sam would be safe, no doubt about that, and he would love staying with Caleb. And time away from Caleb and Sam would give her a chance to process what she now knew: that she was in love with Caleb, to hug it to herself and sort it out. She wasn't sure she could think about it objectively if he was caring for her son.

As well, she had a job to do and her team was counting on her. "Thanks, Caleb. I appreciate it. I'll call my mom and dad to ask them to pick him up when they get home."

"No hurry."

She called Kebra back to confirm the time to meet at the airport and then hurried to tell Sam what was happening.

"I get to stay with Bertie and Mr. Ransom?" he asked, his eyes shining as if he'd been given a magical gift.

She crouched in front of him so they could talk eye to eye. "I expect you to do what Mr. Ransom asks you to do."

He wrinkled his nose. "What's 'spect mean?"

"It means you're going to do it." Her firm tone left no room for question, so he nodded vigorously.

She gave him a hug and a kiss. "I'll go home and get your overnight bag. Is there anything special you'd like me to bring? Books? Games?"

Laney slid a sideways glance at Caleb, who stood nearby, watching in that thoughtful, self-contained way of his. She didn't let Sam play video games yet and she wasn't sure how Caleb would feel about playing kids' board games with her son.

Sam told her what he wanted and she turned toward her Jeep, then paused and looked at Caleb. "What about a bed for him? I have a cot I can bring over, and as far as food, he'll eat most things except salads and…"

"I can handle it, Laney. I've still got a freezer full of the food Karen Bartlett brought over, and I can make him a bed on the sofa, or move the sofa cushions into my room. He'd probably rather sleep on cushions on the floor with Bertie beside him, anyway. I've taken care of kids before. I've got a bunch of younger cousins."

She blinked. This was the first time he'd mentioned anything about his family since his mother had visited. There was a great deal more she wanted to know, but it would have to wait.

"Okay. Thanks." She jumped into the Jeep and hurried home. Quickly, she threw everything together and called her parents to tell them what was going on. Vivian fretted about her banana tree, but said she'd call a neighbor to look in on it. Smiling at the new love in her mom's life, Laney finished collecting her and Sam's gear and rushed back to Caleb's.

The entire time she was getting ready, dropping off Sam's things, reminding him to brush his teeth and obey Caleb, she felt an undercurrent of electricity humming through her. It was partly due to the adrenaline rush she always experienced before going to a fire, but also because she'd discovered she was in love with Caleb.

Tears threatened when she leaned over to kiss her son goodbye. He wriggled away and said, "'Bye, Mom. Are you gonna kiss Mr. Ransom goodbye, too?"

Her gaze shot up to meet Caleb's. The unscarred corner of his mouth kicked up. "Yeah, are you gonna kiss me goodbye?"

She and Sam had been standing on the porch and Caleb was at the bottom of the steps. Laney raised her chin and gave an exaggerated sigh as she said, "If I must."

Caleb's grin widened and one eyebrow shot up as she sauntered down the steps. When she reached him, she made a show of giving a chaste kiss, putting her hands behind her back and leaning forward to peck his cheek.

He was having none of that. His hands came around to grasp her wrists and haul her arms up to encircle his neck. Tilting his head, he spoke to her son. "Sam, is it okay if I give your mom a really big kiss?"

"Yup," the little boy answered on a giggle.

Caleb gave her a wicked grin that made her heart stutter then pound. He pulled her close and fit his mouth over hers.

He tasted sweet, warm, delicious. She would never get tired of this. She pressed herself even closer and wound her fingers up into his hair, knocking his hat to the ground. Completely lost in feeling, she had no sense of space and time.

She was barely aware of Sam bouncing down the steps to pick up Caleb's hat. He tapped it against their legs and said, "Mr. Ransom, you dropped your hat." When he didn't get a response, he tapped harder. "No more kissing."

Finally, when she hadn't a bit of breath left in her, Caleb pulled his mouth away from hers and buried his face in her neck. "Be safe, Laney. Come home to us."

Tears spurted into her eyes. Unable to speak, she nodded, kissed the side of his neck and stepped away as she dragged air into her lungs.

"I'll..." Her throat closed up. She cleared it and tried again. "I'll call you." She wiped tears out of her eyes, gave Sam another hug and kiss, then whirled and hurried to her car.

As she pulled away, she glanced in the rearview mirror and saw that Caleb had picked Sam up. Her son's arm was hooked around Caleb's neck and the two of them were waving. She stuck her hand out the window and waved until she made the turn at the end of the drive and headed toward Tucson.

CALEB HATED TO see her go. He hated knowing she was going to be in danger. He had the same knot in his gut he'd had every time he and his men had gone out on a mission; the same prickle of nerves along his neck and down his back as if he could feel the crosshairs of an enemy rifle locked onto him.

The feeling, once so familiar to him, sent alarm clanging through his head. He knew it signaled danger and he had to resist the urge to look around to check the position of his men. A phantom squad, he'd heard an old soldier say once. Even though his men were long gone to other units or bases, or had left the army, in his mind, they were always together and he always had to look out for them.

He took a breath, then another, steadying himself. He'd been home for a year and a half—closer to two years now. His reactions and his fight-or-flight response had settled down. It should surprise him that it was happening again, but he knew what was going on. His protective instincts were kicking in.

He wasn't even going to speculate on why he felt the need to protect Delaney Reynolds, when only a few weeks ago his goal in life was to keep her—and everyone else— out. But, inch by inch, Laney and Sam had worked their way into his life and now he couldn't even imagine being without them. When he thought about how he'd lived before they'd come along, all he could recall was a big echo of loneliness. Crazy that he'd thought it was what he wanted.

What had really shocked him was his reaction when she'd told him about her marriage; about the college professor who'd obviously seduced and tricked her into marriage and motherhood, and then had dumped her. Caleb had seriously considered finding the son of a bitch and beating the crap out of him. It would have been a real pleasure, but he wasn't sure Laney would have appreciated the gesture.

He hated that he couldn't protect Laney now in her dangerous job, couldn't even be there to know exactly what was going on, but he wasn't in charge. And as she'd pointed out, no one was shooting at her. As much as it galled him, he had to stay behind, mind his own business, look after her son.

Glancing around, he saw that Sam had climbed the porch and was perched on the top step. He was leaning over Bertie, petting him and whispering in his ear. He was probably telling Bertie how much he was going to miss his mom. Caleb knew he was going to have to do something to distract the kid.

"Hey, Sam, how would you like to learn how to rope?"

When the little boy's head bounced up and a wide grin split his face, Caleb knew he'd hit on the right diversion. "Come on," he said. "Let's go see what we can find in the barn."

MONETTE LUGGED THE box up the last few stairs then scurried along the landing and into her apartment. She swung the door shut behind her and checked to make sure the drapes were tightly shut. No one was allowed to take files out of the office without permission, but she knew she could get them back where they belonged before Susan, or anyone else, noticed.

That was one thing she'd learned from her mother; how to be sneaky.

Although Monette had made a point of living her life in an exemplary way—unlike every other member of her family—she now realized that her whole campaign to save little Sean from his mother's neglect would be jeopardized if she didn't make her case airtight. And she had to do it before Susan made her take a vacation.

Picking up the box, she turned toward the sofa, intending to spread her work out on the coffee table, but she paused, staring. The table was piled high with newspapers and magazines. How had those gotten back there? She'd put them in the recycling bin downstairs. Hadn't she?

Frowning, she took the box into the kitchen instead and put it on her small dinette table, shoving aside dirty dishes to make it fit. She stacked the dishes and carried them to the overflowing sink, then stood staring down at the mess. She needed to clean this up, but not right now. She had more important work to do.

"Everything has to be in perfect order," she murmured as she opened the file box and began pulling out papers, which she placed in stacks. She'd been watching Laney Reynolds for years, since before her son could walk, so she had a great deal of documentation.

"Little Sean won't be in danger ever again," Monette said to herself with satisfaction. "And when he's grown up, he'll find me and thank me for saving his life."

Not like the other time, the other Sean. Monette's hands fell into her lap and she sat staring blankly at the work in front of her. She lost the battle to keep the memories at bay. Her mother's voice rang in her ears…

"YOU'D BETTER WATCH HIM, little missy. If something happens to him it'll be your fault. I gotta work and I can't afford no babysitter." Bambi Berkley added another layer of red to her lips, adjusted the too-tight skirt

of her waitress uniform and glared at her daughter.

Monette put her hand back to make sure four-year-old Sean was securely behind her and lifted her chin defiantly. "Well, if you're gonna work, maybe you better bring home some food instead of spending all your money on booze. Oatmeal's all we've had to eat for two days."

"Don't you back-sass me!" Bambi raised a hand as if to strike, but Monette grabbed Sean and scuttled out of the reach of that palm she'd felt far too many times. Bambi started after them, but Monette shoved Sean, who was now whimpering, behind a chair and stood in front of it.

"You're not gonna hit him or me. You gotta get to work or you'll get fired. Again."

Bambi stopped, stared at her daughter. Her lips curled. "You're nothin' but a goody-goody know-it-all, but you don't know nothin'. I'll deal with you later." She grabbed her purse and keys and headed out to the beat-up old Ford sedan that sometimes got her to work.

"Fine," Monette shot back. "But bring home some food."

Monette was relieved when the car started and Bambi pulled away from the remote shack they'd called home for two weeks now. Clouds of dust followed the car as it shuddered over the rutted track leading to the highway into town.

She hated this place. But it was all they could afford and there was a corral by the house where Bambi's new boyfriend, Stanley, could keep his horse—as soon as he bought one. It was too far from town, no close neighbors to ask for help, to beg for milk for Sean, to let the county know that Bambi neglected her children.

There was nothing but desert and a few cows and horses in the fenced area nearby. She didn't know if the fence was secure, had never been around animals like them before, but she knew she had to protect Sean from them. She was his security, and he was hers. She didn't know what she was going to do when summer was over and she had to go back to school. Bambi would have to get a babysitter for him then. It would be easier when he was old enough to start kindergarten. There would be other people to

*help Monette look after him—and he'd get
at least two meals a day at school.*

*Sean came out from behind the chair and
slipped his hand into hers. Monette smiled at
him. "Looks like it's oatmeal again, baby."*

*"I'm not a baby," he insisted. "I'm a big
boy." But when he poked his thumb into his
mouth, Monette laughed and hugged him.*

"Okay, big boy. It's time for oat—"

A DOOR SLAMMED nearby and, with a start,
Monette came out of the memory to discover
tears rolling down her cheeks. Getting up,
she grabbed a paper towel, wiped her face
and blew her nose. She couldn't let this happen, she thought fiercely. Couldn't let the
memories come out of the corner where she
kept them safely locked away or she'd never
be able to work, never be able to save the
little Reynolds boy. She'd never be able to
rescue Sean.

She sat forward and picked up the completed form on the top of the nearest stack of
papers. His name wasn't Sean. It was Samuel. Sam. She had to remember that.

Putting the paper down again, she looked
around her apartment. With an effort, she

wrenched her thoughts away from the Reynolds boy and studied her surroundings. The place was a mess and she didn't know how or when it got that way.

Monette stood and walked over to examine the calendar clipped to the refrigerator door. It still showed the page for April. That was when she'd learned that Laney and her son would be moving. It was also when she'd heard the news about little Lily Morales and realized she'd made a terrible mistake in not being more vigilant in overseeing that case. She couldn't let that happen to Sam Reynolds.

A thrill of accomplishment shot through her. She had remembered to call him by the right name. Maybe she had been a little bit overwhelmed by work. Monette knew she was the best case worker, the best Department of Child Safety specialist, in the county. Susan was wrong. She didn't need a vacation and she would prove it.

The new rules specified the type of meeting she needed to have with Susan before proceeding with the Reynolds case. Monette knew exactly how to present it, and how to present herself, so that the danger to Sam was obvious.

With a clear sense of purpose, she turned back to the file box. Everything about the paperwork on this case would be perfect. She wouldn't fail.

THE MEMBERS OF Fire Team 8 studied the map spread out on the hood of a pickup. Laney and the members of her team were preparing to go in as other teams straggled in off the line. Exhausted, red-eyed and dirty, the captains stopped to share information about the wildland fire that had been started by lightning and, fueled by high winds, had spread more quickly and erratically than anyone liked.

"Here and here," Kebra said, tapping two places on the map. "Laney, Shelley and Marie, you take the west side. Katie, Leigh and I will take the east. We'll work toward each other. There are hot spots everywhere and underbrush that's been drying out for years. Perfect fuel for this nightmare, so watch out and keep within sight of each other."

The team nodded in agreement, checked

their own equipment and each other's and headed out.

Laney was grateful to Caleb for taking care of Sam. It was a relief to know that she wouldn't have to worry about her son. She was even more relieved that this job required all her attention, giving her less time to think about Caleb. She couldn't afford to be distracted.

The team fell to work, setting backfires to clear the underbrush and creating clear areas on each side of the road in the hope that the fire wouldn't make the leap across.

With her partners, Laney worked her way down a slope. Intent on the ground she was clearing, she didn't notice what was happening in the top of the trees until Shelley shouted, "Laney, look out!"

She jerked up her head and saw that the fire was crowning, with flames licking and leaping from one treetop to the next. Whirling around, she grabbed for her radio as she called out to Shelley and Marie, "Let's get out of here."

The three of them started running with Laney attempting to radio a warning to the other half of their crew. She didn't see the tree root that sent her sprawling. As she scrambled to her feet, she heard a loud crack. She looked up in time to see a flaming branch plummeting toward her.

TWO NIGHTS LATER Caleb stood on his porch, staring across the expanse of pasture to Laney's house. He'd moved outside where he could at least hear crickets chirping and the occasional bawling of his cattle, because he couldn't stand the quiet of his house any longer. Forty-eight hours with a little boy who sang at the top of his lungs whenever water was running, who had conversations with his toys, the dog, the horses, anything that stood still for a moment, who noticed absolutely everything and commented on it, made the current silence of Caleb's home unbearable.

Caleb's walking cast had been replaced by a removable brace, which had made it easier for him and Sam to go all over the ranch together, either on horseback or in the truck.

Vivian and Frank Crown had picked their grandson up a few hours ago, and Caleb had been at loose ends ever since.

Normally, he would have found a dozen

different things to keep himself occupied, but none of them appealed to him. He'd had fun looking after Sam, the most fun he'd had in years. He was accustomed to looking after others—his younger cousins, soldiers, cattle, horses—but it had been a long, long time since he'd been responsible for anyone or anything like Sam, with his four-year-old's egocentric view of the world.

Caleb was trying to figure out how he'd stood the silence of his life up until now. Sam's presence had helped him in other ways, too. His nightmares had calmed down, barely troubling his sleep, and he'd been gratified to discover he hadn't cried out in his sleep, something that would surely have awakened and terrified Sam. Now that the little boy was gone, Caleb didn't know how that would affect his sleep. Even Bertie seemed unhappy, following Caleb around and collapsing at his feet with a woeful sigh whenever Caleb stayed put for a few minutes, as if Sam's absence was too much for him to bear, too.

Except for today, Caleb had talked to Laney every day since she'd been gone. She'd called to see how Sam was, but now that the boy was with his grandparents Caleb didn't think she'd call again. He wished she'd get home so he could see for himself that she was all right.

As if his thoughts had conjured her up, a light snapped on at her house. Without even thinking, Caleb turned, shooed Bertie back inside and grabbed his truck keys. He closed the front door behind him as he left.

CHAPTER THIRTEEN

WITHIN MINUTES HE was pulling up behind
her Jeep, knowing that if he'd given himself
any time to think about what he was doing,
he wouldn't have come. But he made a point
of not thinking about it, not analyzing things
as he usually did, and simply went with it.

Hurrying up her back porch steps, he
rapped at the door and then stood back in
shock when she swung it open.

Red-eyed and exhausted, she looked up
at him. "Oh, Caleb. Hello."

"What happened?" he demanded, stepping into her kitchen, his gaze fixed on her
neck. "Have you been hurt?"

There was nothing she could do except
step back hurriedly and let him in. Her hand
shot up to cover the area where he was looking, but he was quicker.

He grabbed her wrist and held it. "No," he
said. "Let me see."

She didn't resist as he turned her toward the kitchen light to better see the long, angry red burn that ran across her neck and collarbone, disappearing below the edge of her white T-shirt. Without a word, he eased down the shirt to see the full injury.

"Caleb," she said, protesting, trying to pull from his grip, to cover her burn.

He again moved her hand, but held on to it this time. "How bad is it?" he asked, his dark gaze piercing hers, demanding she tell him everything.

"First-degree burn. The doctor says it'll probably heal without leaving a scar. The challenge is going to be hiding it from Sam—and from my mom and dad—until it looks better. The bandage was coming loose, so I took it off. I've got to shower and then I'll put medicine on it again. The paramedic said for me to leave the bandage off and let the air get to it as much as possible."

"Go take your shower. I'll doctor it when you're done." Caleb kept his voice low and calm, hoping she wouldn't see how her injury was affecting him. "Have you eaten?"

"No. I was going to get a bowl of cereal or…"

"I'll fix something. Go."

Her eyes flashed at him. She wasn't used to being bossed around in her own kitchen. "Caleb, that isn't necessary. I can take care of myself."

Anger flared. "I don't think so. You can barely stand up."

Her lips pressed together as she looked at him, obviously weighing the merits of continuing the argument. He gave her his best bad-ass-sergeant glare and she backed down, turning in a huff to stalk from the room. The stalking would have been more effective if she hadn't been barefoot and still wearing the baggy pants to her firefighters' turnout. Seeing her sassy annoyance with him calmed him. If she was defying him, she wasn't seriously hurt.

Relieved, he turned to examine the contents of her refrigerator. Luckily, his limited cooking skills stretched to scrambling eggs and making toast, so that's what he did. He also found several kinds of herbal teas in the cabinet, read the labels, and chose one that said it was relaxing. He made Laney a cup, though his examination of the teabag made him think he was brewing chopped grass clippings. He decided that she wouldn't have it in her cabinet if she didn't like it.

He was putting the food on the table when she returned, fluffing her long, damp hair with her fingers. She was wearing a loose, red T-shirt and pajama pants printed with high heels, pouty red lips and perky hair bows—things he knew she'd never wear in the flesh.

His gaze swept over her as he wondered if she had on any underwear beneath that get-up. As if she didn't look luscious enough, a wave of the honeysuckle scent he always associated with her rolled in, nearly sending him to his knees.

Involuntarily a strangled sound came from his throat and she looked up. "Something wrong?"

"Uh, no. No," he said hastily, turning away, picking up a pot holder and putting it down again. "Sit." He hooked his finger through the handle of the tea mug and carried it to the table.

She looked at him again and then at the table. "Oh, this is great."

Her eyes brightened when she saw the tea

and he felt quite pleased with himself to have thought of it.

"Thanks so much, and thanks again for taking care of Sam until my parents came back." Her eyes met his. "I never worried about him for a second."

"It was fun," he said gruffly, wondering when the last time was that he'd used that word. He pulled out a chair and sat opposite her as she picked up her fork and dug into the eggs. "And I didn't have to wonder where he'd gotten himself off to since he was never more than two feet away from me, except when he was asleep on the couch with Bertie."

She smiled. "He loved the whole adventure of staying with you. I don't think he missed me at all."

"Believe me, he missed you. If I didn't read *Goodnight Moon* to him exactly the way you did, he made me read it again." Caleb paused, his eyes on her. "I've got that book memorized."

"Join the crowd."

He watched her take several sips of tea before he said, "Okay, enough stalling. Tell me how you got that burn."

She gave a small shrug and picked up her fork again. "Wasn't watching what I was doing. The fire started crowning, jumping from one treetop to another. We scrambled to get out of the way, but I tripped and fell and a branch landed on top of me. No one else was hurt, so the whole thing was a non-incident."

Caleb thought it was more than that, but he didn't pursue it. He was so pathetically grateful that she was home safe. He relaxed, settling back in his chair and stretching out his legs, then realized with a jolt it was the first time since he'd been wounded that he'd done that without carefully gauging whether or not it would hurt. Another benefit to hanging around this Reynolds pair. They'd made him forget himself, had drawn him out, made him part of their lives.

As she ate the eggs and toast he'd prepared, Laney continued talking, telling him about the fire she had come from, the people on her team and the fires they'd fought together previously. He listened and didn't interrupt. Talking when they were tired, this was something he'd noticed Sam did, and apparently, it was something he'd inherited from his mom. Most people got quiet, but these two talked. They might have dark bruises of exhaustion under their eyes, but they had plenty to say, and he didn't mind listening.

Caleb was fascinated to see Laney so vulnerable. Except for the time she'd fallen off the hay bales and knocked the wind out of her lungs, he hadn't seen her like this. She was always the one in charge, the one taking care of everything and everyone.

As she spoke, she gestured with her hands. He watched them; the graceful way her fingers fluttered as she described how the fire had looked skipping from pine to aspen to oak. He remembered how they had felt running over his skin, not hesitating to touch the scars he'd feared would have repulsed any woman.

But Laney Reynolds wasn't any woman. She went from teaching school to fighting fires to caring for her son to finding ways to improve his life whether he wanted her to or not, yet he had never seen her this spent.

She finally wound down about the same time her cup was empty. She shook her head when he asked if she wanted more tea.

"You need to get some sleep," he said, gathering up the dishes. He washed them quickly and put them in the drainer. "Now, what do you have to put on that burn?"

"The medic gave me some cream. It's in my bag. I'll get it."

"Stay there," he said, hauling out the sergeant's voice again. "I'll get it."

She blinked at his commanding tone, but seemed content to stay where she was. He was back in a few minutes with some cotton swabs and the tube of unguent. Uncapping it, he squeezed some onto a swab and gave her an expectant look.

Laney's gaze shot up to meet his as she reached up and swept her damp hair aside to give him access to her neck. It made him recall what it had been like to kiss her there.

Wondering what kind of sick jerk he was to think about that when she was this worn out and injured, he carefully doctored the burn then stood back. He didn't want to leave her alone tonight. Maybe he should offer to sleep on the couch. He wondered how she would take that suggestion.

"Time for bed..." For some reason his

voice broke on the word. He cleared his throat, frowned and said, "Lock up after me."

Turning, he started for the back door, picturing escape from her disturbing presence and the long night that loomed ahead of him. He heard her chair scrape as she stood. Good, she was going to lock the door after him.

"Caleb?" Her voice was soft, questioning.

Without turning to look at her, he said, "Yes?"

"Why don't you lock the door...but stay on this side of it?" When he looked back at her, she read the confusion in his face and quickly said, "I would feel better if you stayed. You can sleep on the couch."

His mouth went dry even as blood rushed to his head. "Laney, you're tired, don't..."

"Don't tell me don't." She took a step toward him, lifting a hand, palm out, as if to ward off any more of his objections. "I keep saying that, but you won't listen." She smiled. "It's been a hard week and I wouldn't mind some company."

Feeling helpless, exposed, he shook his head. "Laney, this may not be a good idea."

"Caleb, I do everything mostly by myself.

Every day I take care of myself and my son, and everything that needs to be done. I don't mean to seem like I'm coming on to you. I only want to know someone else is here."

She correctly read the hesitation in his eyes. With a gentle smile curving her lips, she said, "Caleb, when have I ever asked for your help?"

"Um, never."

"Even when I needed someone to look after Sam, I didn't ask you. You volunteered."

He frowned, wondering where she was going with this. "And...?"

"And I think we're good enough friends now that I can ask you to stay with me tonight. I only need some company."

He stood, bonded in place as if he had no will of his own. When she reached him, she put out one of those hands he'd been admiring and intertwined her fingers with his. "I don't really know why, but I don't want to be alone in this house tonight. I'll fix you a bed on the sofa."

Caleb felt his breath hitch in his chest. She was right. She had never asked him for anything; mostly because she was so busy telling him what to do.

"Sure, Laney. I can do that. The couch will be just fine," he said and was rewarded with a sparkling smile.

LANEY DRIFTED IN SLEEP, her mind as peaceful as her body was relaxed, until she heard a low, anguished sound of distress and her eyes flew open. Instantly she knew where she was and what was happening. Strangled, incoherent words came from the living room. Caleb was having a nightmare. Scrambling out of bed, she pulled on her robe and tied the belt as she rushed to his side. His arm thrashed around and he called out in his sleep, words she couldn't quite make out, but she understood the urgency behind them.

She snapped on the lamp at the end of the sofa and turned, reaching over to place her hands on his shoulders. "Caleb, wake up."

His eyes flew open, but he didn't see her, only the threat he thought she presented. His hands came up between them and swung outward to free him from her grip. He slammed her backward against the sofa pillows and loomed over her, his arm coming up to press against her throat. The hard set of his jaw and the steel in his eyes were terrifying—and all the more so because she knew he wasn't aware of what he was doing.

"Caleb!"

Her cry of alarm broke through to him. He blinked, focused on her, and his face spasmed. He looked around frantically, as if trying to understand where he was.

He released her immediately. His eyes were dark with lingering trauma and then with sorrow and apology. "Laney, I'm so sorry. Are you all right? Did I scare you? I would never hurt you, I…"

"I know that," she said, scrambling away from him and standing. "I'll get you some water."

"I don't need any, Laney," he said as she hurried from the room.

Maybe he didn't need any water, but she did, and she needed a few minutes away from him. In the kitchen, she grabbed a glass, filled it with water and downed several gulps before her pounding heart began to slow and she could clear her thoughts.

She wasn't afraid of Caleb Ransom, but she was afraid of the ruthless warrior he'd been in his dream and acted out on her.

Knowing she couldn't let him think she was afraid of him, she refilled the glass and took it to him.

He was sitting up, reaching for his shoes. Stricken, she stared at him. "Caleb, don't go." She set the glass on the coffee table. Getting him water had only been a pretext, anyway. She hurried around the end of the sofa and placed her hand on his arm. Meeting his eyes, she said, "Please stay. Tell me about the nightmare."

His gaze skittered guiltily away from hers. "I need to go."

"You need to stay."

"No, Laney," he said in a fierce tone. "I might have hurt you."

"But you didn't."

"I scared you."

"Only for a moment. And you didn't mean to. I surprised you." She smiled. "You're not used to sleeping anywhere but your own house, so on someone else's couch and…" She gave a shaky little laugh, plucked at her serviceable old robe and ran a smoothing hand over her wild bed-hair. "You're certainly not used to be awakened by a gorgeous woman," she teased.

Against his will, his lips twitched. "No, I'm not."

Nervously she pressed her palms together. "Do you want the water? I..."

"No." He took a breath and released it in a gust. "I shouldn't have stayed. It wasn't fair for me to stay here without you knowing exactly what you're dealing with."

Her mouth went dry as another thought occurred to her. "Did this happen when Sam was—"

"No," Caleb answered quickly. "I was fine when he was at my house. I think the nightmare came tonight because I was thinking about you being in that fire. It brought back too many memories. My sleep has been much better lately, but tonight..."

Before he could fall into silence, shutting her out again, she sat beside him on the couch. Pulling up one knee, she turned so that she faced him though he didn't have to face her unless he wanted to. Instinctively she knew he'd be able to talk better that way. Still, several long moments passed until he started talking.

"We were out on patrol in up-armored Bradleys, rolling down a road where troops had been attacked before, so we were on alert—though that doesn't always do much good. We were getting ready to come home. It was supposed to be our last mission. When we got back to base, we were going to start packing up our gear. We were talking about what we would do when we got home. Maybe that made us careless."

Caleb's hands clenched on his knees.

Laney reached over and entwined his fingers with hers. "Go on," she encouraged.

"In Afghanistan, you see people walking everywhere, even down the sides of roads out in the middle of nowhere. We saw a woman and her little boy. The kid—" Caleb paused, cleared his throat "—looked a lot like Sam. Big brown eyes, huge grin, like he was thrilled to see us. He waved and I waved back, then we drove over an IED."

Tears spurted into Laney's eyes. "You don't have to tell me any more, Caleb."

He shook his head. "I have to. Now that I've started, I have to finish it." Still, he waited, gathering his thoughts. "Berman had insisted on riding shotgun and that's what took most of the blast. I was in the seat behind him. I was knocked out, didn't wake up until I was on the way to the hospital. I was lucky. At least they saved my leg. But Berman and that little boy and his mother… They never had a chance."

"It wasn't your fault, Caleb."

"I know that. But why did I live when Berman didn't? He had a wife and baby daughter at home. Showed us every picture and video he had of her, shared every new thing she did, everything she learned…and that little boy…" Caleb paused, his throat working. "He couldn't have been more than six. He'd probably walked miles with his mother that day, but he grinned at us and waved, and in a place where we were often hated, that meant a lot. That's what I can't get out of my head. If we hadn't been there, passed right then, he'd still be alive, playing soccer with the other boys from his village, going to school. Having a life, maybe even a good one. I keep reliving it in my dreams."

"We never know why these things happen," she said, realizing her words were poor comfort. He kept reliving it because he didn't have closure and he might never have it.

He looked down at their clasped hands

and Laney watched the play of emotions on his face, humbled and grateful that he now felt comfortable enough with her to let her see this side of him, see his searing pain. She wanted so badly to tell him how much she loved him, but she knew he wasn't ready for that yet. She would tell him soon, though, no matter if he loved her or not. Love was a gift that needed to be given. It didn't necessarily have to be returned.

"You still can't blame yourself for what happened."

When he didn't respond, she went on. "Things happen in life—terrible tragedies we don't understand. Your problem is that you think you should be able to fix everything, make problems go away, solve issues."

"And that's bad?" He frowned, not seeming to like what she had to say, but at least he was listening.

"No, it's the way you are, so you have to accept it—or accept what you can't change."

He didn't answer. Laney knew she had merely stated what he already knew. It was time to drop this. She watched his face carefully as she asked, "Do you think you can go back to sleep?"

Caleb shook his head. "Not yet."

"Me neither." Laney turned and rested against the sofa cushions. "Do you want to watch a movie? I think I've got every animated one ever made, and some of them are really good. My mom buys them at yard sales."

He grinned. "Sure. Got any popcorn?"

"Coming right up."

While she made popcorn, Caleb looked through her movie collection and chose Disney's *Fantasia* of all things. "Happy dream sequences," he explained when she returned, answering her puzzled look with a shrug.

With him stretched out on the couch and her curled up in the big chair, they watched dancing hippos and magical floor mops. Eventually they both fell asleep.

LANEY WOKE WITH the feeling that things had changed for her last night. She was curled up in the overstuffed chair while Caleb was sprawled on the sofa, still asleep. He was on his back, one leg on the sofa, the other falling off the edge, his foot resting on the floor. His hands rested on his chest, easy, relaxed.

It was the most natural and defenseless pose she had ever seen him in.

Laney thought about all the expressions she'd seen on his face in the weeks she'd known him, and she thought that the peaceful expression on his face now was the one she loved the most. His thick lashes lay against his cheeks, a contrast to the scars she now knew had come from a bomb blast, one that had taken more from him than any man should have to give.

She didn't know what had gotten into her last night when she'd asked him to stay. Maybe it had been the shock on his face when she'd opened the door and he'd seen the state she was in. Maybe it was the commanding way he'd sent her off to the shower while he cooked. It certainly hadn't been his cooking, she thought, smiling. She could teach him how to scramble eggs so they'd be fluffy and moist, not dry.

No, she thought, stretching like a cat. All of those things had contributed, but it was the way he had tenderly applied ointment to her burn that had pushed her over the edge. She had seen this man working to tame a horse, his face intent, his purpose set. She had seen him scared when she'd fallen off the hay bales, and firm and also indulgent with her son. Never had she seen a look like the one he'd given her last night when he'd leaned over her with a delicate cotton swab in his big hand to dab cream on her burn. He'd been so infinitely tender she'd felt her heart roll over in her chest.

Then, when he'd awakened from his nightmare, reacted violently when she had touched him, she had discovered the depth of the anguish that ate at him. It made her love him even more. The question now was…could she help him? She wasn't sure he wanted any help from her. He might regret having told her what he had.

Watching his face as she eased out of the cozy nest of the chair, she acknowledged that even though she felt differently about him, as if something had fundamentally changed within her and between her and Caleb, she didn't know if he felt the same. She gathered up her blanket and pillow and headed for her bedroom. Time would tell.

LANEY MADE PANCAKES for breakfast and after they ate, they lingered over their coffee.

Bright sun streamed through the window, promising another hot Arizona summer day. She'd thought she would feel awkward in the glare of morning, especially now that she knew what was haunting him, but she didn't. She felt at ease, relaxed. Happiness bubbled through her.

To her vast relief, she discovered that her fears were unfounded. Caleb looked more peaceful than she'd ever seen him—and very appealing with his hair mussed and his shirt partly unbuttoned. She could see the scars that laced his chest, but he didn't seem to mind and she was grateful that he didn't hurriedly do up the buttons. She loved knowing that he felt at ease with her.

They talked about their plans for the day. When she'd pick up Sam and when he'd do more "work" for Caleb…mundane conversation that felt right given the dark place they'd been in the night before. There was still much to talk about, but there was time. She didn't know what the future held, but Laney decided she was in no hurry to rush out to meet it.

When her phone rang, she had to locate it, searching her duffel bag, tossing clothing aside and then smiling when she saw her mom's name and number pop up. She carried it back into the kitchen, glad the foolish grin she couldn't seem to wipe from her face wouldn't show through the phone.

"Hello?" She stilled as her mother struggled to speak.

"La…Laney. That woman was…was here. She took Sam."

"Took Sam?" Laney's heart dropped and began pounding. "What do you mean? What woman?"

Across the table, Caleb surged to his feet, his gaze fixed on her face.

"Monette…your old neighbor. The one who works for Child Protective Services. She came here and talked to Sam, then she and a deputy took him away! She said it was for his safety and…and that there was an ongoing investigation. I didn't hear what she told Sam."

"That's crazy!" Laney said. "His safety? There's been some kind of mistake. Did she say why?"

"Child endangerment. That's why she took him without warning or a meeting with you. She said Sam is in imminent danger. That you let him be around a mountain lion and wild horses and that you left him unattended, and that…that someone had independently confirmed your neglect."

"She's saying I'm responsible for the mountain lion? Wild horses? The only horses he's been around are…" She stopped as sick dread filtered through her body. Her stricken gaze sought out Caleb.

"Mom, I'll straighten this out and call you back." Punching the end button, she looked at Caleb. "Monette Berkley took Sam. Said I've endangered him by letting him be around that mountain lion—as if I'm responsible for where a mountain lion would roam. She also said I've let him be near wild horses, but he was never around any—only Addie and her filly. Where did she get that idea?"

Caleb frowned. "How would I know? I've never spoken to her except…" He paused as a vague memory surfaced of the hospital, late at night. "I think she came into my room at the hospital…"

"What did you say to her?" Laney could feel hysteria rising in her voice, but couldn't seem to stop it. "Did you tell her I was endangering Sam?"

"Of course not! I would never say that…" His voice trailed off as he tried to remember. "All right, I don't know exactly what was said, but I would never deliberately hurt you or Sam."

He started toward her. Eyes wide and full of tears, she backed up, her hands palm out to ward him off. "They took him *away*. My baby. He's in emergency foster care. He's probably scared, wondering where I am, why I don't come for him, thinking he did something wrong." She skirted around Caleb and ran toward her bedroom.

He followed her, watching in alarm as she hurriedly brushed her teeth and swept her hair into a neat ponytail, then grabbed clothes from drawers and closet. She dressed in her blue dress with the wide, full skirt and slipped her feet into sandals.

"Where are you going?" he asked.

"To get a lawyer and then to the DCS office. I've got to get him… I've got to get my baby back."

Snatching up her purse, she started for the door.

Caleb snagged her arm as she whirled past. "You're too upset to drive. I'll take you. You don't know what you're doing."

Furiously, she jerked her arm from his grasp. "I know exactly what I'm doing. I've never been on this end of this situation before, but I know what to do."

She ran out, but Caleb followed right behind, grateful he could now run almost as fast as she could. When she pulled open the door of her Jeep, he slammed it shut. "Let me drive you, Laney."

She rounded on him, her eyes furious. "No! You've done enough. How could you have said those things? Told her I put Sam in danger? Couldn't you see she was simply looking for an excuse to take him away?"

Heartsick, he shook his head. "No, I had no idea. How would I have known that? And I'm sure I never said that you put Sam in danger. Laney, at least let me come with you."

Laney only shook her head and shoved him out of the way. "Just stay away from me *and* my son." Climbing into the Jeep, she slammed the door and started the engine. Stomping on the gas, she fish-tailed out of the yard, kicking up gravel that had Caleb scrambling out of the way. She didn't look back as she raced onto the road and disappeared in a screen of dust.

"IT'S DONE. YOU'LL be safe now, Sean," Monette whispered as she drove away from the foster home where she'd taken Laney's little boy. His mother couldn't neglect him now. She couldn't put him in harm's way around mountain lions and wild horses.

Monette was pleased with herself, satisfied with the job she'd done. Even though she had to take a vacation starting Monday, she had done what she'd set out to do. She had saved him. She had saved Sean. No one would hurt him ever again.

Now she had to get ready for the meeting with her supervisor, with Sean's mother and maybe a lawyer. That was okay. She was confident she had all the proof she needed to make Sean safe forever.

CHAPTER FOURTEEN

HEART POUNDING, HANDS CLAMMY, Laney gripped the steering wheel and forced herself to calm down and focus on driving. It wouldn't help Sam if she had an accident. Her thoughts scrambled to make sense of this, to think of the fastest and best way to get her son back. Memories swamped her of being small and scared, left in the care of strangers. The thought of Sam being in that situation panicked her.

Within a few minutes she was at her mother's house. Vivian was still somewhat hysterical, but Frank and Ethan had begun to calm her down. After they had gone over everything that had happened that morning, Laney and Ethan went to see a friend of his who was an attorney practicing family law.

Robert Fernandez met them at his office in town and listened to the facts as they knew them.

"The Department of Child Safety has undergone a complete overhaul in the past year," he told them. "The first thing that will happen is what's now known as a Safety Meeting to work out a plan to ensure Sam's safety at home. We will be present and involved at this meeting. They have up to seventy-two hours to keep him, not including weekends."

Laney did a quick calculation in her head. "It's Thursday, so it might be five days before I get Sam back?"

"Yes." Robert gave her an uncomfortable look. "Maybe longer if she can prove that you've placed him in danger."

Laney fought back tears, trying to understand the enormity of what was happening to her and her son. "When…when will the meeting be?"

"I'll push to have one as soon as possible. Tomorrow even. We need to find out exactly what your neighbor said to Monette."

Laney shook her head. "He says he doesn't remember, that she came into his room in the hospital and questioned him… He'd probably had painkillers and he doesn't react well to them. Who knows what he might have said?"

Ethan gave her a sharp look, but she glanced away, unwilling to explain how she knew this about a neighbor. She was devastated by Caleb's betrayal, painkillers or no painkillers. How could he so carelessly let it seem that she neglected her son.

"Will they let me see Sam today?"

"I doubt it. Since it was an emergency removal, Monette is probably making sure no family members can see him."

"Is that the usual procedure?" Ethan asked.

"It is with Monette," Robert said.

Laney stared at him. "She's done this before?"

"I can't discuss any specific cases with you, but I've seen it happening lately."

That brought even more alarming questions to Laney's mind, but she knew she had to focus on getting her son back.

Robert promised to let them know as soon as he spoke to the DCS clerk. He also said he would talk to Caleb; find out exactly what was said.

Heartsick at the thought of Sam being alone in a strange place, Laney tried to find reassurance in Robert's conviction that she would have Sam back within a couple of days. Ethan drove her to her parents' house where she spent the day, only going home long after dark.

Laney parked the Jeep and sat staring at her house, loathe to go in because she knew Sam wasn't there. She probably should have stayed at her parents' house overnight, but she would have had to come back anyway, to get ready for whatever tomorrow might bring.

She finally stepped out of the Jeep and walked toward her back porch only to be brought up short when a figure rose out of the darkness. With a squeak of alarm, she stumbled back.

"It's me, Laney," Caleb said, stepping forward. "Don't be scared. Sorry, but I didn't think to leave the porch light on when I locked up this morning."

Laney pressed a hand to her pounding heart. "What are you doing here?"

"I want to talk to you."

"No." She skirted around him and darted up the steps. Fumbling with her key, she got the door unlocked then reached inside and hit the light switch.

"I want to know what's happening with Sam."

"Same as what happened this morning!" she snapped. "He's been taken away from me and I'm not sure when or if I'll get him back."

"It can't be that bad, Laney." Without hesitation, Caleb followed her into the kitchen.

"Oh, how do I know that since I don't know what you told Monette?"

Caleb's lips pulled together in a hard line. "There's nothing I can do about that because I don't remember exactly what I said. But I never would have purposely made you look like a bad mother. You're obviously a wonderful mother."

She shot him a swift, angry glance, wrapped her arms around her waist and walked into the living room. Caleb paced along right behind her, turning on lights as he entered. She didn't like that. She would have preferred staying in darkness. Walking across the room, she stared out the window.

Caleb was quiet for several seconds before he asked, "Why do you doubt that, Laney? You do what's best for Sam. You've always had your family to help you, to show you how to be a good mother…"

"Not always."

"What do you mean?" He stepped closer. She could feel his warmth at her back, but she refused to lean into it, to depend on him.

"My birth mother didn't simply drop me off with Vivian and Frank when I was seven. I bounced in and out of foster homes all around Phoenix until then, never knew what was going to happen, if we'd have food, or an apartment, or even a car to sleep in. I think the foster families must have been nice to me, but I don't really remember. I only remember being little and scared and confused."

"But you're not like your mother. Sam is—"

"Gone. Taken away."

Caleb tried to reach for her but she jerked out of his grasp.

He inhaled a ragged breath. "You can't let the past rule your life, Laney."

"Oh, really?" Her chin jutted out as she fixed him with an angry glare. "You're a fine one to talk about not letting the past rule your life. You can't even forgive yourself for what happened to Berman, and that little boy and his mother in Afghanistan. How can you lecture me about it?"

Caleb jerked back as if she'd slapped him.

His face paled, causing his scars to stand out in stark relief.

Stricken, she took a step toward him. "Oh, Caleb. I'm—"

"Stop," he said, holding up both hands, palms out. His eyes were stormy and his jaw worked for a second before he said, "You have to deal with this yourself. I shouldn't have pushed you." He turned toward the door. "I'm going home."

He strode out, closing the door firmly behind him.

Panicked, Laney darted after him. She had to find out what he'd said to Monette, at least try to make him remember. But when she threw the door open, he was already through the gate, stomping across his pasture. He wouldn't talk to her now.

Laney closed the door and sank into a kitchen chair, dropping her face into her hands. She had tried so hard to do everything right, to make up for the fiasco of her marriage to James, to be the kind of mother Vivian was, not like her own birth mother. She hadn't been able to do it, though. And she hadn't been able to keep the man she loved.

ROBERT FERNANDEZ ARRANGED a meeting for late the next morning. Laney's family showed up in force to support her, but had to wait in the lobby of the DCS office.

Laney had dressed carefully in a modest skirt and blouse to look as polished and pulled-together as possible—even though she felt like broken glass on the inside.

When she and Robert entered the room, she took in the solemn faces of the people seated at the table. One man had a laptop computer open on the table, hands poised, obviously ready to take notes on the proceedings. Laney didn't recognize him so she knew he probably didn't live in Sweetsilver, only worked there. He stood to shake her hand.

"Hello, I'm Juan Flores. I'll be recording everything we discuss today and you'll receive a complete transcript."

The woman beside him smiled warmly. "I'm Susan Martinez. I've lived here for many years, but I don't think we've ever met before. I'm the head of this office of the Department of Child Safety and my job is to ensure your son's safety and well-being, which I know is what we all want."

"Of course," Laney agreed. She turned to the third person in the room and was startled to realize that it was Monette Berkley—but an upgraded version. Her hair was pulled back into a neat bun, she was dressed in a charcoal-gray suit that looked new, and she was even wearing makeup. When she looked at Laney and Robert and gifted them with a regal nod, it was all Laney could do not to lunge across the table and throttle her.

Robert must have felt Laney's anger because he immediately took charge of the meeting. "We are here to clear this matter up. Since my practice deals in family law, I'm well aware of the new rules governing the Department of Child Safety." He nodded toward his briefcase. "In fact, I've got a copy of the manual with me."

"We're glad you're so well informed," Monette said, her eyes steady.

Laney stared, taken aback by the change in the woman. She was acting like a normal person, none of the crazy-eyed insistence of Laney's neglect that was her usual routine. Laney pressed her palms together nervously, unsure what to make of this.

Robert ignored the case worker's interruption and continued. "The only reason for the type of removal that occurred yesterday is if the child is in severe and imminent danger—"

"We thought it was best," Monette interjected, "to remove him when he was already out of the care of his mother, who has showed herself to be neglectful of his welfare."

Laney smacked her hands on the tabletop and half rose from her chair. "I have *never* neglected my son!"

Robert placed a calming hand on her arm while Susan Martinez shot Monette a sideways glance and said, "What Miss Berkley means is that recent occurrences at your home, Ms. Reynolds, placed Sam in situations of grave physical danger."

Before Laney could utter any of the furious words she was contemplating, Robert very calmly said, "Let's see your proof."

"Gladly. You certainly have the right to see it." Susan nodded at Monette. "Go ahead."

With crisp movements Monette removed a thick file folder from a box below the table and began.

"Normally we receive notices from concerned members of the public regarding the welfare of children, but since we lived in the same apartment building, I was able to make firsthand observations of interactions between you and your son."

"I'm well aware of that," Laney said tightly.

Robert again touched her arm to calm her.

Monette proceeded to read through a list of incidents, including the time Sam had nearly, according to her notes, fallen headfirst down the stairs on his riding toy. She mentioned a couple of other things that Laney thought sounded very minor like the time Sam cut his knee when he fell on the landing. Laney hadn't been holding his hand that time, either.

Then Monette looked up and Laney saw a flash of the familiar intense purpose the social worker had always showed her. "Matters became much more grave," the social worker went on, "when Ms. Reynolds and her son moved from town to an area where their activities were much harder to observe."

"Not that you let it stop you," Laney pointed out.

This time Robert shushed her and she sat back, fuming, to listen.

Monette glanced up and pursed her lips in the rigid line Laney knew so well. "I had an obligation as a concerned citizen to look out for Sean."

Susan looked over at her. "Sean?"

"Excuse me. I mean Sam." She rattled a fistful of papers. "And here is the evidence I collected." Hurriedly, Monette began listing what she considered dangers to the little boy—the mountain lion, the wild horses, the times when Sam had been too close to these dangers.

"My client can hardly be held responsible for the appearance of a mountain lion in the vicinity of her home," Robert said. "Or for the abused horses her neighbor takes in."

"It shows an inability or unwillingness to put her child's safety first!" Monette's voice was harsh and as she looked from Robert to Laney, her eyes glowing with fervor.

Susan gave Monette a swift look and spoke in a soothing voice. "Let's all keep calm. Remember, our goal is to keep Sam with his mother if at all possible."

"It won't be possible," Monette insisted, tapping her finger on the folder. "Other, more terrible things have happened as a result of Ms. Reynolds's uncaring attitude."

"Uncaring!" Laney nearly choked.

"What things?" Robert asked.

Monette gripped the edge of the table and leaned forward intently. "The fact that she has let her boyfriend severely punish Sean, to the point where he raised welts on his back."

"My boyfriend! I haven't *got* a boyfriend, much less one who would harm my son— whose name is *Sam*!" Laney knew that Caleb had never laid a hand on her son in anger or in harm—and he certainly wasn't her boyfriend. She'd destroyed any possibility of that.

Before Laney could say anything further, or Robert could demand an explanation, Susan and Juan surged to their feet.

"Let's take a break," Susan said, her eyes on Monette's fixed expression. "It's time for lunch, anyway. We seem to be having some miscommunication, which I'm sure we can settle quite easily after a, um, some food. Shall we meet back here at one o'clock?"

Grabbing Monette's arm, she all but catapulted her out of her chair and out of the room. Juan Flores gave Laney and Robert an apologetic smile, picked up his laptop and hurried after the two women.

"What in the world was that about?" Laney asked.

"I don't know." Robert picked up his briefcase. "Why does she keep calling your son Sean?"

"No idea. There is something seriously wrong with that woman."

"Yes, I can see that. Let's hope it works to our advantage. Come on. Go get some lunch. I've got to go back to my office, so I'll meet you back here at one."

Laney preceded Robert from the room and glanced around the office area. She didn't know where Susan had taken Monette, but a low, intense voice could be heard coming from a room down the hall.

Distressed, Laney found her family in the waiting area. Her parents and brother all jumped to their feet, wildly curious about what was going on and still desperately worried about the outcome of the meeting. Laney could think of no words to soothe them.

"MONETTE, WHAT IS the matter?" Susan asked, her eyes searching. "You seemed to be doing better. The file you showed me had everything in order. I trusted your professionalism and the accuracy you've shown in the past."

Monette shook her head, trying to clear the fog that seemed to have filled it. "Everything I said was true," she murmured.

"There was nothing in the case file about physical abuse by a boyfriend."

Looking away, Monette tried to think, tried to remember where she had written that down. "It's in there. I…I guess I just forgot it in my office. Yes. It's in my office. I'll go get it. I'll show it to you. I've got proof." Stumbling a little, she turned toward the door and reached for the knob, but Susan scooted around her and placed a hand on her shoulder.

"Never mind that right now. We can find it later. Right now, you need to eat something and relax for a little bit. We've got plenty of time to find what you're looking for."

Monette looked at her supervisor's concerned face, heard the words coming out of her mouth but couldn't quite understand what they meant. Nodding, she opened the door and went out. Moving as if she was wading through mud, she found her way to her own office, picked up her purse and then left through the back door. Walking to her car, she got behind the wheel and started the engine. A persistent pinging noise wormed its way into her brain, but she couldn't place what it was, so she ignored it.

She was doing the right thing. She knew she was because she was saving Sean.

Pulling out of the parking lot, she turned to the main street out of town. She would go see Sean, just to make sure he was all right. He would be happy to see her. He would thank her for saving him from their mother.

Tears filled her eyes. As she reached up to wipe them away, she crested a rise in the road and saw a truck headed straight for her. She jerked the wheel, overcorrecting as the other vehicle zoomed past. Her wheels left the highway and she bumped down an embankment, coming to rest in a ditch.

LANEY HAD LUNCH with her parents and brother, describing what had happened in the meeting. "I got the feeling there was something going on that had nothing to do with us, that Monette's body was in the room but her mind wasn't. At least, not after the first few minutes."

Vivian shook her head. "You mean like she was disassociated from what was going on?"

Laney nodded. "This can't be good." Her biggest worry was how it would affect the outcome. Would she get Sam back today?

"And I don't know where she got that story about my boyfriend hurting Sam. Caleb would never—" She clamped her mouth shut.

Both her parents stared at her and Ethan chuckled, at least until she glared at him.

"Honey, is there something we should know?" her dad asked.

"The stress is getting to me," she said.

Wisely, no one responded, but three pairs of speculative eyes considered her as they finished their meal and hurried back to the DCS office.

Once again, her family waited in the lobby while she and Robert entered the meeting room.

Susan and Juan were talking together quietly and they both looked up, their expressions unreadable.

"Where's Miss Berkley?" Robert asked.

Susan gave a half smile. "She hasn't returned from lunch yet. I'm sure she'll be here momentarily. I left a message on her cell, so she knows we're starting."

"Well, while we're waiting, maybe you could explain how this new system of dealing with child safety has gone so badly wrong in this case," Laney said. The state of shock she'd been in for two days was melting away with the heat of her growing anger.

"Hmm, well, not every new system works perfectly," Susan began. "And… Oh, here's Miss Berkley now. She said she had further information for us."

The door opened.

Laney didn't turn to look at the social worker, though she saw Susan glance up and do a double take that had Laney swinging around to look at Monette. Her mouth dropped open in amazement.

Monette's earlier good grooming had disintegrated to a state Laney had never seen on Monette before. Her hair was falling out of the bun that had been so tightly wound earlier, her suit jacket was gone, her blouse was dirty and her skirt was torn. Blood tracked down her left leg and into her shoe.

Susan stood and rushed around the table. "Monette. Are you all right?"

Monette looked confused as she set a briefcase, bulging with papers, on the table. "Of course. Why wouldn't I be?"

"Have you been in an accident?"

"I don't think so."

Susan pointed to Monette's leg. "You obviously need medical attention." Glancing at Juan, she said, "Go get help."

"You need to sit down, Monette." Susan tried to guide her to a chair, but Monette jerked her arm from the woman's grasp.

"I don't know what you're talking about. There's nothing wrong with me. Anyway, we're not here to talk about me." Monette's voice rose and she tossed her head. "We're here to make sure this woman loses custody of her son and never sees him again."

Laney gasped. "Monette, that certainly isn't the reason for this meeting."

"You put Sean in danger!" Monette shrieked as she surged to her feet. She pointed a shaking finger at Laney. Her eyes were wild as she said, "You're a bad mother! It's all in my report."

Calm in the face of the other woman's

growing hysteria, Laney sat forward and gently asked, "Who is Sean?"

"You know who he is. He's my little brother and you're responsible for his death."

Laney, Susan and Robert all exchanged shocked looks.

"Monette," Susan said, "we're going to get you some help. You're bleeding."

"No, no, this isn't about me!" Monette shook her head and fell back into her chair. She began sobbing. "She let Sean get trampled by a horse. She can't hurt him anymore."

"Let's make her more comfortable," Robert said, stepping forward and pulling up another chair so they could elevate Monette's feet. Reaching for his hand, Monette cried and clung to him while he awkwardly tried to calm her.

Susan Martinez looked on the verge of tears herself. "I don't know what has happened. I thought she was better. Everything she showed me was in order. But now..." Her voice trailed off as she gazed at her employee in dismay. After a moment she rallied and said, "Ms. Reynolds, please accept my apology for my department's action. I can see we were working on misguided information. So this case is dismissed. Your son will be returned to you today."

"Thank...thank you." Laney felt some of her anger turn to pity as she looked at Monette.

Juan returned to say the paramedics were on the way. He and Susan sat down to wait with Monette who was slumped in her chair.

Laney left the room with the sound of Monette's sobs ringing in her ears.

SUSAN MARTINEZ BROUGHT Sam home that afternoon. Laney, who had been pacing and checking out the window every few minutes, ran out to greet her son. While she kissed and hugged him, checking him over from head to toe, the other woman cleared her throat and said, "I must apologize again for the department's failure in regard to you and your son. We made a terrible mistake."

Laney picked Sam up and held him close. "I'll say!"

"I feel I must explain," Susan went on. "I owe you that." She paused as Laney nodded and then lowered Sam to the floor with whispered instructions to go play with his toys for a few minutes. He trundled off toward his toy box.

"Ms. Berkley was supposed to be closing out her cases," Susan began, "and getting ready to go on vacation starting Monday because—"

"She was having a psychotic breakdown," Laney interjected.

The other woman had the grace to blush. Her gaze darted away but at last she said, "No, exhaustion, we thought. We had no idea... Every bit of paperwork she showed me was strictly in compliance with the DCS regulations, however—"

"It was fabricated," Laney interjected again.

Susan nodded and lifted one shoulder in a shrug. "Not entirely. Every incident actually happened, but more than twenty years ago and to her brother Sean, who died when he was trampled by a horse belonging to their neglectful mother's boyfriend. Sean was four and Monette was ten. Apparently she's buried the incident in her mind for years, but it all came back last April when another child, a little girl, died in a similar way."

"And since she was already fixated on Sam, she became obsessed, thinking I was going to let the same thing happen to him,"

Laney said, her heart breaking for the two children who'd died so tragically.

"Yes," Susan said. "And again, I'm so sorry about what happened to you and your son."

Laney knew the apology was sincere. But there was more she wanted to know. "At lunchtime, Monette was in an accident, wasn't she?"

"Yes," Susan confirmed. "She went into a ditch, wasn't wearing her seat belt. I never should have let her leave the office at noon, especially not in her car. I didn't realize what a bad state she was in."

"I think she must have been covering it up for a long time. Thank God it happened after she'd dropped Sam off and that there were no other cars involved," Laney said.

Sam had left his toys and come back to cling to her thigh. She stroked his silky hair, then shook the other woman's hand. "I'm sorry about all of this, too. I know yours is a hard job and I know you do your best for children. It must have become too much for Monette. I'm glad she'll get the help she needs."

The woman nodded and left.

As soon as her car pulled away, she went into the house where Sam jumped up from playing with his toys and asked, "Can we go see Bertie and Mr. Ransom? They want me to tell 'em I'm home."

Laney stared at him in dismay, not sure how to respond. It was obvious that whatever Caleb had said to Monette had been blown out of proportion by the troubled woman. "Let's have dinner first and you can tell me all about where you stayed last night."

"They had a dog. He wasn't as smart as Bertie, but he let me hug him and the lady let him sleep with me."

Tears filled Laney's eyes and she swept him into her arms again, despite his protests. She buried her face in his tousled hair and kissed him, grateful to the foster mother who had tried to make her son feel at home.

After a quick meal of Sam's favorite grilled-cheese sandwiches, they walked together to Caleb's place. Laney tried to formulate an apology as they went, but words seemed to be inadequate to make up for the way she had lashed out at him.

As they came up the drive, they saw Chet

Bartlett coming out of the barn. No sign of Caleb's truck.

"Hey, Laney," he called. "Everything all right?"

"We're looking for Caleb."

"And Bertie," Sam added.

"I can tell you where Bertie is, Sam. He's at my house. Caleb dropped him off last night, asked us to take care of him for a few days because he had some business out of town." Chet glanced around. "I only stopped by to check on things."

"Did he say where he was going?"

"No. Sorry, Laney. And he didn't say when he'd be back." With a wave, Chet climbed into his truck and drove off.

Sam's small hand crept into hers. "Do you think Mr. Ransom will come back?" he asked in a quivery voice.

Regret was bitter in her mouth as she looked at the ranch through the gathering dusk. Even though she may have squandered the right to tell Caleb she loved him, she at least wanted to tell him she was sorry. "I hope so, Sammy. We'll have to wait and see."

His bottom lip stuck out. "I don't like wait and see."

"I don't, either, honey, but at least we can probably go play with Bertie tomorrow." That cheered Sam up and he gave a little hop of joy as they started back toward home.

TWO DAYS LATER Laney was standing in her kitchen, staring into the refrigerator and trying to decide what to make for dinner, when she heard a scuffling noise on the back porch.

Sam, who'd been sitting at the table creating a structure out of his colored plastic building blocks, scooted from his chair.

"Bertie!" he yelled and dashed for the screen door. Swinging it open, he flung his arms around the dog, who happily returned the love with a mighty swipe of his tongue to the boy's cheek and ear. Sam fell back laughing and then jumped up to wrap himself around the leg of the tall man who loomed in the doorway.

"Mr. Ransom, where've you been? Me and Bertie thought you was never coming home!"

"I had some things to take care of, buddy."

Laney's heart leaped into her throat and began pounding as she watched Caleb hunker down and scoop Sam up. He gave him a hug, then opened the screen and looked at her over the top of her son's head.

His face was in shadow, but when he stepped into the light of the kitchen and looked at her, his eyes were clear and steady. "Hi," he said. "Okay if I come in?"

"Yes, of course," she answered around the lump in her throat.

Sam started to wiggle and Caleb set him down. "Me and Bertie are gonna go play," Sam announced. He and his best friend ran out into the yard, leaving the adults alone.

"Caleb, I'm sorry for what I said and—"

That was as far as she got because Caleb hauled her into his arms and covered her mouth with his. The kiss was long and warm and so right. Then he set her a little away from him and met her gaze.

"I'm sorry, too," he said. "You were right about not facing the past. I should have called you, but there was something I had to take care of before that could happen."

The seriousness in his voice had her searching his face in alarm. "What is it? Your leg?"

"No." Caleb gave a quick shake of his

head. "No. I went to see my old command-ing officer." He paused.

A shiver of apprehension ran up her spine, but she waited for him to go on.

"To find out about that kid's family in Af-ghanistan. I thought if there was any fam-ily left, I could send some money, help them out. Took a couple of days, but my CO got some information for me."

"And?"

Caleb turned his head, cleared his throat, then met her eyes. "He's alive."

"What? You mean that little boy?"

This time a grin broke over his face. "Yeah, turns out he was badly injured, and so was his mother, but they're alive and they're recovering. I sent some money through an aid organization. Maybe it'll help."

Tears formed in Laney's eyes. "I'm sure it will."

"Then I went to see Berman's widow like I should have done long ago. She's doing okay, some days better than others." Another pause. "I met Berman's little girl, Katie. She looks just like him."

He smiled ruefully and went on. "Turns out you were right. I had no business telling you that the past shouldn't rule your life when I—"

"I needed to hear it," Laney admitted. And then she told him about what had happened with Monette. "Seeing her like that, haunted by what had happened to her when she was little, when her brother died… Well, it showed me that I *did* need to deal with the past, to know I'll never put Sam in the kind of situation I was in with my birth mother." She took a breath. "I feel…lighter."

He smiled. "You seem happier."

"So do you," she answered, reaching over and wrapping her arms around his neck. She kissed him, savoring the taste of him. At last she leaned back, smiled at him and said, "I'm so glad you're home."

"Me, too." With gentle fingers he smoothed her hair away from her face. "I'd almost forgotten how beautiful you are. Inside and out." He kissed her. "I love you, Laney, and I love your son."

"And I love you. *We* love you. Well, Sam mostly loves Bertie, but I think he loves you, too."

He grinned. "In that case, I was wondering if maybe you and Sam might like to make your home with me."

Heat washed into her face and her heart did a slow roll in her chest. "You mean…?"

"Marry me, Delaney. I love you and I love Sam. I'd be a good dad for him and for our other kids, too."

"Other kids? You've been thinking about this."

"Not much else to do while I was traveling the past few days, and since you weren't around to pester me."

She laughed. "That ends now. I intend to be around to pester you every day. Sam, too."

"So is that a yes?"

"It's absolutely a yes." She leaned back and gazed at him. "Cowboy, do you realize we're going to get married and we've never even been on a date? So how about you take me out to dinner?"

Caleb swept her hair aside and kissed her neck. "I can do that and we can talk about the day my luck changed and I found your son in my pasture."

Laney turned her head and found his lips with hers as she thought maybe that was the day *all* their luck had changed.

"Um, Laney?"

Lifting the full white skirt of her wedding dress, Laney turned to look at her new husband, handsome in a navy blue suit and silver-gray tie. "Yes?"

"Is this banana cake?" He indicated the small plate on which his new mother-in-law had placed a big slab of their wedding cake.

Her eyes brimming with laughter, Laney nodded. "I'm afraid so. You were hoping for chocolate, maybe?"

"Yeah. But I knew when we cut through the frosting that it wasn't to be, then when I tasted it…"

"Have you tried the punch my mom made?"

"Do I dare?"

She laughed. "It has frozen, crushed bananas in it."

"Of course it does." Setting the plate aside, Caleb took his bride into his arms and began dancing with her to the tune the high school band was playing.

Caleb was thrilled that his leg didn't bother him. All the extra weeks of physical therapy that his doctor and Laney had insisted on had paid off. His leg was much better, probably as good as it was ever going to get. Good enough for him to dance with his wife.

He glanced around the school gymnasium. Laney's parents were dancing and his were sitting at a table with Sam, Shane and Logan. They all seemed to be enjoying the banana cake and punch. "My parents are thrilled about their ready-made grandson. I never actually thought I'd get married, much less have a wedding and reception where the whole town was invited."

"All my students past and present insisted they be invited. Since they offered to decorate, how could I say no?"

He surveyed the shiny ribbons and sparkly decorations that hung from the ceiling and walls. It was winter now, and Christmas was approaching, so maybe that justified the over-the-top decorations, but he hadn't known that much glitter even existed. "It's a simple, two-letter word…"

"And your favorite."

"Not anymore. I've found lots of things to say yes to lately."

She smiled at him. "I'm glad you invited Elysa Berman and Katie. Not so sure about your soldiers. Those guys' only interest seems to be flirting with my fire team."

"Don't worry. They won't try anything. They know how to respect women who can handle a chainsaw and a fire ax." Caleb paused and looked down at her. "I know I've said this before, but I think it was big of you to invite Monette."

Laney glanced over at the table where Monette sat with Susan Martinez and several members of the high school faculty. She wore a simple black dress, hair cut in a flattering style. Her expression was serene.

"It's time to heal and move on. I should have showed her more compassion, been more understanding, realized that there had to be a reason for her nosiness... I was so afraid of being thought a bad mother, I didn't consider anything else. She's supposed to go back to work soon, on a limited basis."

"So she won't be letting her past rule her life, either."

"So it seems. We both know that the past isn't a place to live, or even to visit for very long."

He pulled Laney closer. "I'm happy with the present."

* * * * *

LARGER-PRINT BOOKS!

GET 2 FREE LARGER-PRINT NOVELS PLUS 2 FREE MYSTERY GIFTS

Love Inspired®

Larger-print novels are now available...

LILP15

LARGER-PRINT BOOKS!

GET 2 FREE
LARGER-PRINT NOVELS
PLUS 2 FREE
MYSTERY GIFTS

Love Inspired®

SUSPENSE
RIVETING INSPIRATIONAL ROMANCE

Larger-print novels are now available...